Sleight of Hand

An Alewives of Colmar mystery
Elizabeth R. Andersen

HAEDDRE PRESS

Copyright © 2024 by Elizabeth R. Andersen

All rights reserved.

No portion of this book may be reproduced in any form without written permission from the publisher or author, except as permitted by U.S. copyright law. No generative artificial intelligence (AI) was used in the writing of this work. The author expressly prohibits any entity from using this publication for purposes of training AI technologies to generate text, including without limitation technologies that are capable of generating works in the same style or genre as this publication. The author reserves all rights to license uses of this work for generative AI training and development of machine learning language models.

This is a work of fiction based on historical facts that the author researched to the best of their ability. Any omissions or misrepresentations are unintentional. Resemblance of fictional characters in the book to living individuals is coincidence.

Contents

1. A devilishly good brew — 5
2. The brewers in the tanners — 11
3. A not so ordinary evening — 19
4. Jorges goes to work — 25
5. A Franciscan among wolves — 31
6. The perpetrators — 43
7. The scriptorium gang — 51
8. The time to act — 57
9. Appel's excellent adventure — 65
10. Cat and mouse — 77
11. The lost dowry — 87
12. Trials and tribulations — 99
13. Brothers will be brothers — 107
14. The journey — 115
15. A rare meal — 121
16. The gate yard — 131

17.	A parcel tied with string	137
18.	The suspect	145
19.	Witch-hunters	153
20.	Honey cake treachery	163
21.	Return to Vogelgrun	173
22.	The minstrels' tale	183
23.	Falling out and falling back in	193
24.	An interview with an entourage	203
25.	The witch of Vogelgrun	215
26.	The visitor	221
27.	The accomplice	229
28.	A splash in the dark	239
29.	A most unwanted helper	249
30.	The ale must flow	259
31.	Alewives and fishwives	265
32.	Banished	277
33.	A bounty of suspects	283
34.	Loaves of mystery	291
35.	Rising suspicions	299
36.	Bloodstains	305
37.	True love burns	311
38.	Up in smoke	315

39.	Fresh air	321
40.	Author's note	335
41.	Join me!	339
42.	Acknowledgements	341
Also by Elizabeth R. Andersen		343
About Elizabeth R. Andersen		345

To my mom, who taught me to enjoy the ridiculous things in life.

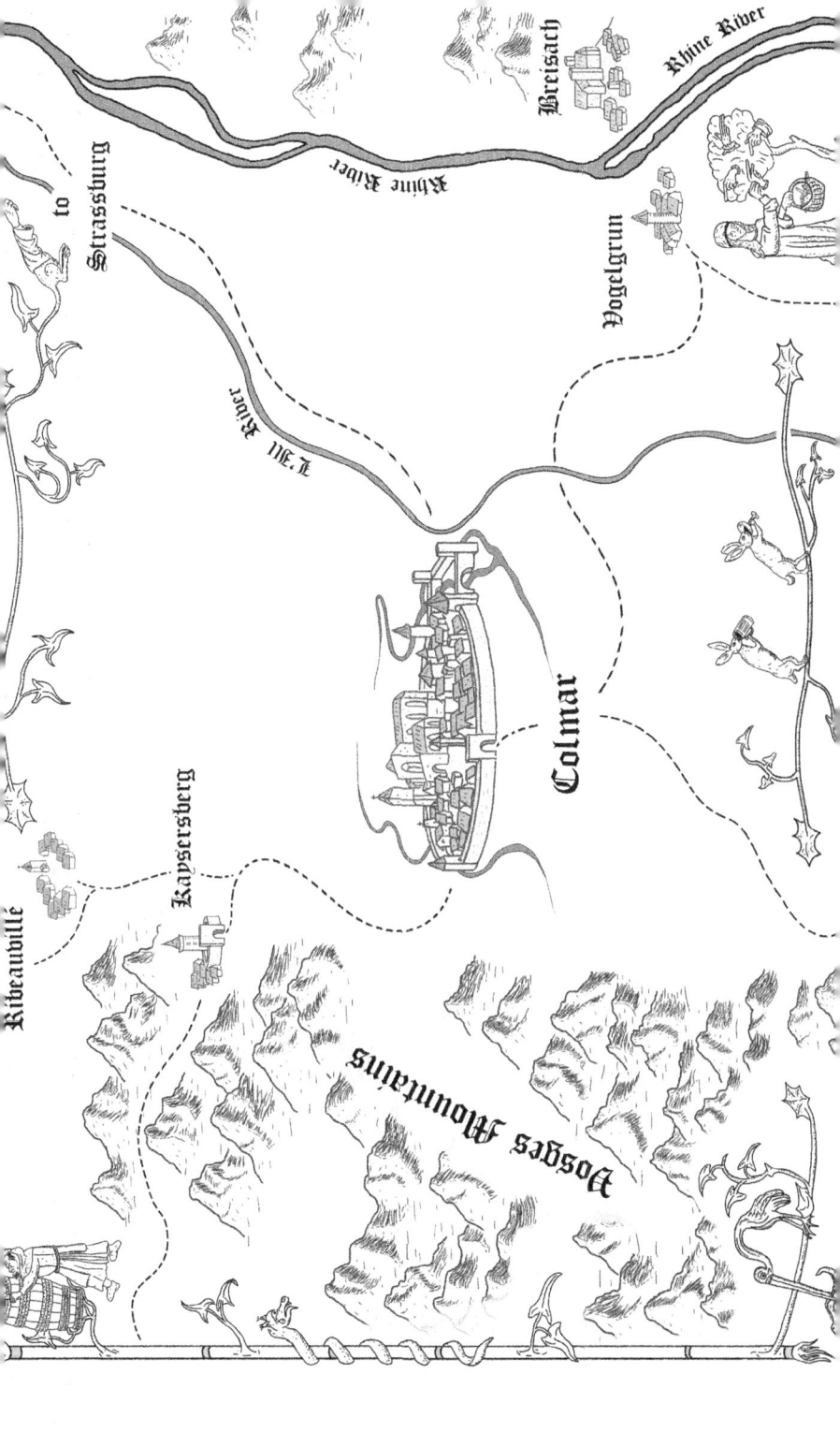

A devilishly good brew
In which an unusual ingredient is discovered

I T WAS EFI WHO made the gruesome discovery.

All morning she had worked at a new dark ale, coaxing the water to boil in the large pot that sat atop the fire in the yard on an iron trivet, then carefully adding scoops of malted barley to make a fine, frothy mash. The ale that she and her friends, Appel and Gritta, concocted was so fine and sweet that travelers and merchants passing through the district often stopped along their way to see if a green branch hung on a peg near the door of Appel's house, signaling to all that ale was available to purchase.

There were no travelers this afternoon, however, and Efi worked in silence with deliberate movements. She was the youngest and least experienced of the three alewives of Colmar, a fair-faced woman of twenty years, or perhaps twenty-one. Although she and her late husband both survived the horrors of the Great Pestilence that had ravaged the world with death and suffering only a few years before, misfortune struck when Harald died the summer prior, leaving her widowed and penniless. Were it not for the friendship of Appel and Gritta, she would most likely be washing linens in a lord's house or picking and sorting scraps to sell in the market. Brewing ale was so consistent that she and her friends were not even obliged to take extra work in the fields, like many of her neighbors.

She hummed a tune to herself, a mixing tune, she called it, for her mind was willing to drift when she was stirring the mash, and her singing kept her hands moving and her thoughts quiet. The off-tone sound stopped when she felt a slight bump against her long-handled paddle. Something was in the brew. Efi pulled a face that wrinkled her pretty features.

"If one of Gritta's children has lost another plaything in the mash again, I will throttle the little beast myself," she grumbled. Searching around in the muck of water and grain with her paddle, she felt the slight thump again and chased it through the thick brew until she had it pinned against the side of the pot. Her annoyance knew no bounds, for now she must start a whole new mash, which would cost the three alewives a week of lost wages and time. With the price of grain these days, throwing away an entire mash and starting over would mean she was that much further away from saving for her dowry so she could remarry.

Efi and her friends lived in Les Tanneurs, the quarter of the city where tradesmen cured and tanned hides that would eventually become saddles and halters, gloves, belts, buckets, jerkins, waterskins, and anything else that required leather. The tanners were well respected as a guild, for their work resulted in wares essential to daily life, but the work of taking the freshly removed hide of a cow or pig into something pliable enough to last for years was a smelly business. Only those who lived in

Les Tanneurs could walk through the neighborhood without their eyes watering from the stench of the urine, feces, and rotting flesh that wafted through the streets. One could pretend they were safe from the stench inside the house, but today, Efi brewed in the open air. She glanced at the side of the house and clucked her tongue at the gaping hole in the wall. Frau Appel had commissioned a new hearth to accommodate a larger fire that could heat two pots at once for the brewing, and the stonemasons she had hired – feeling it was an excellent time to take a break – were eating their bread and onions in the warmth of the spring sun in the garden. As they ate, they shared raunchy tales and a bowl of small ale between themselves.

Efi looked left and right. After her husband Harald died, Frau Appel took her in, and the two widows lived together almost as mother and daughter. The older woman's husband had been a prosperous tanner before he died during the Great Pestilence. The house had a sort of shabby, neglected grandeur. There was evidence that Appel had once lived a fine and comfortable life, but the yellow plaster flaking from the walls and the moss creeping into the thatched roof were signs of growing poverty. Although Frau Appel was entitled to take over her late husband's tanning business if she desired, the work was strenuous, and finding workers was difficult since so many had died when sickness swept through the city. Brewing ale wouldn't make her rich, but it kept the loneliness at bay. Unfortunately, it did not prevent the whispers, rumors, and suspicion about what the three alewives got up to in their spare time – or what they might be putting in their brew.

Efi heard a voice approaching, and her friend Gritta breezed into the fenced yard, sending a small flock of hens scattering through the gate.

"Infernal birds!" Gritta yelled. "Following me about as if they think grain and grubs will drop from my apron like manna from heaven. They have even less sense than you, Efi."

Efi nodded absently as she tried to fish the hard lump from the mash pot. The insults the old housewife flung in Efi's direction no longer rankled her.

Frau Gritta Leporteur, wife of Jorges Leporteur, lived across the lane in a crumbling old warehouse and was the mother of twelve children, who – along with her drunkard of a husband – vexed her daily. Everyone told Gritta that she shouldn't complain. After all, her whole family – she, good-for-nothing Jorges, all the children – and the animals had survived the scourge of the Great Pestilence, and no one else in Colmar could say the same. She was a hard woman, with no fat on her limbs and care lines that carved chasms in her sun-dry face. Some called her callous, but Efi knew that under the exterior of epithets and complaints, Gritta was a loving and fiercely loyal friend.

Gritta paused her complaining and sniffed the air. "Efi, the mash smells too rich."

"Frau Appel says that for a darker ale, we cook it longer," Efi grunted as her paddle chased the foreign object in the pot. Whatever was in the mash, she almost had it. "But I've found one of your children's toys again in this brew, and so it is ruined."

"The Devil's got those children of mine in his taloned grip!" Gritta whirled and stomped toward the gate. "I shall teach them never to put their playthings in the brew again! Which child was it? Egilhard? Wina? Don't tell me you let my lack-witted son Lonel anywhere near this house, did you?"

But Efi didn't answer. She was leaning forward, looking at the object that had risen from the murky water on the end of her paddle. Her face paled, and she shrieked, scurrying away from the pot.

Gritta rushed to her and examined the object, which had fallen to the hard-packed dirt. A hand lay there, dark red and bloated from being boiled with the malted grain. A long, dark spot stretched from the base of the thumb to the first knuckle. She blinked and looked around, expecting to see an arm and an elbow lying somewhere, perhaps behind the stack of firewood, but this hand appeared to be unaccompanied by the rest of its body.

"Well." Gritta smoothed her dress with satisfaction as she spoke. "No, Efi, I feel confident that my children did not put this hand in the ale mash."

"Well then, who did put the hand in the ale mash?" Efi wailed. "It looks like the hand of a demon! And see there, it even has a mark upon it. The Devil's work!"

"They do say that our brew is devilishly good," Gritta mused, and Efi shot her a horrified stare.

"Gritta, how could you!"

Gritta shushed her quickly. The stonemasons had finished their meal and filed past Efi and Gritta back into the house, shedding dust and small chips of stone and mortar from their clothing. There were three of them, all brawny and tan-skinned from spending days atop a scaffolding in the sun and wind.

"I heard a yell," the head mason growled. "What is the problem now? Disturbing my men's work twice in one day means it will cost more for this hearth, you know."

"Twice?" Gritta quirked an eyebrow.

Efi blushed. "My frock caught a'fire this morning." She lifted the skirt of her apron, and Gritta saw a blackened patch of fabric near her left foot. She glanced at the masons again, noting the way the muscles of their arms filled out the shape of their untied tunics and the tight places in their dusty leather hose. Efi and Appel both had a weakness for handsome men. Gritta narrowed her eyes.

"And would this little fire have been an accident or an attempt to find a husband?"

The head mason leaned forward, squinting, at the hand lying on the packed dirt floor of the yard and pointed, his mouth agape.

"What in the name of Jesu's bloody wounds is that?!"

The brewers in the tanners

In which the presence of alewives is a problem for the men of Colmar

THE RESIDENTS OF COLMAR took abundant civic pride in their city, which boasted an expansive market and walls of mica-flecked sandstone that glowed orange in the light of the setting sun. The stately spire of Saint Martin's church, encrusted with carpenter's scaffolding for as long as anyone could remember, rose above the half-timbered houses like a calm and reassuring patriarch, spreading its shadow across the grand courtyard of the Place de la Cathédrale. It was always loud and busy outside the church, as burghers, ox-drivers, merchants, and goodwives bustled about with commerce and conversation. Shallow streams, some lined with stones and others not, crisscrossed the streets, and flat-bottomed boats slipped languidly in the current from one end of the city to the other, carrying baskets of fish, bales of brightly dyed wool, and crates stacked with brilliantly glazed pottery. Some of the goods would be placed on boats in the mighty Rhine River to eventually grace the households in Strassburg. Others would travel west over the deep green ramps of the Vosges mountains to the great fairs at Troyes and beyond.

All was orderly and calm in the city. Its leaders, men of high esteem and responsibility, stood a little higher on the toes of their pointed shoes when they talked amongst themselves of the accomplishments of their fair ville, for they were a free city – not under the direct control of a baron, and in good standing with their neighboring towns. Being allowed to manage their own affairs was not a burden – no, indeed! It was an honor. The men attended to city business during the day and then met at the hearth of Herr Schlock's weinstube in the evenings to discuss important matters and exchange gossip over mugs of crisp, white Alsatian wine and plates heaped with steaming pork knuckle stew.

On this particular evening, there was a matter that puzzled them, and it was what to do with Les Tanneurs. It was an old part of Colmar, and as the city flourished, the land around the shabby houses and smelly canals grew increasingly valuable. The tanneries brought economic benefits that could not be ignored, and the councilmen had gathered to discuss the possibility of moving them further downstream to allow the city to grow beyond its current borders. For, as Herr Bertram, the city's wealthiest grape grower, commented, the stench of the tanners was beyond belief. Indeed, a perceptive nose could even catch the scent of rotting meat and urine wafting through Saint Martin's during the recitation of the mass. Herr Bertram assured the others that he possessed such a nose and could not concentrate on his prayers when the wind blew in from the east. The other men at the table nodded their graying heads in agreement. When summer came, and the heat of the sun and many bodies warmed the inside of the church like a bread oven, no amount of priest's incense could cover the smell.

"What about those women?" Herr Gilgen asked, and a few council members stopped tipping their mugs back mid-sip. Herr Gilgen smiled, emboldened by their reaction. "You know the ones I mean. The alewives who brew in Les Tanneurs. What shall we do with them?"

"A mighty fine brew they make," said Herr Mortimer, licking his lips in appreciation. "It would be a shame to shut their aleworks down."

"You drink their brew? I refuse since it is befouled with tannery water! I am amazed that you have not shit yourself to death, Herr Mortimer."

There was silence at the table for a moment while Herr Mortimer blushed furiously. He was the youngest of the council members and the most easily embarrassed. None of the men thought to mention to Mortimer that the water for the ale came from the clear, cool water of the stream that flowed past Saint Martin's church by special permission from Father Konrad himself. No, it was too much fun to watch the young man squirm.

"Those women are a scourge, even upon Les Tanneurs. They are loud and uncouth, and Gritta Leporteur is birthing babies out of anyone's control. Soon the whole of Colmar will be populated with drunken churls, just like her husband, Jorges." The men giggled into their mugs as Herr Schlock placed another trencher of stew studded with soggy wheat dumplings before them.

"Colmar needs no aleworks!" Herr Schlock declared, stamping his foot and wiping his hands on his greasy tunic. "Our wine is superior here, even to Strassburg and Kaysersberg. Ale will only weaken our market for fine drink. Let them brew in their homes for their own families like other women do. We had made a name for ourselves as the city of fine white wines before those three came along. Did they consider what this would do to our businesses? No!"

"But what will those women do if they have no employment? Only Gritta is married, and Jorges does not earn enough money at the docks to support such a large family. Young Efi has still not remarried after her husband Harald died," Herr Mortimer asked.

"It ain't as if Efi is at a loss for offers of marriage," Hans, the baker, grumbled. He had sat silent all evening and was well into his third mug of wine. "She just has no sense, and we all know it."

"Hans is just sore because he asked the fair young widow to warm his bed and bear his children, and she turned him down," Herr Gilgen teased. "And why not, eh? Your stomach is as large and round as a boule of bread." He leaned over and gave Hans a whack on his ample midsection while the rest of the room roared with laughter.

"Ah, Efi is strong enough. She's young. Put her to work in the fields. She will be too tired to cause trouble at the end of the day," Hans said, slamming his mug on the table and sloshing drink on the floor.

"Seems a cruel thing to do to a woman whose only crime is being widowed," Herr Mortimer mumbled.

"I'll wager Herr Mortimer regrets that he married the daughter of Karl Gasthaus before Efi's foolhardy husband died," Herr Gilgen quipped. Again, the room broke out into roars of laughter, with Herr Schlock laughing the hardest because he considered Karl Gasthaus, who owned the largest inn in town, to be his rival.

"Ah, but the widow Appel is a good and pious woman," old Herr Frankbert declared, and the other men jerked out of their collective revelry. "I believe she can keep an eye on the other two. And do you really want to drink naught but the ale your wives make? You know that those three from Les Tanneurs make the finest brew from here to the Rhine and perhaps beyond."

Herr Mortimer was nodding vigorously. "Indeed. And since it is Appel's house used for the brewing, and she is the widow of a tanner, we cannot turn them out. The tanning guild would turn our hides into shoe leather."

"No, we mustn't turn them out." Herr Frankbert stabbed his walking stick into the straw-covered floorboards. "Well then, it appears that the alewives can stay where they are for now, but, sirs, the city must expand, for we are bursting with people and straining against our walls."

"To the northeast, then?"

"But what of the River Lauch? The floods will surely destroy anything that we build. They already have – dozens of times!"

Herr Gilgen sighed. "I do not see why we cannot simply move the alewives. Certainly, a group of recalcitrant women is not intimidating enough to change the course of the entire city! Put them outside the city walls."

Nearby, Herr Schlock stopped cleaning a table and nodded his head in enthusiastic agreement, for if there was anyone he hated more than Karl Gasthaus, it was the three irreverent women who dared to presume themselves equal citizens.

"Unless they do something against the laws of this city or God, they stay, and the tanners with them." Herr Frankbert's walking stick punctuated his statement as it smacked against the table, sending the wooden trenchers and clay cups jumping and clattering. "Wine is fine enough, but I'll not go drinking ale from another city again, and if I keep drinking that weak and flavorless brew that my wife makes, I shall die from a bored stomach."

"But…b-but," Herr Schlock stuttered as he realized his opportunity to banish the alewives was draining away as fast as the wine from the men's cups.

Herr Frankbert cleared his throat loudly. He was the oldest and sagest of them all and the head of the winemakers' guild besides.

"They stay."

The other men looked at each other and shrugged their shoulders. What could they do? The matter was settled.

A not so ordinary evening

In which it is necessary to produce assurances about the future

WHEN FRAU APPEL, WIDOW of Old Schneider the tanner, returned home from her nightly routine of conspicuous piety at Saint Martin's church, she stood in amazement at the scene before her. Efi sat outside on a bench, crying prettily into her hands, but this did not surprise her. Unlike some women who screamed or fainted when the situation called for particular urgency, Efi perfected her tears as a clarion call to all young and available men around her. She was flanked by Ingo, the glover's son, on one side, and Hervé, a newly widowed and prosperous tanner, on the other – both eligible men.

Frau Gritta, Appel's long-time neighbor and hard-bitten mother of twelve unruly children, stood by, hands on her bony hips, arguing hotly with Herr Werner, a low-ranking lord who served as the sheriff. Nearby, the stonemasons milled about amongst the chickens in Appel's yard, kicking at the dust and making crude jokes to one another. The vignette was one of confusion and dismay, filling Appel with dread. But she composed herself, adjusting her dingy white wimple devoutly on her brow, and walked forward into the yard, a picture of calm, grandmotherly control.

"Greetings to you, Lord Sheriff." She curtseyed. "Has there been an accident?"

"Indeed, Widow Appel, but to whom the accident occurred, we do not know," Sheriff Werner huffed.

Appel cast a questioning glance at Gritta, who was grinding her teeth nearby.

"There's a hand in the mash," Gritta said tersely.

"Whose hand?"

"We do not know, but he was abominably rude to place his hand in our mash because now we need to start a new brew."

"Well, tell him to take it out!"

Efi shook her head, sending her wimple tumbling to the ground and setting her blonde curls bouncing. The eyes of all the men in the yard swiveled in her direction. "No indeed, Frau Appel. Whoever possessed the hand is no longer attached to it."

Appel, who thought herself wise, found she was at a loss for words. Her mouth opened as she considered what she had just been told, but all she could do was gape.

"That's days of work gone and a full basket of good grain. Thank the Virgin I had not added the gruit yet, for that would have been a real tragedy, what with the amount of money in taxes it costs us." Gritta spat on the ground to mark her disgust, and the sheriff jumped back.

"Foul woman! Grind that spittle into the dust and go home to your family. It's time for you to serve them their supper!"

Gritta grinned at him, kicking a tuft of dirt over the glistening glob with her foot. Appel knew that her friend would do whatever she could to annoy the sheriff, and whether or not the hand had been placed in their mash by its original owner, now was not the time to irritate the representative of the law.

"Sheriff, please come inside. I have a new red ale that you will enjoy, and then we can put this matter to rest. I am sure the hand was an accident."

"An accident!" Sheriff Werner's mouth moved silently with apoplectic shock. He snatched his cap from his head, slapping it on his thigh. "Hands do not wander upon their fingertips and drop themselves into ale cauldrons! I want to know where this appendage came from!"

"And we shall determine that in good time. Come, have a cup, and let us discuss the matter before it's too dark outside to see."

Efi had stopped her crying now and watched Appel through red-rimmed eyes, and Gritta flounced inside, tossing a few chickens out the door behind her as she went.

"I will not drink ale made of a person's finger meat, Appel, and I think that goes for everyone in this city. If I catch you selling that to any godly citizen of Colmar, then it will be the pillory for you."

"Of course, of course. But you see, I have another, finer ale put by, and this brew is free of body parts. I assure you, Sheriff, I made it myself two days ago." Appel favored him with her most serene smile and clutched her hands behind her back. If the sheriff did not come inside and have a drink, she would need to find another way to soothe him into compliance, a chore which she did not relish. "And if I am not mistaken, Efi brought some rosemary cakes from the market. Surely you will stay."

"Well, I uh…"

Appel took the sheriff by the arm and urged him into the house. Turning at the doorway, she cast an eye over the masons, who, instead of loafing about, had lined up behind her, each holding their wooden cups with eager expressions on their faces.

"Small ale for the rest of you when you've completed your work for the day. Now off you go."

Their groans and curses followed her inside, and she smiled to herself.

"But, Frau Appel, what will we do with him? If someone finds the sheriff here, drunk and all a'snoring on your ruined hearth, we are sure to be called prostitutes, and he a scoundrel!"

"Do not question your elders, Efi," Gritta commented from where she sat near the smoking, sputtering rushlight. She had Wina, her youngest child, upon her lap, and two of her other children chased the cat through Appel's house.

"Indeed, Efi. It would be unwise for the sheriff to suddenly find himself the center of a scandal, and so I think he might be willing to discuss the matter of the hand in the mash without casting accusations too quickly. Gritta, I wish you would tell your whelps to leave my cat alone."

"Mattheus! Anstett! Leave the beast and go home to your father. Make sure he's a'bed," Gritta yelled, and the sheriff startled from his sleep with a snort.

"Good evening, Sheriff. You fell asleep, and we did not wish to wake you," Appel said in a genial voice. She might as well have been greeting a merchant on the street.

Sheriff Werner sat up with difficulty, clutching his head and looking about him wildly. The masons had left, the light was gone, and he woke up the only man in a house full of women. Appel could see him calculating the predicament in his head as he slowly staggered to his feet.

"Good evening to you, Frau Appel…" He hesitated and nodded in greeting toward Gritta and Efi, who crossed their arms and watched him. "I would uh…appreciate your discretion. I don't know how I managed to fall asleep. That's a powerful brew you have there…"

"You must be exhausted from the good work that you do in our fair city, Sheriff." Appel laid a hand on his shoulder, and he flinched. "I am sure you only meant to rest your eyes, and the heat of the fire overcame you."

The sheriff mumbled in agreement, failing to notice that the still-unfinished fireplace was a cold pile of rubble in the center of the room.

"Of course, we wouldn't dream of doing anything to harm your reputation among the townsfolk or the council, would we, my dears?" Appel asked innocently.

Efi and Gritta nodded, and the sheriff, now thoroughly flummoxed by his situation, slunk to the door and disappeared into the night.

Appel dusted her hands against each other, as if to scrub away the man's presence.

"That ought to keep him quiet for a day or two. Now, girls, tell me everything that happened."

Jorges goes to work

In which we learn that this is an event of great proportion

WHEN GRITTA AND EIGHT of her twelve boys and girls lined up to see her husband Jorges off to his week of work at Vogelgrun, she kissed him on the cheek and leaned forward seductively. Nearby, her various children who were in the throes of puberty either blushed or gagged according to their temperament.

"You had better bring back coins, and breath as sober and sweet as a mountain breeze, Jorges Leporteur, or I'll throttle you!" she whispered, keeping a smile frozen upon her face. Jorges grinned crookedly and tried to place his lips upon his wife's, but she sent him along his way with a smack on the back of his head.

No sensible tradesman or farmer in Colmar was willing to employ Jorges, a notorious drunk, so he had to search further afield, sometimes leaving for days or weeks at a time to find work. In Vogelgrun, on the banks of the Rhine River, he rented a room with seven other men while he labored at the docks as a porter. If the weather was fine and the coins scarce, he sometimes slept beneath a tree on the riverbank. But work as a porter was hard to come by. After the pestilence, the shipping commerce slowed on the waterways, and more men drifted along the roadways, looking for unskilled labor.

As Jorges' scrawny profile finally disappeared over the horizon, Gritta turned and assessed her children. "Well now, you lot. There's work to be done!" she called out, and immediately her children scattered. Lonel ran down the street, laughing. Anstett and Matteus, her mischief-making twins, leapt a fence and trooped off through the onion patch while Rosmunda slipped quietly behind the house and into the shadows. Egilhard, Urbe, and Maragret immediately began to holler their complaints, slapping each other and walking toward the creek so that Gritta was left alone with little toddling Wina, who tugged at her skirts and whined.

"The Devil take those demons back to hell and their father with them!" Gritta yelled at the sky. She stood for a moment, her thin frame shaking with rage and indignation. Around her, the neighbors paid no heed to the noise, accustomed as they were to the loud sounds of domesticity coming from Gritta's house at all hours. "Ah well, at least Jorges is out of the house and working." She turned and appraised the lane in which she stood.

Somewhat narrow, it was, with the upper stories of the half-timbered houses leaning crookedly into each other and hunching over the dusty road. A shallow trench cut a ragged splice down the center of it all, earning the street its name: Trench Lane. Appel lived on the other side of the trench, and a few paces past their houses the street opened into a small square with a few other crooked houses and several ramshackle stalls for selling oil, scraping knives, leather punches, and other tools that might come in handy for the recipient of a finished hide. The dung collectors were at the far end of the tanning quarter, barely visible through their cloud of flies. Urine and dung were an essential part of the process for softening hides and the main reason for the dubious reputation of Les Tanneurs as a necessary olfactory nuisance.

The spring rains had transformed the lane into a mire of horse dung and muck, and brown water trickled through the trench to the nearest canal, which was swollen to the top of its banks. The stench of the tanners was so pungent that some said you could see it in the air, but Gritta had been born and raised in the tanning district, where the poorest and meanest could still afford to put a roof over their heads inside the protection of the walls, and she did not notice the smell. If anything, the fresh air near the wealthier, more well-heeled parts of the city made her uneasy.

Other rushing streams crisscrossed Colmar, shunting the marshy water across town to be used for moving water wheels, carrying shallow-hulled boats, and washing waste away. There was always motion in Colmar, as the sun sparkled on the water or the currents and eddies of the swollen streams swirled fallen leaves in the autumn months. Pilots pushed their small boats up and down the waterways with long poles, carrying people and parcels. Colmar was never still, and neither was Gritta, for there was always work to be done.

She glanced across the lane. Her family lived on the bottom floor of a warehouse owned by one of the council members. Once meant for drying hides, the building was so old and unstable that no tanner would risk losing his business in a collapse, so the rent was cheap. Appel, who had long been her closest friend, owned her house outright after her husband died. It leaned crazily over the lane as if trying to be closer to Gritta and whisper a secret. Appel's husband had built it on the canal where the refuse and pollution from his trade would drift downstream and eventually out of the city through a water gate in the wall.

Gritta trotted across the street to her friend's house with Wina still clinging to her dress. Inside, Appel and Efi stood near the vat of hand-flavored brew, their heads bent together in a clandestine conversation.

"Ahem!" Gritta cleared her throat, and the two women jumped. "And look at you two, whispering like cats who have found some cream. Whatever tales you're telling, I want in on it."

"We were just discussing this hand and wondering how long it had sat in the cauldron before Efi discovered it," Appel said calmly. On the table lay the offending appendage, still bloated and now turning gray on Appel's great wooden serving platter. Despite the decay, a large birthmark in the shape of a loaf of bread stood out in stark contrast to the rest of the rotting skin.

"Phew! Long enough, for it is beginning to putrefy. Take it outside and throw it in the canal!"

"Can't," Efi said, wrinkling her nose. "The sheriff says he needs to come and get it as 'evidence.'"

"What does that mean?"

"Don't know. But Appel couldn't convince him otherwise. He went to fetch a friar to say some last rites over it and is returning from the church now."

"Last rites? The owner of this hand might not be dead."

"But you never know, do you?" Efi asked.

"Very well. But finding a hand in our brew doesn't mean that we stop working. We must procure more grain. Efi, you go around to Herr Gilgen for some more barley. Appel, you and I will take the waterskins on the old wagon and fill them from the priory canal. God knows how much this will cost us."

Appel and Efi were quiet, and Gritta looked from one guilty face to another. "What?"

"Well, it can't have done much damage, can it have? The hand? It is intact, and it's not as if I discovered a foot or a head."

"Are you saying that you mean to —"

"Hush now, the sheriff is here!" Appel hissed as the silhouette of the big man darkened her doorway. He walked inside, but instead of a friar from Saint Martin's to say the last rites over the rotting hand, two townsmen armed with cudgels followed him in.

"Greetings, goodwives," the men all mumbled.

The women bowed in response. Appel presented the hand on its plate with the flourish of a squire at a lord's feast. "Here is the hand of evidence that you wish to take, Sire!"

"I no longer need it because a townsman from Vogelgrun recognized the mark upon the thumb," the sheriff said, his face hard. "Gritta Leporteur, I am arresting you for the murder and dismemberment of Gilbert of Sundhoffen, the owner of this hand."

A Franciscan among wolves

In which an argument is resolved with a most unpleasant solution

"And furthermore, Brother Wikerus also took more than his share at the morning meal, and I saw him nodding off to sleep during prayers at Prime two days back. And you know what the Lord our God says about gluttony and sloth."

Brother Tacitus rubbed his parchment-dry hands together as he finished speaking, raised his chin in triumph, and cast a cool gray eye at Friar Wikerus, who stood next to him. Wikerus was not sure how long it had been since Brother Tacitus marched him with a hand on the back of his shorn neck to the chambers of Father Konrad, the prior of Saint Martin's church and spiritual leader of the Dominicans in Colmar. It felt like hours. Through this recitation of his sins, Wikerus kept his hands tucked into the too-long sleeves of his brown habit; his fingers were clasped together tightly so he would not fidget. If Brother Tacitus suspected weakness in Wikerus, he would press further, like a dog at a bone.

The two friars stood before Father Konrad, who, on this day, looked distinctly world-weary as he sat behind his weathered oak table. "Did you take more than your share at the pottage this morning, Brother Wikerus?" he asked, his tone displaying his exasperation.

Wikerus took a breath to speak and then caught himself. His first instinct was to lie, and he hated himself for it. His second instinct was to turn and strike Brother Tacitus across his beak-nosed face, but he felt less remorseful about that. His fingers gripped each other tighter in his woolen tunnel of sleeves.

"I took one dipper of pottage to fill my bowl, as we are instructed, Father Konrad."

Father Konrad began to nod his head, clearly relieved that the matter could be settled easily.

"But…"

The old prior could not manage to stifle his exasperated sigh. Wikerus lowered his large blue eyes to the floor. He was humiliated, but his anger superseded all other feelings. Brother Tacitus had been bullying him for months, and Wikerus intended to call the man's bluff.

"But I did take a heaping dipper of the pottage, Father. And two pieces of boiled turnip instead of one."

Father Konrad opened his mouth to address the two men, but Wikerus continued.

"And I did season my pottage, Father Prior. With spice."

"Spice? Wherever did you get that?"

Wikerus took a deep breath. He must not lie, but he would rather not profess his gluttony in front of Tacitus of all people, who seemed to relish every additional sin.

"I acquired a small twig of cinnamon in Strassburg, Father."

"What were you thinking? Are you a nobleman's first son that you would break your fast in the morning with spices from the east?"

"This is what comes of allowing so many young and untrained brethren into the flock," Brother Tacitus commented, shaking his head. "And was it worth it, I ask you? We servants of God may have required more help during the pestilence, but because the foul affliction was brought about by the sin of man, do we not perpetuate that sin by allowing weak-willed young men into our midst? And a Franciscan besides!"

"You have made your point, Brother Tacitus," Father Konrad interrupted, holding up a hand. "I am sure Brother Wikerus will not commit this gluttony again. And his status as a Franciscan on loan from Breisach does not make him more or less culpable than you or any of the other men inside my walls."

"But the sleeping, Father Prior? I heard him snoring at Prime!"

"Oh, come now, Tacitus. Cast a stone at your fellow brother only if you have never once fallen asleep during the earliest prayers in the morning." He held up his hand again as Brother Tacitus tried to speak. "No more, please! Brother Evart blackened his eye this morning whilst hanging the wet linens on a tree branch, and Brother Humbert insists upon his shaved tonsure that he witnessed the holy spirit settle upon his favorite mule in the stable, and now he stoutly refuses to let anyone else ride the beast. I cannot abide another one of you acting foolish and petty today. Give me a moment's peace!"

Tacitus turned his mouth down into a deep frown, which did his name credit. Wikerus felt his sweaty grip release in his sleeves, and he slowly lowered his hands to his sides and wriggled his clammy fingers.

"Go with God," Father Konrad said, waving an impatient hand at them. "Go!"

Wikerus bowed and hurried out, followed by Tacitus, who stalked from the room with a disdainful sniff. In the hall outside the prior's solar, Tacitus turned to Wikerus and eyed him sourly.

"I have tried to correct your willful ways and poor habits, Brother Wikerus. You should give thanks that I am here to ensure you do not slip too far into sin, though I know that, as a Franciscan, you have a weak will."

"We both serve God, Tacitus – Franciscan and Dominican the same. And it's not a sin to put a little cinnamon in my pottage. Especially since I came by it honestly, using my own means."

"And what means would those be, Brother? You are not supposed to have any worldly possessions that you could trade for a stick of cinnamon. How could you come by such a prize with your ascetic, Franciscan lifestyle?"

Tacitus said the word "Franciscan" as if it were a piece of spoiled meat in his mouth. Wikerus knew that his status as a Franciscan in the Dominican priory had already raised eyebrows. After all, considering the existing rivalry between the two orders – and Wikerus's questionable record of obedience and humility, it would be easy to assume that Wikerus being sent to Colmar by the prior at Breisach was a joke. But among his many faults, Wikerus had a knack for solving difficult questions and for acting as a bridge between the poor and those fortunate enough to give alms, which was precisely what Colmar needed last year when gold and relics began to disappear from the reliquary of Saint Martin's. Although Father Konrad and most of the Dominicans at the priory had been kind and accepting of a Franciscan in their midst, Brother Tacitus seemed to find Wikerus distinctly reprehensible.

But back to the matter of the cinnamon. Wikerus cleared his throat and squared his shoulders. "I did a favor for a friend. He gave me the cinnamon as a gift in return."

"What favor would this be?"

Friar Wikerus clamped his lips shut. He should have kept a tighter rein on his tongue earlier, but his mouth was always getting him in trouble. He forced himself to look Tacitus straight in the eye.

"More secrets, I see. The prior will be made aware that he has a man in his midst who is keeping company with someone in Strassburg." Tacitus's thin lips curled into a smile. "You know, it is not unusual for a woman – or a man – of ill repute to be paid in items other than coin. And we are all aware that there are paying customers in the big cities with all manner of deviant appetites."

This was too much to bear. Wikerus took a step closer to his rival and balled his hands into fists. Brother Tacitus was taller and looked down the length of his narrow nose.

"Say it one more time, Tacitus, and just you see what happens."

Tacitus favored Wikerus with another thin-lipped smile. "I said, Brother Wikerus, that you must have received that cinnamon as payment for —"

For the second time that afternoon, Father Konrad sat at the table in his solar, facing the two sullen friars, his head gripped in a weary hand.

"And here we are again. In less time than it takes me to pray the beads, you have already committed an atrocity inside these walls!"

Before him, Brother Wikerus lowered his gaze in penitence, and Brother Tacitus held his head high despite the bruises. Before Tacitus had time to even finish uttering his insult, Brother Wikerus had landed a good blow to the underside of the man's chin. Sometimes, being shorter carried an advantage.

"Brother Wikerus!" Father Konrad barked at him, and Wikerus jolted his eyes up. Father Konrad's angular face was stormy.

"What have you to say about this? Tacitus here says you started it."

"Indeed, Father Prior. I started it."

"Fighting in the priory!" Father Konrad shouted. "What next? Minstrel shows? Alehouses?"

Wikerus opened his mouth to speak, but Father Konrad held up a warning finger. "No. Don't answer that. I am ashamed of you both."

"He made insinuations about my chastity," Wikerus muttered under his breath.

Father Konrad shot a look at Brother Tacitus, whose expression remained stony.

"That is a serious accusation to level at another man of God, Brother Tacitus. What would make you suspect such a thing?"

"I suspect that he came upon his stick of cinnamon by ill-gotten means, Father Konrad," Tacitus said, his voice wooden. "All I did was ask, with the purest of intentions, for Brother Wikerus to reveal the source of his spice, and he struck me."

Father Konrad turned to Wikerus and sighed heavily. "Ah. I think I understand. Did Father Anselmo of Strassburg give you the cinnamon?"

Wikerus nodded. The movement sent his brains knocking about in his bruised skull, for after Tacitus recovered from the blow Wikerus bestowed, he chose to retaliate in kind.

"Father Anselmo is well intentioned, but his actions have caused this misunderstanding. Brother Tacitus, it is no business of yours where Wikerus received his cinnamon," Father Konrad said.

Brother Tacitus gasped and pointed vaguely toward Les Tanneurs with a long, thin hand. "But he spends most of his time with those immoral ale-women in the tannery district. And you know what the men say in the confessional about that old crone Frau Appel."

Father Konrad slammed his palms upon his desk. "That is enough, Tacitus!"

This was surprising behavior. Father Konrad was known to be severe – sarcastic, even – but never hot-tempered. Wikerus stood perfectly still while the prior took a few heavy breaths to calm himself.

"I can see the two of you are not the best of friends. In truth, I do not require you to be friends with each other, but you must work together. That is why we call ourselves 'Brothers.' Sometimes, the brethren in a holy commune argue among themselves just as brothers of the same earthly mother do, but we must display the forgiveness and tolerance of Christ in all our actions. This manner of bickering and disunion between you two will spread to the others. Quarreling is like a pestilence that kills slowly. Therefore, I am sending you out together. You will work in a pair to minister to the population."

"What?!" Wikerus and Tacitus both said together.

"I feel that this is the right decision. Brother Tacitus, as of late, you have been staying close to the priory and spending all your time in the scriptorium, therefore you will accompany Brother Wikerus as he works in Les Tanneurs, ministering to the poor and the widows. And, Brother Wikerus, you will take on the work that Brother Tacitus does. When you are not in Les Tanneurs, you will be in the scriptorium making copies of the scriptures."

Brother Wikerus cast a baleful eye on Tacitus. He hated copying texts. He could read a fair bit but disliked writing in all its forms. The cramps in his fingers, the pains in his neck and shoulders from hunching over a slanted writing table, and the strain on his eyes were enough to drive him to madness. He would much rather be on his feet out working with the poor than sitting in silence all day with a quill.

He could see by the twisted snarl of disgust on the face of his rival that working in the pungent quarter of Les Tanneurs was equally distasteful to Brother Tacitus.

"Well, now that you both appear to be equally unhappy in your tasks, let us start immediately. Brother Tacitus, please make your way to Les Tanneurs after your prayers tomorrow morning. Wikerus, I expect to see you in the scriptorium copying the sacred texts when I visit after my morning meal. Then, we shall all meet together at the end of the day to discuss your findings. You are both dismissed." Father Konrad stopped to think for a moment. "Please spend the rest of the evening in contemplative silence. You are not to speak until prayers at Prime tomorrow. If you both have your mouths shut, perhaps we will have no more complaints about the two of you for an evening, at least," he muttered.

Brother Tacitus and Brother Wikerus exchanged a look of loathing, marched back into the hall, and went their separate ways. Tacitus stalked toward the dormitory building nearby, but Wikerus made his way into the church. It was late by now, but the candles were still lit, and the nave was warm with their flames and the heat from the bodies of the faithful who stood in silence or knelt near the altar in prayer.

Wikerus found a dark corner and sat on the straw-strewn floor with his back against a cool stone wall. He closed his eyes and breathed deeply. The nave, with its towering ceilings, still smelled faintly of incense from the previous day's service. The straw dampened the sound of people coughing and shuffling or muttering their prayers aloud. It wasn't like his home church in Breisach, which was smaller.

He should feel some longing for his home, but he didn't. Father Guillaume of the Breisach Franciscans had lent Wikerus to Father Konrad in Colmar to assist in the investigation of church treasure that had disappeared from the storerooms of Saint Martin's, and although he had thought the decision mad at the time, Wikerus was grateful. He closed his eyes, breathing in the scent of the lingering incense and the warm, oily smell of bodies. It was a blessing that he left Breisach, but at any time, Father Guillaume could call him back again, or worse, Father Konrad could send him away.

"How can I leave this place?" he whispered into the silence of the room. "I can't return to Breisach." There were too many memories of hunger and sadness in Breisach. Memories of mistakes made. Sometimes, Wikerus felt like the human embodiment of mistakes.

A patron of the church turned at the sound of his whisper, and Brother Wikerus clamped his mouth shut, pulling himself further from the puddles of light cast by the candles. Father Konrad said he was not supposed to speak, and here, he had already broken his promise. Further evidence that he couldn't do anything the right way. Wikerus turned his mind to the challenges of the morrow, and he groaned, causing more heads to turn. This time, he did nothing to hide his outburst.

The evening vow of silence did not bother him, but the thought that Brother Tacitus would be responsible for the spiritual health of the community of Les Tanneurs made a chilly feeling of concern creep down his spine. This could turn out badly for everyone.

The perpetrators

In which Gritta and Jorges embrace their predicament with the grace and charity of two people who have had twelve children together

G RITTA SAT WITH HER arms crossed on a pile of straw in the corner of the small room in the gate tower, her saddle-bagged eyes boring holes into her husband Jorges as he sat across from her. Jorges cleaned his fingernails with his teeth, studiously avoiding his wife's gaze.

"I still don't understand how you ended up with me in this tower." Gritta's voice cut through the silence. "Last I saw of you was your flat backside when you were walking towards Vogelgrun."

"Sheriff took me when I was on my way home, returning to my children and to you, my beloved wife."

Gritta rolled her eyes.

"It's all a misunderstanding, my dove. As soon as we explain the situation to Sheriff Werner, he will see that neither of us was anywhere near Gilbert of bloody Sundhoffen when he died. We'll be freed before Vespers, I am sure of it," Jorges said, flashing her his best gap-toothed grin.

They were sitting in a small, damp room in a tower that flanked one of the city gates. For a time, a thin beam of light penetrated the darkness of the room from a narrow, arrow-slit window, but now the light had faded and been replaced with the cool glow of a full moon. Somewhere in the city, a bell rang out, and Jorges turned his head to listen. It was the evening bell, calling the faithful to Vespers. Jorges shot a glance at Gritta like a cur who had eaten the porridge. Gritta glared back at Jorges, unblinking.

"I don't know what happened to make Sheriff Werner snatch us both into this tower, but one way or another, you are going to tell me why I was implicated in a murder!" She rose to her feet, stabbing an accusatory finger at her husband. "And if we're taken before the council, I will ensure they know that this is solely your fault!"

Jorges threw his arms over his head and cowered. "It weren't me, my dove! I swear to you, I never saw Gilbert of Sundhoffen at the docks yesterday, nor his confounded hands, the Devil take them!"

"Well, I never heard of the man in my life! So, unless I removed his hands in my sleep, it couldn't have been me, could it?!"

They were interrupted by sharp banging on the wooden door of their prison. "Shut up!" the guard shouted. "I have to go home to my own woman after my duties, and this tower is the only place free from her nagging tongue."

"I pity your wife for being yoked to a man who keeps innocent goodwives locked in a tower!" Gritta screamed back.

There was a scuffle and a scraping sound as the guard hefted the bar away from the door and yanked it open.

"Jorges, control your woman!"

"Never could, and neither can anyone else, I assure you," Jorges said with a chuckle. He leaned back against the cold wall of the tower and folded his arms across his skinny chest.

Gritta threw herself into the pile of straw. At least it was fresh and not crawling with vermin. For a moment, she reminded herself that she could have been worse off. She would stand trial before the council, and they probably wouldn't hang a woman. Probably. She buried her face in the straw a little further, breathing in its sweet, dusty scent, and wondered why the council would want to execute anyone at all, considering how many had been lost in the Great Pestilence only a few years earlier. There were hardly enough people left in Colmar who were willing or able to plant and harvest the fields, and the price of food had gone sky-high.

The guard had slammed the door, barring it behind him, and Jorges slouched toward the arrow-slit window, trying in vain to push his head through.

"Gritta, I just don't think we're going to be able to escape this way."

Gritta groaned and flopped onto her back in the crackling straw. Jorges was not terribly clever, nor was he a good provider or an attentive father. And one of his ears was distinctly lower than the other. And his breath smelled bad. She wondered, as she had wondered for twenty years, why she remained married to him. In truth, she had been in love once when Lisette, her eldest, was conceived. Jorges was handsome back then – a tanned, strapping porter at the docks with a head of dark wavy hair and his own mule. But as the years passed, younger men like the ill-fated Gilbert of Sundhoffen took work as porters. Other men moved on to higher paying and less strenuous labor, but not Jorges. The day-long walk home from Vogelgrun provided him with ample time to finish a jar of wine before he arrived back in Colmar, at which point he relinquished the rest of his coins to Gritta.

She heard a snuffling in the dark as Jorges felt his way over to her on his hands and knees, eventually laying his head in her lap. She stroked his thinning hair and looked out the window at the narrow rectangle of starry sky.

"Jorges," she whispered, "you didn't kill this man Gilbert, did you?"

Jorges lifted his head, obviously affronted. "I ain't no killer. I'm a lot of things, Gritta, but I ain't no killer."

"No," she sighed. "It's true. You're not a killer. So, if you didn't do it, then who did, and why did we catch the blame?"

Jorges rolled over, and she could see a glint where the starlight reflected off his dark brown eyes. "Dunno, but this could be our last night together, and I would hate to leave this world a virgin."

"Jorges, whatever are you talking about? You stopped being a virgin when you were thirteen years old."

"A virgin of this night."

"I don't want any more babies, Jorges. Twelve is quite enough."

"Won't matter if they hang us."

Gritta gave it some thought. "Right you are," she said.

Jorges grinned.

Outside the door, the guard stuffed his fingers in his ears and wished himself back in his own home.

"Gritta! Gritta dear, wake up!"

Gritta blinked the grit of sleep from her eyes and opened them reluctantly. Next to her, Jorges snored, his arms wrapped around her waist. Appel's gently wrinkled face peered down at her in the dawn light. Efi stood nearby, her uncovered hair a halo of blonde curls around her head. Gritta sat up and felt the stickiness of her mouth after a night of slack-jawed sleep.

"Girls, what are you doing here?"

Appel jerked her thumb over her shoulder toward the door. "He was easy to bribe. A pint of my nice strong red ale put him in good spirits quickly enough."

"It worked on the sheriff, too!" Efi chirped.

Gritta's limbs were stiff from lying in the lumpy straw. She slid Jorges' arms off her and rose to her feet, picking fragments of fodder from her loose hair.

"Here, Frau Gritta, allow me to help you with that!" Efi sprang forward, withdrawing a small wooden comb from the bosom of her dress.

"Vanity will be your downfall, Efi," Appel said dryly. "Gritta, tell us everything. What happened? Why under the heavens did the sheriff arrest you, and how is Jorges also ensnared in this mess?"

Gritta told them everything. Admittedly, it wasn't much. When she was finished, Appel and Efi sat silent and still next to her in the straw. Jorges still had not stirred.

"And you have never heard of this Gilbert before he didn't show up for his work at the docks? Did he work alongside Jorges?"

"Indeed, they both lifted crates and baskets from the ships at Vogelgrun since the beginning of the winter, although Jorges insists that he did not even see Gilbert at the docks of Vogelgrun this week. The man may have been working in Breisach or elsewhere. I do not even know which day Gilbert went missing from his work, and I begin to suspect that the sheriff doesn't either."

"Do we know anything about him? I have certainly never heard of Gilbert Sundhoffen before."

"Gilbert of Sundhoffen," Gritta corrected her. That is why you never heard of the man. He wasn't from these parts."

"Is there anything else that you know of him?"

"Nothing at all. Jorges!" Gritta elbowed her sleeping husband, and he snorted loudly, blinking at the wood-beamed ceiling of the room. "Know you anything else of this man Gilbert of Sundhoffen?"

Jorges snatched at his hair as if to remove his cap, but upon finding none there, he dipped his head from where he lay. "Greetings, goodwives. I wasn't expecting to fall asleep next to one angel and wake to two more. Ow!"

Gritta slapped him on the stomach, and he leapt to his feet. "Gilbert was a boor and a nuisance! Always bragging of his conquests and cheating at dice. There were none in Vogelgrun who liked the man, young and comely as he was. Anyone would have taken a swipe at him, given the right opportunity, for he owed money to almost everyone at the docks and never repaid them!"

"But why you, Jorges? Why did they think that you, and not someone else, killed Gilbert? Did he owe you money, too?" Appel asked, and next to her, Gritta narrowed her eyes.

At this moment, their disgruntled guard tapped on the door with the butt of his sword and wrenched the bar up. "Alright, that's enough. Appel, Efi, get out of this tower before someone catches you here."

Efi squeezed Gritta's hand for reassurance, but Appel grasped her friend and neighbor by the back of her head and whispered into her ear.

"We will find out what happened, Gritta, make no mistake. And whoever truly did this will dangle from the gallows, not you."

"Thank you, my dearest friend," Gritta whispered back.

The scriptorium gang
In which we learn that Friar Wikerus has poor penmanship

"Excellent, Brother Tacitus. As always, your work is superb. A true example for us all!"

Brother Isembard, who had the run of the scriptorium in Saint Martin's priory, dragged a liver-spotted hand along the crisp sheet of vellum at Tacitus's desk. Tacitus smiled his most learned, serene smile.

"Your praise is appreciated, Brother Isembard...and most accurate, for I have excelled at copying manuscripts since my youth." He shot a sly look toward Brother Wikerus, hunched over a wobbly writing table in the corner. "My father provided an excellent tutor for my brothers and me when I was just a boy."

Wikerus knew the comment was directed at him – an orphaned child, penniless and forgotten. The kind that seeks out the church more for a bed and regular meals than for the pursuit of learning or for God. He drew in a deep breath to calm himself. It was early afternoon on his first day doing penance in the scriptorium for fighting with Brother Tacitus, and Wikerus was feeling flummoxed and embarrassed. The room was uncommonly hot because it contained glass-paned windows, the kind that let in heat and light but no cool draft. The smell of ten men sweating in their dark wool robes was decidedly musky. He straightened and felt the bones in his back and neck crackling as they rearranged themselves into some semblance of a spine.

Brother Isembard's knees creaked as he shuffled around the room, his hands clasped behind his back, peeking over the shoulders of the friars and commenting or giving direction. The man was as old and dry as the parchment that he worshiped.

"Oh no, this will never do, Brother Wikerus. Your writing looks like a child's at school!"

"Well, Brother, I never had much practice at writing when I was a child, so it stands to reason..." Wikerus stopped speaking when it was clear that his attempt at making a joke was going over the old friar's head. He cleared his throat. "I shall endeavor to try again, Brother Isembard."

Brother Isembard thought for a moment. "Perhaps you would be of more use in the kitchens, Brother Wikerus?"

A gentle snort of laughter erupted from the side of the room where Tacitus sat with his cronies – a short, narrow-eyed friar with no hair on his head and a young, handsome monk on loan from the abbey at Basel. Wikerus seethed.

"Well, I am no good at cooking, Brother Isembard."

"And what skills has the Lord gifted you with, Brother Wikerus?"

The old friar was staring hard at him, and the whole room had gone more silent, if that were even possible. Wikerus swallowed hard. He wished to be anywhere but here in this moment. Right away, he was back in his uncle's smithy as a small child, feeling the shame of not being considered worthy of a trade – another mouth to feed, who would soon be tossed out, along with his brother. But he had put that life behind him. It was time to move on.

"Well, I —" he began, but the wide sleeve of his rough brown robe caught the dish of ink at his table, and it overturned, spreading a glistening black pool across the vellum and dribbling onto the floor.

"Oh, by the Virgin's —!" Brother Isembard quickly stopped himself before he shouted out something truly blasphemous. He drew in a deep breath. "That is a whole vellum leaf ruined. Young man, you shall apply to the kitchens for a bowl of milk, and then you shall soak, scrub, and scrape these leaves yourself until the stains disappear. After that, you shall begin again. In my scriptorium, nothing is wasted!" The man whirled, his black robes swinging around his ankles, and stalked to another part of the room to sulk.

Wikerus felt bowed down by shame. His usual disposition was cheerful. He was always the first to laugh and had the quickest smile of all the brothers. But sometimes, his baby-faced expression of peace hid a sort of despair. All his life, he had never felt genuinely skilled at any kind of work.

He wiped his table clean with a few fistfuls of straw, then took the soiled vellum to the kitchen and sat heavily on a three-legged stool near the oven.

Parsnips and other tubers sat on large stones around the perimeter of the oven's great mouth, glistening with oil, their skins beginning to sizzle and blacken. The cooks, both brothers and laypeople from the community, worked in relative quiet, each focused on their task. Not only would their efforts feed the friars of Saint Martin's, but they would also provide meals for travelers who sheltered in the long dormitories provided by the Dominicans. Any remaining food would be distributed to the poor. All of this was an expensive undertaking of labor and money, but each man and woman in the kitchen knew their task, and they completed their work with practiced efficiency until they flowed around each other. Wikerus loved to sit in the kitchens and watch the dance unfold.

Someone sat next to him on a stack of firewood, and Wikerus jumped. He was so entranced by the choreographed movements of the kitchen workers that he didn't notice Hans, the baker, enter with a tray of loaves. Hans wiped a sweating brow with the sleeve of his tunic and sighed.

"Well then, Friar Wikerus. I see you are also taking your ease in this insufferable heat."

Wikerus looked at his lap. The bowl of milk was balanced between his knees, turning a rather pleasant shade of blue from the ink that slowly lifted from the vellum. He pressed the thick material under the milk.

"Not taking my ease, Hans Bäcker, but enjoying myself as I watch these good people do the lord's work in such a pleasing fashion. They are true proficients."

"Pro-what?"

"It is a word that means they are experienced and skilled in their work – much like you at baking. Since you supply much of the city with your baking, and I am told you never burn a loaf, I will also call you a proficient baker." Wikerus smiled kindly, and Hans glowed with the compliment. He gave Wikerus a good-natured jab on the shoulder, which set the bowl of milk sloshing. Wikerus could feel the lukewarm blue milk soaking into his robe, but he stifled his dismay so the baker wouldn't feel embarrassed. His clothing would stink by the day's end.

"I always liked you, lad. Don't much believe what they say about you in the weinstube when the men are in their cups. You're just fine, in my opinion."

Wikerus opened his mouth to ask precisely what the men said in the weinstube, but Hans had already leapt to his feet and was joking gregariously with the head cook.

The door to the kitchen slammed open, and a surprised hush descended on the hive of activity. Brother Tacitus slowly descended the three steps from the courtyard into the room, his back as straight as a soldier's pike.

"Brother Wikerus," he said, his lip curling in his angular face. "I am to accompany you on your rounds in Les Tanneurs tomorrow."

Finally, something to smile about. Wikerus grinned and dipped his head. "I shall be glad to introduce you to those I feel to be the finest citizens of Colmar," he said, his eyes twinkling. Tacitus turned and walked stiffly from the room. Wikerus heard a long whistle behind him.

"Wonder how far the stick goes up his arse before it comes out the other end?"

The kitchen staff tittered quietly but didn't dare laugh out loud. Hans Bäcker could say such things because he was a layman who worked in the town, but everyone else knew that the bony fingers of Brother Tacitus extended far in the priory.

Hans turned to Wikerus. "You goin' to Les Tanneurs tomorrow, then?"

Wikerus nodded.

"Give my regards to the fair Efi, will you? Now that she no longer has that harpy, Gritta Leporteur, standing guard, I might have another chance at her if you get my meaning." He winked and swaggered from the kitchen, his wooden baking tray tucked under his arm.

Wikerus blinked. *Efi no longer has Gritta guarding her?* he thought. *Where has Gritta gone?*

The time to act

In which the gossips descend upon rumors of scandal

Efi sulked and dragged a twig broom across the packed earthen floor of Appel's house. Nearby, Appel slowly poured a jug of new ale through a skein of linen and into a clean tun to filter out the remnants of grains, herbs, and stray insects before she would cover it and put it away to ferment for a few days. Efi cast an annoyed glance at the older woman. Appel's serene expression insulted her.

"Appel, this is unjust. We cannot allow Frau Gritta to stay in that horrid tower a day longer than she must, especially not in the company of her repulsive husband!" Efi stamped her foot, but Appel was not in the least bit startled.

"I rather think it will be good for Gritta and Jorges to spend some time locked in a room together."

Efi wrinkled her perfectly shaped nose and snorted her disagreement. "Surely not. Frau Gritta is wise and discerning, and Jorges is...is..."

"An oaf?"

"Aye, an oaf! And a drunk, and a coward, and a fool!"

"But Gritta has borne twelve children by him, and what does that tell you?"

"That he forces himself on her."

"Ha!" Appel unleashed an unusually crass peal of laughter. "I would like to see some man try to force his way on Gritta. He will find himself with a piece of crockery broken over his skull."

It was a balmy evening, and Appel had her door propped open to let a fresh breeze blow the stale winter smell from her house. So, it was noticeable when a figure stood on the threshold and blotted out what little light of the day remained.

"Get on! Get out of here! Appel, I wish you would control your patrons," an irritated voice called out. Frau Ditmer, a woman of about thirty years, with the smooth skin and colorful clothing of someone who didn't live entirely inside Les Tanneurs, breezed through the door. Appel looked past her neighbor and saw several disgruntled men holding their clay mugs and standing in her dooryard.

"Ah, I forgot to remove the branch. Such a day it has been." Appel walked outside the door and grasped the limp bundle of barely green willow branches from where they hung on the wooden peg next to the door. A green branch above or near the door signaled to passersby that there was ale to sell, although in the winter – when there was very little green to be had other than pine branches, which required a trek to the hills – Appel was known to hang a twist of brown grapevines interwoven with a bit of red yarn. Appel thought the yarn looked cheery and friendly in the bleak months, but some whispered that it was a spell of protection over her house or some such nonsense.

When she removed the willow sticks, the men protested, and Appel waggled the limp branches at them.

"Quit your groaning. There will be more tomorrow."

The men disappeared into the gloaming, and Appel appraised her uninvited guest. Frau Ditmer was wealthy by Les Tanneurs' standards. She didn't live in the neighborhood – just on the cusp of it and, most importantly, upwind. Her husband, a second-tier cooper in the city, also managed the apprenticeship of Noe, Gritta's middle child. Of course, Gritta had ten middle children, but no one, not even Gritta, could remember their ages, birth order, and, sometimes, their names. Appel dropped the twigs to the floor and nodded in Frau Ditmer's direction.

"Good evening, Marta. What brings you over my threshold? I just sold the last of the strong red ale, but I do have a bit of a fine wheat small ale left if you want to purchase some for your family."

Efi wrinkled her nose, puzzled. Appel had not kept the sarcasm from her voice, and this was unusual. In Efi's mind, Appel represented all that was admirable and good about a woman growing into her crown of gray hair. Rarely uttering a cross word to anyone, Appel's calm and genial temperament balanced Gritta's fiery disposition and made it possible to be in the same room with the two of them. However, if Marta Ditmer noticed Appel's chilly reception, she gave no indication.

"Well, Harald is all a'flutter about the news."

Efi gave a little squeal at this. Frau Ditmer's husband was called Harald, but that had also been the name of Efi's husband, who died a season past. Appel reached over and patted the girl's hand. "It is a common name," she said in a low voice. "You will have to become accustomed to hearing it now and again."

"What was that?" Frau Ditmer yelled, being slightly deaf from a childhood fever.

"I was saying that I cannot imagine what would upset your husband, Frau Ditmer. Surely the barrel-making business is strong these days?"

Frau Ditmer dropped her basket as a means to illustrate her shock.

"Well, of course the barrel-making business is fine! I came here to find out about Gritta! Noe's sister fetched him from the coopery, and I overheard that the sheriff put both his parents into the gatehouse." She leaned forward, lowering her voice. "On an accusation of murder!"

"There is no need to spread rumors, Marta."

"Oh, I assure you, Appel, they are not rumors. News of this has gone around the entire city! I knew that it would happen someday. Frau Gritta is a weak-willed woman. Just look at the number of children she bore!"

Appel stood, and a saccharine smile spread across her mouth but did not reach her eyes.

"It is late, Frau Ditmer. I am sure your family needs you."

"But are you really going to throw me out without telling me what happened?"

"Yes, I really am going to do that."

"Come now, Appel. We are friends!"

Appel stiffened, and Efi's eyes darted wildly between the two women.

"I will not discuss the circumstances of my friend Gritta until I know more. And you, Frau Ditmer, never cared a jot about her in your life until she became a gossip sensation. Nor did anyone else in this town."

Frau Ditmer stood, sniffed, and retrieved her basket. "Well, I must be off. I have a girl minding the children while I take care of my responsibilities, but I must pay her and send her home."

Appel watched the woman as she let herself out the door and vanished into the street, now lit only by the faintest glow of the recently set sun. She turned to Efi, whose eyes were wide.

"Before you ask, Efi, I do not want to explain my friendship with Frau Ditmer to you."

Efi nodded. "Frau Appel, what are we to do? We must prove Gritta's innocence."

"Indeed, Efi. Indeed." Appel tapped her chin for a moment. With the lowering of the light, a breeze arose and blustered through the open door.

"If we do not help them, no one will. We must get to the bottom of their accusation. So, what do we know?"

"We know that a man named Gilbert of Sundhoffen was murdered because only that man had a long dark spot upon his thumb."

Appel nodded. "Aye. We know that the murdered man, Gilbert, was from Sundhoffen, and Gritta says that he was not well-liked amongst his coworkers."

Efi wrinkled her head in thought. "I've never been to Sundhoffen before, have you?"

"No, I haven't," Appel said. "And we know that he worked as a porter at both Vogelgrun and Breisach and was handsome. Such a shame to lose a beautiful man to dismemberment." She clucked her tongue.

"None of those facts are enough to imprison Jorges, and especially not dear Gritta!" Efi said.

"No, indeed. What we do know is not enough. What do we need to know?"

"Perhaps there are others who have long birthmarks upon their thumbs," Efi said tentatively.

"Unlikely."

Efi wrinkled her forehead again. "Very well. We should determine if Gilbert of Sundhoffen had family or if they all died in the pestilence."

"People die for reasons other than the pestilence, Efi," Appel chided, but for a moment, both women fell silent. The Great Pestilence had only faded from their daily lives a few years earlier, and although life was returning to some sort of routine, there was no way to forget the horrors inflicted upon them. The disease ravaged every city and town with an almost incomprehensible appetite for death. It required a moment to find one's bearings and reorient the mind to the present.

"Well, I'm not sure there's any use in knowing if this Gilbert fellow had people or not." Appel turned back to her work, and for a moment, Efi looked at the thin shoulders bunched together, the straggling lock of gray hair that slipped from beneath Appel's bonnet, and the deep, steadying breath that filled the older woman's lungs. Some people hid their pain better than others. Efi laid a hand on her friend's shoulder.

"I am sorry I brought it up."

Appel wiped at her eyes with her sleeve and sniffed loudly. "I do not blame you, my child. Sometimes, though, the grief —" she hiccoughed a small sob "— the grief comes upon you like a bandit. It grabs you by the throat and threatens you. Efi, we are alive by the grace of Jesu Christi and our Lady Mary. We must not allow ourselves to forget our great blessing." She was clutching Efi's hand now. "Live your life, girl, and don't let a single day pass that you do not appreciate." Appel's tears fell freely, and Efi pulled her into a hug.

"I will, Appel. I will live my life to the fullest. But I want Gritta to live, too, and she is in peril. We must act."

Appel set her jug of new ale down and wiped her eyes with the threadbare sleeve of her wool dress. "That we must. And I know where I must go."

"Go?" Efi's eyes widened.

"I must go to Vogelgrun. The answers are there. Whoever this Gilbert of Sundhoffen was, someone in Vogelgrun will have known him."

Appel's excellent adventure

In which Appel reunites with an old friend

Unlike Gritta, who had never ventured further from Colmar than Ribeauvillé, Appel had gone on a pilgrimage or two in her past – once to visit the birthplace of Saint Odile near Barr, and once she undertook the long journey to Conques to pay homage to the golden statue of Sainte-Foy. She would have completed her pilgrimage had her daughter not been born only a day's walk from Colmar. She considered herself worldly, but there was a vast difference between traveling with a group of shoeless pilgrims who were zealous with wine and holy vigor, and the task she was about to attempt to help free her friend Gritta. Vogelgrun, a bustling river port town, was an entirely different matter.

The morning she set off on her journey, she stepped outside and was surprised to find Efi dressed in a wool cloak and bonnet for traveling, with a bit of bread and hard cheese wrapped in a kerchief and a walking stick at her side. The young woman's cheeks were rosy, and her clear blue eyes twinkled with anticipation. It was just dawn, and no one was in the streets yet except a few snoring drunks in the hedgerows and a cart driver urging a drowsy ox down Trench Lane. Josse, the new night watchman, ambled past and tipped his hat, but Appel only narrowed her eyes in return. She distrusted night watchmen.

"Oh no you don't, Efi. You will stay here in Colmar to mind the brew and Gritta's children while I am away."

"I shall not," Efi said. "You need a traveling companion, and I need to find a husband who wasn't born or raised in Les Tanneurs. There are no eligible men here, so I shall try my luck in Vogelgrun."

"While the brew sours and we lose profit? While Gritta's babes cry out for food?"

"Rosmunda is perfectly capable of minding the children."

"Who's that?"

Efi growled and stomped a dainty foot. "Rosmunda is Gritta's daughter. One of the older ones. Honestly, Appel. I think you are growing forgetful in your advanced years."

"I have a mind to slap you, girl! You shall stay here while I investigate in Vogelgrun, and I will hear nothing more on the matter from you."

"But —"

"I will hear no argument from you!" Now it was Appel's turn to stomp her foot. Across the lane, the shutters of three houses flew open, and the faces of their neighbors appeared in the windows, their eyes alight with vicious anticipation. Entertainment was difficult to find in Les Tanneurs, and two women arguing in the street would do in a pinch. The sleepy ox and cart had finally made it to the end of the lane, and the driver, Herr Fuhrmann, gave a low command to the beast. The empty wine barrels tied into the cart bumped hollowly against one another as he rolled to a stop.

"Well there, Frau Appel. Are you ready, then?"

Appel nodded, snatching the kerchief of bread and cheese from Efi's hand before she grasped Herr Fuhrmann's hand and stepped into the cart. With a terse command to the ox, the cart lurched forward, and they were on their way, leaving Efi fuming – and without her dinner – in the middle of Trench Lane.

Appel felt a little guilty. Efi could do with a change of scenery. But the ale needed tending, and unleashing the girl into a port town full of rivermen was a recipe for disaster.

Herr Fuhrmann turned to Appel and flashed his most beguiling gap-toothed grin.

"How about a tickle, then?"

Vogelgrun was a muddy town; its streets choked with two-wheeled carts, painted wains pulled by ponderously slow oxen, porters with baskets and bundles on their shoulders, and stalls set up alongside the main thoroughfare, each occupied by vendors shouting over each other.

"Money-changing here! Money-changing and scribe services!"

"Mountainous transport! I shall find you a caravan of good Christian men at a price you can afford! Find a way through the Vosges in security!"

"Guards! Armed men to watch your goods for you – overnight and on the road!"

Appel did not relish the thought of stepping from the wagon into the mire of the street, but her ride with Herr Fuhrmann was far from tolerable, and so as soon as she spied a relatively dry piece of ground, she asked him to pull the wagon aside and let her down.

"Here then, old girl. Did I upset you?"

Appel straightened her wimple and adjusted her shawl on her shoulders. "One mile of listening to you talk about your recipe for veal sausages is well enough, Herr Fuhrmann. But an entire day of it is simply rude. Good day to you."

She stomped away before he had a chance to respond. Somewhere in Vogelgrun lived her childhood friend Margitte – if she'd survived the pestilence, that is. Margitte had married a prosperous young man who ran a warehouse on the ground floor of his large home, and Appel would be well pleased to stay there instead of an inn. After some inquiry, she found the house of someone named "Margitte the Witch" – a three-level affair of rotting wattle and daub at the south end of the town and only a short distance from the river. Appel rapped loudly on the door and, receiving no answer, set her shoulder against it and pushed her way in.

The lower floor of the warehouse should have been crowded with baskets, parcels, crates, and stacks of goods waiting for transport along the trade routes, but instead, the room was empty, the dirt floor bare, and cobwebs veiled the rafters. A hole had been cut in the ceiling at the back of the room, and a rough ladder led to a higher floor.

"Intolerable," Appel huffed. She stalked out the door and around the house, smiling when she found what she was looking for – a crumbling but serviceable staircase clinging to an outer wall. This was much more civilized.

"Margitte?" Appel called out at the door. "'Tis I, Appel Schneider of Colmar, your friend from many years ago! We were maidens together!"

She heard the scrape of a chair across the wooden planks of the floor, a slow, uneven footfall, and a struggle to lift the bar from the door. It opened a crack, and a face peered out.

"Appel?" The voice that belonged to the face sounded old and wheezy.

"Margitte, my dear! Do you remember me?"

The door opened wider, and Appel got a good look at her former bosom friend. Margitte had not aged well. Already quite short, she was now bent over with a hunched spine and a pronounced tremor in her limbs. Her cratered skin bore the scars and wrinkles of an episode of pox many years ago. Her uncovered hair hung like lank gray ropes, matted and unwashed. Appel's revulsion at the sight of the old woman was immediately replaced by compassion. Her childhood friend had clearly suffered in the years since they last met.

Margitte squinted, reached out a shaking hand, and pulled Appel closer. "Let me get a look at you. My eyesight isn't good. Well, now, you have aged terribly, Appel! I hardly recognize you."

Appel held her tongue and laughed lightly. "Ill looks come for us all eventually, and we wear our wrinkles and snowy hair with pride and wisdom." She smiled, but the wrinkles on Appel's face were around her eyes and mouth from years of laughing and loving. The lines on Margitte's face emphasized bitterness and suspicion. "It is good to see you, Margitte," she said.

Margitte just stared. Appel cleared her throat. This was all very awkward and uncomfortable.

"I am in Vogelgrun for a few days on business, and I would prefer to stay with a good Christian woman rather than at an inn. I immediately thought of you, my friend. Could I trouble you to let me sleep under your roof for a few nights?" Appel said with a smile, all the while thinking to herself that the very notion that she even had to ask for hospitality was atrocious.

Margitte nodded and pulled the door open, waving Appel into a dim room, sparsely furnished, with more dusty cobwebs spanning the rafters of the ceiling like banners at a banquet. A few embers glowed in a hearth in the corner. The house was large and had once been grand but had now clearly fallen into disrepair.

"You can sleep on the mattress with me. I'll have a boy fetch some fresh straw." Margitte pulled a piece of copper from the small drawstring purse that hung from her girdle, but Appel stopped her.

"Allow me to pay for it, Margitte."

Margitte shrugged, hobbled to her seat by the open window, and sat heavily. Appel waited for a beat, but since it seemed that the conversation was over, she set out to find some fresh straw for her bed that evening while unease prickled in the back of her mind. She wasn't sure what she expected, but a minor show of hospitality would have been nice to see. If any of her neighbors received her in their home in Colmar she would have been welcomed with a small dish of wine or some bread with good butter.

"Hm!" she grumbled as she navigated the streets of the unfamiliar town. "Well, there is no excuse for bad manners. This muddy town has addled Margitte's brains."

Ahead of her, a boy drove a herd of sheep to the slaughterhouse, their braying loud enough to drown out the voice of God Himself. She strolled behind the herd until she located a towering, wooden haybarn on the edge of town and inquired within. She decided on some fine golden straw for sleeping, some coarser fodder to cover the floors, and a few bundles of rosemary that she hoped would combat the musty scent of Margitte's house. When she had paid the proprietor and told him the delivery address, he paled and handed her coins back.

"I don't deal with no witches, Madame, and neither should you."

"Whatever are you talking about? Margitte of Vogelgrun is no more a witch than I am a horse in your stable."

The hay seller looked left and right, lowering his voice. "Pestilence got Margitte's whole family, and she had it too. Turned all black about the throat an' everything, just like they all do before they die. But she still lives! Tell me, how is that possible? No one survives the pestilence, and you know it as well as I. She's a witch, I'm telling you."

Appel's skin prickled. She had once heard a tale of another person who had come close to death with the pestilence and survived. She thought it had been rumors and hearsay. Those who never contracted the disease often wondered if they were blessed or cursed, but someone who survived, well, that was the work of the Devil for sure. No matter what the priests and bishops said, there was no evidence that God could save a person from the pestilence.

"Witches do not know how to survive the pestilence any more than holy men or kings," she stammered.

"Oh? And how would you know what witches can and cannot do, eh?"

"I know what my eyes tell me, and I saw many men and women of my hometown accused of witchcraft who died in agony, as well as priests and Jews who not only died of pestilence but of murder by their neighbors. Now, will you sell me straw for my bed or not?"

The hay seller stuck out his chin, ready for a fight, but a third voice interrupted.

"Oh, just sell the woman some bedding, Steppen! If her coin is solid, what do you care where she sleeps?" A tall man sauntered into the barn. He was well dressed, with dark brown hair that grayed slightly at the temples. His deep brown eyes crinkled at the edges when he smiled.

"I ain't taking money from no witch," Steppen grumbled. "If hers is the last hand to touch it, that evil will rub off on me!"

The newcomer turned to Appel and held out his hand. "Madame, will you allow me to purchase one cartload of straw and these bundles of rosemary on your behalf from my friend Steppen, here?"

Speechless, Appel handed her coins over, and the stranger turned to Steppen.

"I would like to purchase a cartload of straw and three bundles of rosemary, please."

Steppen grumbled but took the money, then waved the two of them off as he turned and disappeared into the back of the barn to find a boy to deliver the goods. The stranger turned to Appel, his dark eyes sparkling with amusement.

"It was a pleasure doing business with you."

"And what is your name, good sir?"

"Heinrik of Strassburg, Madame," he said, bowing elaborately. "I am a merchant and often here on business. Steppen and I are old friends."

Appel flashed her most demure smile, conscious suddenly of the crookedness of her teeth and the grayness of her hair.

"Well, I thank you, good sir, for your help. I am only here in Vogelgrun for a few days, but if you ever find yourself in Colmar, please inquire after Appel Schneider in Les Tanneurs, and I should be happy to receive you with a good meal in thanks for your kindness."

Heinrik of Strassburg bowed again, winked at her, and strode away on long, well-shaped legs. Appel felt her own legs growing weak. The men of Colmar were familiar, often rude, and sometimes quite smelly, but this Heinrik of Strassburg carried himself with self-assurance and a whiff of lavender oil. She was intrigued. Steppen returned, and his nasal voice pulled her back to reality.

"Alright then, you have your straw. Now go back to your witch friend, and don't tell anyone where you bought it."

A chilly nod was all Steppen deserved from her. Appel marched back to Margitte's house, where she found the woman sitting in the same place and posture as when she had left. Appel put her hands on her hips. This was most tiresome. She was here to learn more about Gilbert, the man whose hand was in her ale, not to become entangled in a witch conspiracy. She looked around the large, empty room.

Aside from the sagging bed frame with its straw-stuffed mattress, there wasn't much furniture other than the chair Margitte sat upon. One table with a broken leg was propped up on a small pile of kindling. An iron pot sat near the fire, crusted with dried pottage. A few articles of clothing were strewn about on the floor. Even overworked and underappreciated Gritta didn't keep her house in such disarray. Appel clapped her hands loudly, and Margitte startled from her place near the window.

"Alright, Margitte. On your feet. I am hungry from my journey, and you look as if you haven't eaten in days."

Margitte rose slowly from where she sat, and Appel couldn't tell if the cracking and creaking she heard came from the dilapidated chair or the woman's joints. Margitte hobbled to a shelf and felt around until she found a heel of bread, green and fluffy with decay.

"What in God's name is this?" Appel said. "Margitte, have you nothing to eat in your house?"

"Lad used to live here with me. Never paid me his lodging fees when I asked, but he did go out and fetch bread and wine," Margitte said in her papery voice. Appel narrowed her eyes.

"Where is this young man now?"

Margitte shrugged. "Went out a few days ago. Never came back."

"What was his name, Margitte?"

"Curse his name! I never liked him. He stole from me, he did. Told everyone I was a witch!" Margitte seemed to come to life with this little outburst of anger.

Appel was quickly losing patience with her old friend. Whoever Margitte of Vogelgrun had become, she bore no resemblance to the light-hearted young woman she had played with in her youth.

"Have you no people here in Vogelgrun? No family?"

"Pah! Family is dead, and this town has no friendly faces. Did my neighbors help me when my husband died? Did they give me grain when I was starving? No, I haven't any 'people,' as you call them. Never could call them friends."

With a sinking heart, Appel realized that she knew the answers to her questions, which Margitte's bitterness prevented her from saying outright. The troublesome young man who disappeared without paying his rents was most certainly Gilbert of Sundhoffen, and Margitte's family all deceased. She wanted to know more, but it would take time to extract the information locked away in the old woman's tortured mind. Appel knew what she had to do, and she didn't want to do it. "Well, Margitte," she said. "When I leave here in two days, I am taking you with me. You're coming home to Colmar."

Cat and mouse

In which Les Tanneurs meets Brother Tacitus

E**fi Kleven had always** known what she wanted in her life, and for a while, she had it. Back in her hometown of Kleve, her father had been not a wealthy man, but neither was he poor. Papa had enough money from his wool business to ensure that the births of his children were recorded – even those of his three daughters. Efi knew that she had lived for nineteen years already, and that was more than either Gritta or Appel could say, for those two could only guess at their ages.

"Oh, Papa…" she sighed, and she wiped the starchy remnants of the day's pottage from the last of Gritta's carved wooden bowls and put it away in a cupboard. Other than the large trestle table with its two long benches and the three-legged stool where Gritta did her spinning by the fire, the cupboard, with its carved wooden doors set on iron hinges, was the only piece of actual furniture in the house.

It was a spacious room, built many years earlier to cure the finished hides from a now-defunct leather tannery, with a wooden partition separating the animals from the rest of the family during winter. Right now, only a pregnant nanny goat was in the house, resting quietly in the straw while she waited to give birth. Gritta's large family did not have stuffed mattresses or raised pallets; there were simply too many people who needed a bed to sleep in at night. Everyone found space on piles of straw covered with thick wool blankets, like a nest of kittens. Efi found it quite sweet. She and her two sisters had shared a bit of straw at the foot of her brother's cot in the house where she grew up. Although she and Appel shared a bed on the top floor of the house, she missed having the warmth of many other bodies at night.

The youngest of Gritta's children, little Wina, was just starting to toddle about the house on chubby legs. The child stumbled across the room and caught herself in Efi's skirt.

"Ma," the girl said and pointed a finger in a vague direction. "Mau!"

Efi smiled and picked her up. "Ah, are you trying to call me 'Mama'? Your mama isn't here, poor darling." She felt the tears prickle behind her eyes when she thought of her friend Gritta, locked away in a tower with the odious Jorges. Wina pointed again and said louder. "Maaaau!"

Efi felt a nudge at her ankle and looked down. Appel's striped ginger cat was there, playing with Efi's skirts. She felt something plop onto the top of her foot and then the tickle of little claws.

"Eeeeeeeee!" she screamed. A battered mouse staggered a few steps before Appel's cat pounced again. Efi snatched a twig broom and stabbed at the dirt floor with it.

"Get out! Get out!"

She looked at her arms, only then realizing she had dropped the baby onto the table. Wina giggled and stomped her bare feet on the tabletop. "Maaaaaauuu!"

"Of course." Efi's voice shook. "You said 'mouse,' not 'ma ma.'"

Appel's cat purred now, weaving in between Efi's ankles. She wrinkled her nose.

"Oh, go away, you...you...bringer of pestilence!" For everyone knew that cats were responsible for the spread of the horrible affliction that was responsible for the deaths of nearly half the citizens of Colmar.

Efi chose to ignore the chatter about Appel from the other goodwives of Les Tanneurs. Some said she was a prostitute. Efi snorted. She slept in the same bed with Appel every night, and the woman never had company. What Efi knew that the neighbors didn't was that Appel took a very long walk each evening, and when she arrived home, her eyes bright and cheeks flushed from the exercise, she had a quick wash, and then the two women would lie next to each other on the one large platform with the straw-stuffed mattress, talk of their day, and then fall asleep. If Appel were up to any kind of lascivious behavior, Efi would know.

But there were the other rumors, that Appel was a witch, and Efi denied those with a bit less force. She didn't put stock in the gossip about things that Appel had done in her youth. What was in the past, was in the past. But the fact that Appel insisted on keeping a cat, even though everyone knew that cats were responsible for spreading the pestilence, well, that gave Efi pause. She had even brought it up a few weeks ago, but Appel snorted and waved Efi's concerns away.

"Cats are no more responsible for killing half of Colmar than the Jews."

When Appel saw Efi hesitate, she followed up quickly, shaking a finger in Efi's face. "It weren't Jews, neither! Burned all of 'em in this city, and what did that accomplish? The pestilence didn't stop killing folks, and hundreds of souls needlessly died just because we were afraid. Now leave my cat to do his job, otherwise we will be overrun with rats."

As far as Efi could tell, Appel's cat was one of the few who still lived in a home in Colmar, the rest having fled to the fields or hollowed out their homes in the thatch of the rooftops where they could escape the murderous touch of humans. He was petite for a tomcat, but without the modifying force of other felines around town to take care of the rodent population, Appel's cat had as much food as he could stomach, and this afternoon, he was in a sharing mood.

Efi wasn't entirely sure if cats brought the pestilence or not, but she would rather be safe than dead.

"Get out! Get back to Appel's house where you belong, you fiend!"

She swiped at the cat with her broom, and he hissed, arching his back at her. Near the toe of her shoe, the little mouse lay panting. Efi picked it up by the tail and went to toss it out the window, but she saw Friar Wikerus walking up Trench Lane with a stern-looking friar at his side. Looking around wildly, she opened Gritta's cupboard, flung the mouse inside, and slammed it shut again. Friar Wikerus tapped on the lintel of the door and poked his face into the house.

"Greetings, alewives! Oh, hello, Efi. I stopped at Appel's house first, but no one was in."

Efi curtseyed and pulled her dingy white wimple over her head.

"Good day, Friar. Frau Appel is out visiting, but she shall return tomorrow, and I am here tending to Gritta's house and children while she is...indisposed." She couldn't bear to utter the word 'imprisoned.'

The other friar snorted loudly. "Yes, I have heard all about Frau Appel's so-called 'visits.'"

The pleasant features of Friar Wikerus scrunched into an irritated scowl, and he shot the man a reprimanding look. "Frau Efi, Brother Tacitus here will accompany me for a few days as I minister to the community. I know you will show him the same kindness you have shown me."

Tacitus was strolling around the large, shabby room, his thin hands clasped behind his back. He paused at the pile of flattened straw where the family slept.

"I already know about your work, Frau Efi. It is true that you live with Frau Appel now that your husband has died?"

Efi's eyes clouded for a moment as she blinked back her tears. "Yes, sir, I did move in with Appel after I lost my Harald."

"And do you know where she goes every day on her visits?"

"She is a kind soul, Friar Tacitus. I believe she visits the widows in Les Tanneurs. Those who have lost their families from the pestilence."

"Mmm. I am sure she must spend time with the widowers who lost their wives, as well, doesn't she?"

Wikerus cleared his throat. "Well then, I am here to introduce Brother Tacitus to the neighborhood." He shot Tacitus another scathing look. "And to inquire if there is anything you need."

"And also," Tacitus interjected, "I expect to see you at services and at your confession this week."

Efi nodded. The two men stood and looked at her, and for a moment, no one spoke. Wikerus cleared his throat again.

"And where, uh...where is Frau Gritta today, Efi? I am surprised you are keeping her house while she and the children are away."

"Oh, Friar Wikerus, we need your help! Sheriff Werner took her away and locked her up in the gate tower!"

"Locked her up? But why?"

Tacitus, who had taken a seat at the table, snorted loudly. "Doubtless she was arrested for her irascible language, or for her uncontrolled childbearing." He looked around the room. "Where are all those children, anyhow?"

"Out and about. Rosmunda took the three youngest to the marshes to search for catkins. They taste very fine when cooked in a pot with a bit of lard."

"Efi," Wikerus said gently. "What happened to Gritta?"

Efi huffed, sat down with her face in her hands, and told the whole story as she knew it. Wikerus listened carefully, his brow furrowed.

"A hand taken from a dead man! I can see no way that Gritta could be implicated in something so foul. Not even Jorges. Honestly, I just don't think Jorges could do it."

"Couldn't stay sober long enough to do it, you mean," Tacitus said. "Wikerus, let us continue on our way. I am hot and thirsty, and the morning grows stale."

"Indeed, we have many more in Les Tanneurs to greet this morning, but I can help you with your thirst, for if there is one thing that is always in ready supply here, it is a fine, crisp ale to refresh you."

"I hope it is not ale that has been made with a man's severed arm," Tacitus remarked as Wikerus reached for the cupboard where he knew that Gritta kept a jug or two of ale for household consumption.

Efi's eyes widened. "No, don't!" she screamed, but Wikerus already had the cupboard door open, and the battered little mouse tumbled out and staggered on unsteady legs into the center of the room.

Tacitus leapt to his feet with an ear-shattering scream. Snatching up the hem of his robe, he dashed toward the door but did not notice Appel's ginger cat, who, spying his missing prey, tried to dart between the friar's legs. Leaping about the room, Tacitus stepped on the cat, which let out an unholy yowl. Efi and Wikerus watched in horror as Tacitus tripped and crashed against a barrel of new ale, which toppled and broke open, sending a wave of golden liquid across the floor and out the front door.

"What in the name of the Devil's ice-cold teats is going on in here?!" A man's voice yelled from outside the house.

Efi staggered to the door, her skirts heavy and wet with ale. Behind her, Wikerus was helping Tacitus to his feet. The older friar was sputtering with outrage. "That animal tried to kill me. Wikerus, did you see it? That cat was sent from hell! Where is it? I shall roast it on a spit!"

Efi turned back to the man at the door. "Pardon us, good sir. We're just brewing. Why are you here, if you please? As you can see, I have no ale to sell today, as most of it is soaking into the ground."

"I came to inquire if Frau Appel was at home, but her house was empty and the door wide open, so I came to ask here instead. I met her in Vogelgrun, and she told me to visit should I ever come to Colmar."

"Appel has not returned yet from Vogelgrun," Efi said with another curtsey, and she noted that the man was tall and handsome, with a blush of gray at his dark temples. She felt her cheeks flushing with heat, and she tilted her chin down demurely.

"Well, I am only passing through on my way to Ribeauvillé. Are you her friend? Will you please tell her that Heinrik of Strassburg came to call upon her? I shall try again if I am ever in your fair city again."

"By the eyelashes of Saint Paul, I shall kill that creature!" Tacitus screeched from inside the house, and Efi blushed again.

"That is quite a foul-mouthed fellow you have there, miss. It's no way to speak in front of a fair young woman."

He winked at her, and Efi blushed harder.

"Until next time," Heinrik said, and as he strode away from the house and hopped over the ditch that gave Trench Lane its name, Efi watched the muscles in his back moving underneath his leather jerkin and felt a few lusty thoughts rise to the surface of her mind.

Wikerus had helped Tacitus to his feet, brushed the mud from his robes, and was leading the furious friar away by the elbow.

"Good day to you, Frau Efi. Give my regards to Appel." He leaned in closer and whispered in her ear. "And thank you for the entertainment! Send for me when Appel returns, and we shall discuss how to free Gritta and, hopefully, Jorges, too."

The lost dowry

In which a new visitor to Les Tanneurs causes havoc

IT WAS A COLD, gray day when Appel returned to her house on Trench Lane. Efi had just finished carrying water from the priory to Les Tanneurs and settled in to relax and listen to the mice in the rafters and the sounds of the street outside. She lay on the pallet that she and Appel shared on the upper level of the house, reveling in the rare moment of solitude.

It was never quiet in Les Tanneurs. The sounds of children playing and fighting with each other, animals braying, or the slap-slap-slap of the tanners as they rinsed and threshed the hides in the canal were always in one's ears. In the morning, the roosters screeched, and in the night, the dogs barked. Efi wouldn't have it any other way, especially now that she was a widow. She drank in the noises of daily life. Although she had only lived in Colmar for a few years, and although her husband had died and left her a widow, this was her home.

"Efi? Where are you, you daft girl?" She heard Appel's muffled voice calling her from downstairs, and she jumped up and ran down the steps that clung to the side of the house. She flung herself through the front door and crushed Appel in a tight embrace.

"You're back! And none too soon, for I have so much to tell you!"

Appel disentangled herself from Efi's arms and scowled at her.

"Well, now, and just look at the state of you! Walking about with your head uncovered in the middle of the day! And where are my workers? Why is the hearth not finished? I came home hoping for a roaring fire and a bowl of soup, but all I see is rubble and an empty cooking pot."

Efi hung her head. "No one will come near the house, Appel. Not since the news of the hand began to spread. No one will buy ale from us, either."

Appel muttered some choice words under her breath and set her parcels on the floor. Efi noticed another woman standing in the doorway. She was short and wrinkled, with a face like an onion left in the cellar for too long. She was so stooped that the front of her threadbare dress was ragged from dragging against the ground.

"Efi, this is Margitte. She shall be staying with us for..." Appel glanced back at the woman, who stared straight ahead, mouth agape like a gargoyle. "She'll be staying with us for a while. I am not sure how long. Margitte knew the owner of the hand you found in our mash, and I brought her here to help us. She might have some information that could free Gritta from her tower." She lowered her voice and leaned forward to whisper in Efi's ear. "She ain't in her right mind, poor thing. I feared for her, living alone in a place like Vogelgrun."

Efi looked at the woman again. Her posture and expression had not changed. "I hope your friend will not make things worse for us than they already are, Appel. No one will buy ale from us, and we lost one of our fermenting tuns when Friar Tacitus destroyed it."

"Friar Tacitus did what?" Appel exclaimed. "Come on, girl, you had better tell me everything."

Appel had soundly scolded Efi for destroying the mash tun and sent her off to find Gritta's son, Noe, who was apprenticed to the cooper, to have another one made. There was just enough coin stashed away from ale sales that they could afford it, but Appel knew that there would be no more money for grain. Pushing these worries aside, she marched to the stonemason's workshop and demanded to know why her hearth was still unfinished.

"We're brewing in Frau Gritta's house until you complete the work on my hearth, and it is a situation I would prefer to stop as soon as possible, for her hearth is little more than a circle of stones and a hole in the ceiling."

The head mason looked at Appel sourly. "I don't do business with murderers and women who do witchin'. Find someone else to complete your hearth."

"And who, I might ask, has murdered in my household? There is nothing to prove that Gritta killed a man. She isn't even strong enough!"

"Could have poisoned him with your ale. Poison is how women kill."

"Poison is how women are killed, is what you mean! All the people in Colmar who died of murder in my lifetime were done away with at the hands of men. And how do I know it ain't you or one of your ox-headed workers who killed that man and put him in my brew?"

The stonemason crossed his arms over a broad, sweat-stained chest. "Words like that could have you placed in the pillory, you old hag. Go on then, try and accuse me or my men. See what happens to you and your whole filthy operation!"

Appel shook a finger in the man's face. "I ought to warm your buttocks with a willow switch like I did for your mother when you were a little boy! You will not receive a single coin from me until my hearth is finished and working properly!"

The stonemason snorted. "Off with you then. I heard from Herr Schlock that you've let another witch move into your house, and she's even battier than you." He pulled on a leather cord that encircled his thick neck. A small rock dangled from it. "I have protection against your spells. This stone came from Jerusalem, carried from the hill of Gethsemane by the pilgrim who sold it to me. It is from where Jesu Christi died upon his cross, and it has been doused with his holy blood. Nothing can harm me, not even you!"

Appel looked skeptically at the stone. It was orangey-pink sandstone with a subtle glint of sparkling mica, just like all the other stones in Colmar.

"I would expect a stonemason, of all people, to recognize rocks from his own hometown," she said. "How would Herr Schlock know anything about the guest who has come to stay at my house? She has not yet been here for one full day."

"And enough fuss she has already created. The whole city is talking about her."

This was concerning. Why would Margitte be a topic of gossip when she had only just arrived? And she, a daughter of Colmar, who had spent her youth in Les Tanneurs. Appel flounced from the stonemason's shop without another word and headed straight home.

As soon as she returned to Trench Lane, Appel noticed something amiss. Faces peered at her from their windows, and heads drew closer together to whisper into ears. The gossip around her was so palpable that she could practically smell it over the stench of the tanning pits. Down near the square at the far end of the lane, a crowd of people had gathered outside her house. Appel forgot propriety, and her steps quickened into a trot, her mind racing with fear that something terrible might have befallen Efi. When she drew closer, she heard a man's voice shouting as if preaching a sermon.

"And, good people of Les Tanneurs, the Lord God does not wish for these women to fall into sin and slovenly behavior! An unmarried woman who will not commit herself to chastity and the service of the Lord in a convent should marry when she is still of age because if she will not, her idle hands will seek out the worst kinds of work, and you know what kind of activities the womanly sex is drawn to, do you not?"

Heads nodded, and a few voices raised in agreement.

"That's right! Giving their bodies over to tempt men. Married men! Joining forces with the very Devil himself to pull innocent, God-fearing men down into the torturous pit of hell with them."

More voices called out their agreement, louder now and angry. Appel pulled her wimple and bonnet closer to her face and pushed her way through the crowd. When she finally saw who was speaking, she groaned.

"For too long, this has been allowed to continue. These women, who do not have the skill and strength to take up their dead husbands' trade, have chosen to brew – not just a noble small ale, which gives sustenance and relief after a day of honest work, but strong brews that intoxicate! They brew far beyond what they can use in their own homes, which is the sin of gluttony!"

Friar Tacitus paused and wiped his brow. Despite the spring chill in the air, his shaved pate sparkled with sweat as he stood in the dooryard of Appel's house. He took a deep breath and continued to shout.

"And now, here is the consequence because you, the people of Les Tanneurs, failed to put appropriate pressure on these women. Frau Gritta has killed a man. She, who was once a goodwife, whose only thought was for her family's and husband's well-being, has done this horrible deed. And what happened as soon as Frau Gritta was locked up? They bring in another unmarried woman, clearly a witch, to complete their triumvirate of sin! That woman!" He stabbed a finger toward the house. "She is a known practitioner of devilry in Vogelgrun! I heard of her myself when I was there on my mendicant duties many years ago. And now she is in your city, corrupting your neighborhood!"

The crowd shouted now, full-throated and bloodthirsty. Friar Tacitus nodded along to them, and Appel shoved her way to her front door where the friar stood.

"Go on! Get out of here, every one of you!" she shouted. "If you cast your stones and accusations at me and my friends, then I shall sell my ale to people more worthy than all of you – in Mulhouse!"

The crowd quieted, and Appel cast her disapproving glance across them, meeting the eyes of as many of her neighbors as she could. Then she turned to Friar Tacitus.

"Kindly pack up your altar of fear and condemnation for the day, Friar Tacitus. We have had our fill."

As the people slowly shuffled back to their homes, one figure pushed through them, huffing and sweating. Friar Wikerus had run so hard from Saint Martin's priory to Les Tanneurs that the knot of his hempen rope belt had come undone and was dangling loose around his hips.

"I just heard..." he gasped. "Brother Ignatius just said... Tacitus, you didn't, you didn't denounce the alewives, did you?" He bent over, hands on his knees, and gasped to catch his breath.

"It looks as if you have been spicing your food so heavily with cinnamon that it causes you ill health, Brother Wikerus," Friar Tacitus said with an icy tone.

"I was copying the texts as Father Konrad asked. So much sitting is not good for a man's health. Now, please accompany me back to Saint Martin's and leave this woman in peace." Friar Wikerus squeezed Appel's hand and then turned and followed Tacitus, whose thin, angular frame was fading with the light as he walked away.

Appel pushed her way inside the house. The first thing she saw was Margitte lying on her back on the hard-packed earthen floor.

"Oh no, God, no!" Appel hurried to her friend and dropped to her knees. "I thought they only meant to denounce her. God, don't tell me they have killed her!"

Margitte stirred and farted loudly. Appel straightened up. Her nose wrinkled.

"Don't worry about her, Frau Appel. She's no worse for wear than Jorges Leporteur after a long day in the weinstube." Efi's voice spoke from the semidarkness of the room, and Appel looked around. The young woman was sitting in the shadows with her arms crossed. Appel sniffed carefully over Margitte's open mouth.

"Is she drunk?"

"Sleep-drunk. She is so drunk that I doubt she will remember she proposed marriage to one of Frau Gritta's chickens this afternoon, or that she stole sticks of firewood from Herr Schlock's woodpile, and he threatened to send Sheriff Werner down upon her."

"Why would she need firewood when the hearth is still unfinished?" Appel asked, slowly becoming aware of the faintly acrid smell in the room. In her panic to check on her friend, she hadn't noticed the bluish haze of woodsmoke hanging in the air. Appel looked at the hole where her hearth used to be but saw no evidence of a fire.

"She told me she wanted to light a fire to boil water for a stew." Efi rose to her feet, and now that Appel could see her more clearly, there were obvious signs of scorching on the young woman's dress.

"Oh dear, did she hurt you? Did she hurt someone? What has she done, Efi?"

Efi set her jaw, took a few breaths to calm herself, and then stomped her foot. "She's gone and burned down the privy; that's what she's done!"

For a moment, Appel did not understand. "The privy? To boil a pot of water for soup?"

"Aye! 'Tis made of wood, and since you have no wood stocked at your house while your hearth is in disrepair, your inebriated friend concluded that we wouldn't need the wood that made up the walls of the privy, and so she set it alight and then dragged out our fine iron cauldron for boiling the water when we brew. She filled it with the water I had gathered from the priory, tossed in the last of the turnips, set the privy alight, and the whole thing went up in flames. I arrived just in time to see the smoke drifting in the lane." Efi huffed and sat down again. Then she buried her face in her sooty hands and wept.

"There now, my dear. What a fright you must have had. You must have thought the whole house was burning to ashes and your livelihood with it!" Appel sat beside Efi and put her arm over the girl's shoulders. "It is only a privy. We can use the communal privy near Gritta's house."

"It's not that," Efi sobbed. "I would have found another living situation if the house had burned. But my dowry is gone. Gone!"

Across the room, Margitte snorted loudly, scratched herself, and rolled over. Appel was perplexed. "Efi, there's no need to cry over a burned privy. I shall commission a carpenter to build us a new one. Wait a moment, did you say your dowry is gone?"

Efi couldn't answer. The tears flowed freely from her eyes, and her nose dribbled. Appel offered a square of sacking for the girl to wipe her face.

"What in the name of the Virgin's toes are you talking about?"

Efi snuffled into the sacking and wiped at her nose until it turned bright red. "You see, it was the safest place, the privy. The safest place to keep my coins so that I can tempt a man to marry me."

"Well...this is no trouble at all. We will simply wait until the ashes are cold and retrieve your coins."

But Efi shook her head and would not be consoled. "They were at the bottom of the water bucket that we kept next to the seat in order to clean ourselves. But I forgot, Appel! I picked up the bucket of water and flung it onto the flaming privy to douse the fire, and then what do you think happened? My entire dowry fell into the pit, and after the privy burned, the whole thing collapsed. Everything is ruined!" She wept harder, and Appel sat back, stunned.

"Of all the turnip-headed things you could do, Efi! We need to focus on getting Gritta out of her imprisonment, which might mean paying a bribe to the sheriff, and now you have lost everything because you were too stupid to even ask me if I have a safe place to keep money in this house?"

Efi sniffed and wiped her nose. "Do you have a safe place to keep money?"

"Of course I do! All you had to do was ask!"

Efi cried even harder now – a full-throated wail. Still on the floor, Margitte woke with a snort and stood on wobbly legs.

"I'm off to bed. Tell that young woman to stop making so much noise, will you, Appel? It will ruin my sleep." Then she staggered out the door, and Appel could hear her tripping up the stairs to the second floor.

"Perhaps we shall just sleep down here tonight, Efi," she whispered.

Trials and tribulations
In which Gritta loses faith in her neighbors

It wasn't the first time that the city council had compelled Gritta to attend her own trial, but instead of a small gathering and a quick acquittal, she found herself in the great room of the wine traders' hall, facing a crowd of agitated neighbors. She had only been here once before, as a young child, when an out-of-town merchant paid her a copper to deliver a message to a wine seller in the market. Like that first time, the room was clean, well organized, and smelled of grape must and the thick reek of alcohol. The barrels and casks had all been pushed against the whitewashed walls to make room for the attendees, many of whom were from Les Tanneurs and stood on the earthen floor in their bare feet and scuffed leather slippers.

Gritta glanced at Jorges, who stood next to her in stoic silence. Since their incarceration in the tower, it had been harder for Jorges to acquire strong drink, and a few days of sobriety had changed not only his demeanor but also his appearance. His face, usually dark red and grinning lopsidedly, had returned to its usual pallor. No one who scraped their existence from manuring fields and lifting crates at the docks could ever really grow fat, but the slight paunch that usually clung to Jorges' skinny frame had shrunk, and he almost looked trim and fit. The whites of his eyes were white again.

Gritta looked at all this and felt something she hadn't remembered – a stirring in her gut. A flutter of...attraction? Before she had time to ponder these feelings, Lord Frider, the beleaguered nobleman whose small château crouched on a small hill outside the city, walked to the front of the hall and cleared his throat loudly. When this had no effect, he smacked his hand against the wall behind him, sending the rafters trembling and eliciting a sharp cry from the members of the winemakers' guild. Lord Frider smoothed his iron-gray hair from his forehead and glanced malevolently at the assembled audience. If it were up to him, he would never leave his comfortable estate. He also had a house in town in case an attack or a business deal made it necessary for him to live inside the protection of the city walls. Colmar was a free imperial city, which meant that Lord Frider had very little meaningful authority over the townsfolk. Most of the important matters were managed by the city council. A militia of able-bodied (and not-so-able-bodied) male citizens defended the city, supplemented by the emperor's own troops when necessary. Lord Frider had, or at least felt he had, some authority over the stubborn townsfolk, given his lands, title, and status as a second cousin to the emperor, but most days, he resented this privilege.

"Alright, settle yourselves, all of you!" Lord Frider shouted. The hubbub in the room dimmed, but by no means did it grow silent.

"We are here to determine, as a council of citizens, the circumstances around the murder of..." He paused for a moment, turned to the sheriff, and shrugged. Sheriff Werner jumped to his feet, whispering loudly into Lord Frider's ear.

"Ah yes." Lord Frider cleared his throat and prepared to shout above the din again. "The circumstances around the murder of Gilbert of Sundhoffen!"

At the word murder, the chatter and bawdy laughter finally quieted. Lord Frider waved impatiently, and Sheriff Werner jumped from his seat again, grunting as he climbed atop a large wooden box.

"Here is what happened as I understand it," Sheriff Werner shouted. "Young Frau Efi, the widow of Harald of Kleve, did find a well-poached hand in her mash cauldron as she prepared to brew the day's ale. She was brewing outside, in the dooryard, because Appel's hearth is under repair."

"And how'd a tanner's widow find enough coin to commission a new hearth? That's what I want to know!" a voice called out from the crowd. It was Otbert, the stonemason.

"Be thankful you have a customer, you goat's arse!" Appel shouted back.

"You're no longer a customer of mine, you witch!"

"Silence!" Sheriff Werner shouted. "Let me finish."

"Out with it then, windbag!" a woman from the crowd snarled.

"'Tis nearly time for supper!" another voice yelled.

Sheriff Werner, who seemed ruffled by the ire from the crowd, adjusted his leather girdle more comfortably across his belly. "Frau Gritta, the wife of Jorges Leporteur, was there when Efi discovered the hand, and according to the stonemasons in the house, she registered no shock at seeing such an, ah...ingredient in her ale. Good folk and members of the council, I ask you, would not an innocent woman scream at such a gruesome sight, as Efi did?"

Gritta crossed her arms. "I wouldn't scream. I don't have the same constitution as Efi."

"Oh, and what kind of constitution does young Efi have?"

"A feather-brained constitution."

"Peace, Frau Gritta." Sheriff Werner wagged a finger at her. He turned to address the crowd again. "Now, Gritta probably didn't know Gilbert of Sundhoffen, but Jorges did because they worked together at the docks in Vogelgrun. According to people present on the last night that Gilbert was seen alive, he and Jorges were playing dice, and Jorges lost his day's earnings to Gilbert. However, when he returned to Colmar after his week of work, Jorges went directly to Herr Schlock's weinstube and ordered a jar of wine."

Gritta felt herself grow cold. She leaned close to Jorges. "You told me you hadn't seen Gilbert in days," she whispered. "Why did you lie, you fool?"

"Didn't want you to kill me in that tower before the sheriff had his chance," Jorges whispered back.

"I won't have to kill you," Gritta snarled, gesturing to the sheriff and Lord Frider. "They will do it for me!"

"What kind of wine was it?" Appel asked, and all eyes turned to Herr Schlock.

"My foulest," he replied. "So thick and sour that I have to serve it with a spoon and a bowl."

"And how much does that cost?" Appel demanded.

Her Schlock shrugged his shoulders. "Two copper bits. I am usually pleased to get rid of it. The stuff was so close on to vinegar by the time Jorges bought it that he couldn't even get himself into his normal state of drunkenness."

Sheriff Werner cleared his throat loudly, and the muttering crowd settled again. "It is easy to see what happened. Jorges was enraged after losing his day's salt to Gilbert, so he killed the man after their bout of gambling. Then, he gave the body to his wife to dispose of. Gritta, as I think we can all agree, is the only one of the three alewives who has the stomach to dismember a man."

Around the room, heads nodded knowingly at their neighbors, and Gritta shook with rage.

"It should be obvious by now that Gritta meant to boil the meat from the body and bury the bones later. Her mistake in all of this was in allowing someone else to take control of the mash paddle." And here, Sheriff Werner paused, his small piggy eyes twinkling at his own cleverness. "However, one of the stonemasons heard Gritta scolding Efi that morning for stirring the mash. It is clear that Gritta wanted to keep Efi away from the cauldron so that the foul stew of grain and hand could cook enough for her to hide the bones."

"I scolded her for stirring it too fast, you lumbering dummkopf!" Now Gritta was enraged. "She was ruining the brew. And what does a stonemason know about brewing, anyhow?!"

"Who brought the pot to boil? Who added the grains to the mash to cook it?" Sheriff Werner snapped back.

"I did!" Gritta said. "It is what I always do. I seem to have the knack for getting the measurements just right."

Sheriff Werner leaned in closer to her. "And who was with you, Frau Gritta? Who watched what you did?"

"I, well...no one was with me. Appel had already gone out, and Efi was above stairs, probably rouging her lips or curling her locks."

Sheriff Werner straightened and addressed the crowd. "No one saw Gritta prepare the water and measure the grain." He declared this in a loud voice and squinted at the room. A murmur of voices rose as the people put their heads together and discussed the facts.

"No one saw except Gilbert of Sundhoffen's hand!" Frau Eisner shouted from the crowd, and Gritta shot her a look that could kill.

"Hands can't see, Frau Eisner! And neither can you, else you'd realize your husband has been tupping Hansel the sheepherder all winter!" Gritta screamed.

Frau Eisner's mouth dropped open, and she turned to Herr Eisner, who stood next to his wife, pale with shock. The crowd roared, drowning Sheriff Werner's pleas for calm and quiet. A man called for Gritta to have her hands removed. Another shouted that Gritta ought to be whipped at the post. Someone else said she should be burned. Gritta's eyes darted across the faces of her neighbors and only saw hatred. Standing to the side, Herr Schlock, the weinstube owner, was quiet, his arms crossed, a small smile on his lips.

The crowd surged, and Gritta felt something tug at her dress. It was a woman from the burgher's quarter. "Is my husband next, you filth? Who will you kill next if you go free?"

"I didn't kill anyone!" Gritta said, but the shouts of her neighbors drowned her voice. She turned to look at Jorges. His eyes stared straight ahead in a face white with fear. My God, she thought. They might actually kill us.

Lord Frider climbed to the top of a wine barrel and raised his hands for silence with the gravitas of a priest. When that had no effect on the crowd, who were all talking amongst themselves, he bellowed, "Silence, all of you!"

As soon as he had their attention, he returned to his bored demeanor. "I do not see any evidence that Jorges or Gritta killed this Gilbert of Sundhoffen person," he said.

The crowd erupted into complaints and shaking of fists, but they refrained from surging forward again.

"Shut up!" Lord Frider screamed. "I also do not see evidence that Gritta and Jorges did not commit this vile sin. Since Gilbert is not from Colmar, this trial should not proceed until we can procure a representative from Vogelgrun. The people of that town must be allowed to participate. Someone should ride to Vogelgrun and confer with the council there to see what is to be done. Until then, Gritta and Jorges shall remain locked in the tower, and you all will return to your work, for idle hands are the very origin of sin."

He paused, and his shoulders slumped in resignation. "And I suppose it is I who ought to go to Vogelgrun, damn it all." His warm hearth and fine food would have to wait.

Sheriff Werner dismissed the crowd and ordered Gritta and Jorges back to their tower. The onlookers groaned. For a while, they mingled about, talking amongst themselves, but the work of prepping the fields for planting was long and exhausting in the spring, and the plowing would be waiting for them in the morning. Slowly, they shuffled and pushed their way out of the wine warehouse and to their beds. The day's entertainment was finished. Only one person pushed against the crowd and fought through the throng to Lord Frider and Sheriff Werner. It was Friar Wikerus.

"This will likely involve the church, Lord Frider," he said firmly. "And therefore, I am coming with you."

Brothers will be brothers

In which two friars have not learned their lesson yet

"UNBELIEVABLE. WERE IT NOT for the fact that the report of your antics came from several sources, some of them reliable and some less so, I would have thought the whole thing fabricated by someone intent on ruining your reputation!" Father Konrad's face was purple with outrage.

Standing before him, Brother Wikerus and Brother Tacitus both stared straight ahead, their expressions stoic.

"Lord Frider's steward happened to be passing through Les Tanneurs on an errand for his master, and he described to me a wave of ale 'as tall as from the sea' that swept Brother Tacitus straight out of the house and deposited him in the waste trench!"

"I doubt Lord Frider's steward has ever even seen the sea," Tacitus grumbled.

"Silence!"

Father Konrad's voice was so loud that he had managed to miss the sound of the bell for Vespers, the evening prayers. As the tirade continued, Wikerus began to fidget. When that didn't work, he tentatively raised a finger to stop his prior from speaking.

"What is it, Brother Wikerus?!"

"Pardon, Father Prior, but 'tis the hour for Vespers. We must pray."

A low growl rose from Father Konrad's throat.

Next to Wikerus, Tacitus shifted on his feet; his eyes darted from one man to the other as he calculated the consequences of missing prayers versus missing the tongue-lashing that was bound to be directed at his rival.

"Oh, you can be assured I will not miss prayers. I shall pray at every hour that Jesu Christi may someday relieve me of the responsibility for such ill-behaved and pernicious brothers. Indeed, the both of you are a plague on my sanity!"

Father Konrad stopped himself and took a deep breath. Then he shook his head and sat heavily in his chair. "No. I shall not invoke the title of plague, even on the likes of you two. We have had enough real pestilence to last all of us ten lifetimes. This priory lost seven good men..." His voice faltered, and his eyes grew moist. The two friars standing before him both hung their heads. Some men grew drunk in the alehouses and inns, making dark-humored jokes about the devastating effects of the Great Pestilence, but many still felt they could not speak of the horrors they had seen. Not yet. Perhaps never.

"Father...the prayers at Vespers..."

"Yes, yes," Father Konrad put his head in his hands. "We shall pray. I shall pray for God's wisdom, for I truly do not know how to manage the rivalry between the two of you."

Wikerus and Tacitus bowed shallowly and turned to go, but Father Konrad caught Wikerus with a pinch of his brown robe.

"Brother Wikerus," Father Konrad mumbled. Wikerus observed that the man's face suddenly looked older than his fifty-two years. "I am fond of you, lad. Truly, you have brought only good things to this city. You have managed to form a friendship with some of the most insignificant, some of the most intractable residents of Colmar, especially those in Les Tanneurs. I've found your service there valuable beyond measure. But you must remember that you are a Franciscan among Dominicans, and if you cause too much trouble, there will be little I can do to prevent you from being sent back to Breisach. Unless you wish to return to the town of your birth."

Father Konrad's words hung between them, frozen in the air. A year ago, when Father Guillaume removed Wikerus from his cloistered life in Breisach and commanded him to travel to Colmar, all Wikerus could feel was resentment and apprehension. Those feelings quickly turned to relief. Ghosts of his past haunted him in Breisach – memories of a drowning brother he could not save became voices that constantly asked him why. Hiding from the world had taken the blame for a suspicious death from him, but it also took away his joy. He loved people – talking and laughing, being out among the poor, and trying to ease their burdens. Being cloistered in an abbey was not for him. And so, he embraced his new life in Colmar with all his heart, even though he knew his tenure would be short. At the time, his abbot had told Wikerus that he was being sent to Colmar to live among the Dominicans to help Father Konrad solve the mystery of who was stealing the church's relics and treasures. But lately, he wondered if Father Guillaume had sent Wikerus away to save him from himself.

"I will be good, Father Konrad. I promise I shall."

"You must because there are those in this city who would like to see you return to your home. Some powerful people here do not like that you stand up for the rights of the poor."

"But why?"

"Brother Wikerus!" Tacitus's sharp yell interrupted them. "You will be late for prayers again!"

"I think you know why, my son," Father Konrad said quietly. "Come. Let us pray."

In the dim chapel, the final note of the last song of Vespers rose to the arched ceiling, and the men, standing in two rows facing each other, bowed their heads in individual prayer before turning and shuffling through the nave. Some peeled off to complete various tasks assigned to them, others went to their small, sparsely furnished rooms to continue their prayers, and a few meandered out the doors and into the cool evening outside.

Brother Wikerus made his way to the nearby priory that housed the cloisters, the hospital, and the lodgings for weary travelers. Walking on his toes, he stole inside and made his way to the cloister garden, which was surrounded by an arcade of arched stone. It was dark in the arcade, with only a few oil lamps flickering to light the way. In the dancing shadows, his eyes rested on the rich colors of the murals painted on the walls. He knew of a stone bench in the darkest corner of the arcade, where he wished to sit and think.

Placing a hand on the wall to steady himself, he groped for the bench, but instead of finding the smooth, worn sandstone, his hand brushed against flesh and fabric.

"I beg your pardon!" a man's voice snarled. Wikerus was so surprised that he stepped, and then fell, backward.

"Who is that? Why are you out here at night?"

Wikerus groaned inwardly. The voice belonged to Tacitus. "I might ask you the same thing, Brother," he said, climbing to his feet and rubbing his bruised buttocks.

"I am contemplating the mysteries of God and the guiding hand of his discipline and justice," Tacitus responded.

Wikerus snorted. "I think you would do well to contemplate his mercy and Jesu Christi's devotion to the poor. Why did you join the Dominican Order if you do not wish to serve those in need?"

From the darkness, Tacitus sighed. "Right now, I am the one in need, Brother Wikerus. In need of silence."

"Very well." Wikerus turned to go, but his mind prickled with that old feeling, that wickedness that he knew would manifest some way or another. He was about to do something terrible, and he was helpless to stop himself. "You do not need to be ashamed, Brother Tacitus, if you had to join the Order because you had no inheritance from your father."

It was a wicked thing to say. Wicked and cruel. Moreover, Wikerus had joined the Franciscans for that very reason when he and his younger brother found themselves orphaned as boys. He regretted his words immediately. He turned to apologize to Brother Tacitus but was shoved backward with such force that he tumbled over the low wall that separated the arcade from the plants of the garden and found himself lying on his back in the dark for the second time that night. The sound of retreating footsteps clicked on the stone. Before he could think clearly about his action, Wikerus had scooped up a handful of the thick, sticky mud from a recent spring rain and launched it at the dimly outlined silhouette of Brother Tacitus.

Tacitus gasped. Over their heads, the clouds were beginning to thin and part, and as the bright face of a round, full moon revealed itself, Tacitus could see Wikerus still sitting on the soft, wet ground. With a yell, the older friar charged. Wikerus darted out his foot and managed to kick Tacitus off his feet. Then, with the glee of an errant child, Wikerus took a handful of muck and smeared it on Tacitus's face. Tacitus responded by heaping two great scoops of mud atop Wikerus's head, covering his shaved tonsure.

"Well, now you look a little more handsome!" Tacitus snarled.

"Enough!" a voice shouted, and the wavering flame of a torch bobbed toward them from the cloister. "In the name of God, stop what you are doing at once!"

More torches and oil lamps approached, and the two men sat up, dazed and ashamed of themselves. Both their faces were smeared brown, and Tacitus had bits of grass and weeds stuck to his robe. A novice brother reached them first, flooding the area with light from his torch. Father Konrad followed close behind.

"Well," Father Konrad said. "I thought I would find someone tussling with a thief who was trying again to steal our gold, but I see now that someone has stolen your senses instead!" He reached out and slapped each man on the back of his muddy head.

"Brother Wikerus started it, and he should return to Breisach immediately," Tacitus declared, somehow managing to look cold and arrogant even in his filthy state.

Father Konrad's eyes narrowed, but he ignored the older friar's comment. "Brother Wikerus, you asked for permission to accompany Lord Frider and Sheriff Werner to Vogelgrun to investigate the death of one of their citizens..."

"Yes, Father." Wikerus spoke to the wet ground. He couldn't bring himself to look up.

Father Konrad's lips curled upward, but it was not a comforting sort of smile.

"I've been considering the matter," he said. "Your request is granted."

The journey
In which Friar Wikerus gleans some important information

Friar Wikerus trudged along the rutted, winding road from Colmar to Vogelgrun, setting one foot in front of the other and focusing on each step as a meditation on God to distract himself from his misery. Next to him, Brother Tacitus took a deep breath and continued his soliloquy. Having spent the first mile from Colmar preaching about the sin of gluttony, his favorite topic, he now professed that the wrath of God for man's sins was responsible for the Great Pestilence.

"And furthermore, I do believe that this town in particular suffered from the scourge of the pestilence because of our compulsion to eat pork sausages," Brother Tacitus intoned. He paused a beat, waiting for Wikerus to acknowledge him.

"And why are pork sausages such a great evil, Brother Tacitus?"

"They coat the stomach with temptations of the sweet meat, and it causes men to want to eat more than their fill. It was gluttony, Brother Wikerus." Tacitus cast a pointed glance at the round belly beneath Wikerus's robe and rope belt.

Wikerus ground his teeth and wished he was eating a pork sausage instead of walking to Vogelgrun in his rival's company.

"Ah yes, we've come around to gluttony again," Friar Wikerus said.

When Wikerus first asked for permission to travel, Father Konrad expressed reluctance, but when his two most stubborn and hot-tempered friars demonstrated that they still required discipline, the old prior granted the request on the condition that Tacitus accompany him. It was to be a final point in their punishment for fighting in the priory, but Wikerus thought it might be the thing that finally killed him. For his part, Tacitus was not keen on the idea of leaving Colmar for any reason. It had been years since he traveled the roads as a mendicant friar, but when he realized he had a captive audience, he took it upon himself to pontificate.

Lord Frider had accompanied them for a time, riding astride his horse with a clenched jaw, but when he realized that Tacitus would most likely continue the sermon for the entire trip, he dug his heels into the flanks of his mount and trotted ahead, humming to himself and smiling with relief.

"Brother? Brother Wikerus, did you hear me? I asked you a question."

Wikerus gave Tacitus a withering look. "Please repeat the question, Brother Tacitus."

"I asked your thoughts on the state of Frau Appel's mortal soul, considering all that we know about her."

"Frau Appel is a pious parishioner and a kind woman who cares for those in her community."

"Hmph. Well, I wish she would cease caring for the members of other communities. Margitte, that woman she brought back from Vogelgrun, is certainly a witch."

"Perhaps, Brother Tacitus. But without evidence, I will not accuse Appel's guest of witchcraft or any other sin. Ah, look, I can see the river ahead." Wikerus didn't hide the relief from his voice. "We had best approach Vogelgrun in silence and temerity. Do you not agree, Brother Tacitus?"

Tacitus was not finished with his speech, but he nodded, and they walked on in silence. Ahead of them, a veil of mist hovered over the dark ribbon of the Rhine. Foot and wagon traffic on the road increased as they approached Vogelgrun. Wikerus walked a little higher on his toes, trying in vain to see over the tops of the trees with their vibrant green haze of spring buds. Somewhere on the other side of the river rose the bluffs of Breisach, his hometown.

When they reached the gate of Vogelgrun, Tacitus was in a full pout, sparing only a few terse words for the guards.

Lord Frider waited for them just inside the town gate, leaning against the wall of a crude, open-air weinstube and sipping from a cup. "Well then, let us get on with this and try to be home by dark. I have no desire to stable my horse here overnight, and I imagine you men will want to be back by Vespers."

Tacitus held his chin high and glanced down the prodigious length of his nose at the town, which bustled with activity and commerce. Wikerus, by contrast, wore a large smile, and his eyes took everything in. It wasn't his first time in Vogelgrun, but it had been a few years. Across the vast green water of the Rhine, he could see the church steeple of Breisach. From this distance, it looked like a peaceful place.

"Now, where does that vile little sheriff live again?" Lord Frider muttered. He slammed his cup on a rickety table and left the weinstube without paying, walking several paces ahead of the two friars. When they arrived at the sheriff's house, the sounds of raucous cheers and protestations erupted from inside.

"Ho, Sheriff Vogel!" Lord Frider called out as he pushed through the doorway uninvited. Inside, three men sat on barrels in the main room, tossing stones and bones. The sheriff, a thin man with a purple blush to his florid cheeks, stood watching the gambling. He swayed slightly, and his breath radiated fumes of stale wine. At the sight of three strangers, his eyes widened briefly, then narrowed with malice.

"And who are you, fancy man?"

Lord Frider straightened and pulled in his paunch. "I am a lord of Colmar, and I am here to inquire about the murder of Gilbert of Sundhoffen. You are aware that a man of yours was murdered in my city, yes?"

The sheriff waved the comment away. "Ah, yes. Someone finally did young Gilbert in. Only a matter of time, I suppose."

"And why is that?" Wikerus asked, earning himself a scandalized glare from Tacitus.

"The man was a scourge and a rogue. Don't know anyone who liked Gilbert, do you, boys?" Sheriff Vogel turned to the other men in the room, and they responded with enthusiastic nods.

"Owed money all over the place, he did!" one man said.

"Didn't do much to help his neighbors in Vogelgrun, neither."

The other men of Vogelgrun all grunted in the affirmative. Wikerus dragged a three-legged stool to the circle of barrels and sat down, resting his chin on his hands.

"What do you mean when you say he didn't help his neighbors?"

"Well, he barely lived here, really. Spent all his time either at the docks or roaming. Spent a lot of time in Colmar, that's for sure."

Lord Frider frowned, and Friar Wikerus leaned forward. "By his description, I don't recall seeing him in Colmar. Are you sure that is where he went? Perhaps he lied."

A younger man with a round, genial face and a mop of dark hair stood. "I traveled with him to Colmar more than once when I had business for my master, who sells white wine. He was in your city, I saw, sure as sheep's shit."

Sheriff Vogel elbowed the young man in the ribs, and he bowed slightly, mumbling. "Begging your pardon, m'lord."

"Where did he go when he was in Colmar? Did he have friends there, or family?" Wikerus felt he was on the cusp of solving the unanswered question about the young man's death, and apparently, so did Tacitus and Lord Frider because they both leaned forward too. But the young man shrugged and took a swig from his cup.

"Don't know. We always parted ways just after passing through the gate, and Gilbert usually traveled back alone, as I did not wish to stay the night in Colmar."

Wikerus looked at Sheriff Vogel, perplexed.

"Lukas here has a new wife and no motivation to stay in any bed other than hers."

Behind them, Tacitus sighed heavily and raised his eyes heavenward in an expression of pleading to God for patience.

"Well," Wikerus said quickly, "where did Gilbert sleep when he was here in Vogelgrun? I think it would benefit this investigation if we could speak with his family."

"Gilbert didn't have no family here. They all lived in Sundhoffen, and then they all died of pestilence. He came here seeking work," the sheriff said. "But if you're looking for his landlady, you had best go home, for she left town for Colmar just a few days ago and hasn't been back since. The house is empty."

At this, Tacitus perked up and looked closely at the sheriff. "What is his landlady's name?"

The sheriff cleared his throat, and the rest of the men suddenly looked uncomfortable.

"Margitte, the witch of Vogelgrun."

A rare meal

In which Margitte does little to win people's affection

WITH NO HEARTH AND now no privy, Appel and Efi moved into Gritta's house with the nine children who still lived there, dragging a reluctant and complaining Margitte along with them. Gritta's house was smaller than Appel's, with unplastered walls on the interior, and the upper floor was occupied by another family. With twelve souls inside the walls, including Appel, Efi, and Margitte, it was necessary to take shifts at meals because there were not enough spoons, knives, and seats to go around at the table. Appel was accustomed to sleeping on a large, raised bedstead with a straw-stuffed mattress, but Gritta, Jorges, and the children slept on a mound of straw between rough wool blankets, their shared body heat keeping them warm at night.

Appel had known all of this, of course, but knowing a thing and experiencing a thing were very different.

Every morning, Appel and Efi rose before the children and groaned as they stretched the stiffness from their limbs after a night of sleeping on lumpy straw. The groaning and cracking of bones usually woke Wina, who was a light sleeper. While Efi took Wina into the privy to make her morning water, Appel shuffled to the small, blackened hearth, which was hardly more than a firepit and a stoned hole in the side of the wall, and poked at the sleeping embers with a twig until she could elicit a feeble flame. Efi would return and nudge the other children awake, giving terse orders for some to fetch water and others to feed the animals. It was always Lonel – Gritta's sixth-born son and aspiring wastrel – and Margitte, who did not rouse in the mornings. Both snored loudly, and no amount of shouting and shoving could wake them.

With the warming weather, most of the animals no longer slept in their winter space behind the half-partition, but Gritta's pregnant nanny goat remained inside, her belly so swollen it nearly dragged on the ground. Having a kid goat would mean milk for the family and possibly some meat or extra income if they could sell the animal. Appel and Efi understood how important it was to treat the mother goat gently, to ensure that she had the freshest food and that someone was around when she gave birth in case of complications.

Efi gave Lonel a powerful kick in the shins until he snorted and sat up. Bits of straw stuck out crazily from his lank hair, and he blinked with bleary confusion.

"How'd I get back here?"

"Your sister, Rosmunda, found you sleeping in the trench. Be glad it just rained and the horse dung was not too deep."

Efi was referring, of course, to the shallow trench that ran the length of Trench Lane. In the finer parts of town, streets were named for saints and kings, but the people of Les Tanneurs were practical, and naming the lane for the waste-removing trench was fine with them.

Lonel pulled a face, wrinkling his nose and running his hands along his filthy tunic. "The trench? How did I end up in the trench?"

"I am sure I do not know, and I do not want to know, Lonel Leporteur. But your stench was so foul that none but old Margitte would share a bed with you. I think her sense of smell left with her wits."

"You're not one to talk about being witless," Lonel muttered. "I once saw you hold a conversation with my ma's cloak for as long as it takes a pot to boil until you realized you were holding forth with a garment."

Efi sniffed and tilted her finely shaped nose to the air. "It was dark in the house that day, and as it hung on the wall, it looked like one of your sisters. Anyone else would have made the same mistake."

"No one else would have made that mistake, Frau Efi."

"Hush boy, and don't talk so to your elders," Appel interrupted, giving Lonel a gentle slap on the back of his sleep-tousled head as she walked by. Although everyone acknowledged Lonel as a scourge to the neighborhood and a useless helper around the house, she had a spot of affection for him. Only a few months ago, the two of them saved his mother and Efi from the clutches of a foul murderer who was killing the poor women of Colmar. Although one could argue that Lonel had been partially responsible for Gritta's brush with death, his guilt and penitence afterward redeemed him in the eyes of the community.

Appel glanced down at the hand she'd used to smack the boy and squinted. Her palm was coated lightly in fine, whitish dust. She looked at Lonel and noticed some more dust on his shoulders. Yes, the boy was usually in a filthy state. He was a discredit to Gritta, who might be careworn but was always clean and kept the younger children scrubbed and brushed to the best of her abilities.

"Well then!" Appel addressed the room loudly. Most of the children were all in states of bathing, dressing, or laying out trenchers on the table for the morning meal. "It is a fine day today, and since there's little to do with the ale while it rests, let us all venture outside the walls to hunt for asparagus."

The younger children cheered, for Appel had made foraging sound like such fun! But the older ones – Noe, Margaret, Lonel, Rosmunda, and Urbe – furtively edged their way to the door. Efi darted to it first, blocking their escape.

"Food," she said to them. "We need to find food, or else you all will starve. Now fetch your baskets, and let's go."

"But what about her?" Urbe asked, pointing to the flattened pile of straw where Margitte still snored loudly.

"She is an old woman," Appel declared. "She can stay home if she wants to stay home."

The waning sun cast long shadows across the lane when Appel, Efi, and most of Gritta's children trudged home. Anstett and Mattheus giggled as they skipped ahead, taking turns swinging a long black snake by its tail and occasionally making forays back to the group to taunt Rosmunda with it until she screamed. Lonel had disappeared as soon as they entered the forest, much to the irritation of his older brother Urbe. Noe, who was apprenticed to the cooper, was not required to go, although a day in the warm spring sunshine sounded more enticing than fetching water and stoking fires at the cooper's workshop all day.

Their baskets were loaded with vegetables and greens foraged from the verge near the river Lauch – the tender roots of new catkins, spring garlic, a few wild shoots of asparagus, and herbs that Appel identified for use in the brew.

"Catmint! Now, this is most fortunate that I discovered these growing, Efi, because I may be able to subvert the gruit if I can find the right plants," she said, her face glowing with excitement. Gruit, the carefully curated blend of herbs that all brewsters were required to purchase and use, was heavily taxed by city officials.

Efi knit her brow. "But, Appel, it would be sinful to make our own gruit instead of paying for it by the regular means, would it not? That would be stealing."

Appel felt the joy leave her face as a deep flush rose to her cheeks. In truth, the lines between sin and necessity had blurred after the Great Pestilence. Sometimes a person had to commit a little wickedness or else starve.

They passed through the city gates, nodding curtly to the guards and each looking up at the darkened arrow-slit window of the gate tower, hoping to catch a glimpse of Gritta. Wina, who sat atop her brother Urbe's shoulders, squirmed and kicked her feet against his chest. "Mama!" the child cried out, reaching a small, plump hand toward the tower as they passed. "Want Mama!"

A sun-weathered hand clutched at the lip of the narrow window, and Gritta's face and a few stray locks of graying blonde hair drifted out.

"My babies!" she yelled, and all activity in the gate yard stopped. Gritta thrust an arm through the window, the ledge filthy and crusted with bird droppings. She reached as far as she could, as if she could will her arm to stretch down to the street and touch the faces of her children. Looking at it, the hand waving and grasping from the tower, Appel felt a chill crawl down her spine. This wasn't the first disembodied hand she had seen lately. As Gritta's hand waved and clawed above her, she considered the irony that this innocent woman had been falsely accused of severing the same appendage.

At the sound of their mother's voice, all of Gritta's children began to wail while the merchants, farmers, soldiers, and goodwives in the square looked uncomfortably at the toes of their leather shoes. Efi crossed her arms and glared at each onlooker in turn. Spying an empty hay wagon, she stomped to it, pushed the startled hay seller aside, and climbed into the wagon's bed.

"You!" she yelled at the gathering crowd. "Listen to this woman's children as they cry for her! All of you were at the wine market when Sheriff Werner and Lord Frider determined, with no proof of guilt, that Gritta should remain locked up. Now look at what you are doing – creating twelve orphans."

One of the city's many drunks, his face covered in grime, swayed to his feet and stabbed a finger at Efi. "If Gritta kept her legs crossed, we wouldn't have twelve orphans!"

Efi grew blind with fury. Hopping from the hay wagon, she ran to the man, who trotted away in a crooked line, trying to escape.

"I shall show you how a woman removes a hand from its owner!" she screamed, not realizing that two of the guards had grabbed her until they lifted her from her feet. The men began to drag Efi toward the tower, and Appel panicked. Horses were nickering and raising their hooves. The people of the gate yard clustered around the walls to watch the spectacle, their eyes glistening with malicious joy. The loud, uncultured women of Les Tanneurs were always good for a bit of entertainment.

"Where are you taking her?" Appel asked, and when she received no answer, she grabbed the sleeve of one uniformed man. "Jan-Peter, I changed your shit rags when you were a lad, and I know what you have down there!" She looked pointedly at his legs, and Jan-Peter blushed. "It would be a shame for others to know, too!"

Jan-Peter gave his companion a reluctant nod, and they both released Efi's arms. "Weren't gonna hurt her or nothing," he grumbled. "Just scare her a bit."

"I think you have scared enough people for one day!" Appel snarled. "Now be gone before my tongue forgets itself and blurts out your secret." She turned to Efi, who shook with fear and anger, her fists balled at her sides. "Come now, girl, let's get you back to Gritta's house and lay you down to rest your brains."

"What was it?" Efi whispered in a trembling voice. "Jan-Peter's secret? Is his twig malformed?"

Appel shrugged her shoulders and led Efi by the hand toward Trench Lane, with Gritta's sniffling children trudging behind her, single-file, like ducklings.

"How should I know? He seemed a perfectly normal-looking boy when I changed his nappies, with all of his appropriate parts."

"But why...?" Efi began, and Appel winked at her.

"Every man has made up his mind that he's not as good down there as he could be, and as long as you assume that about all of them, you don't need to know the specifics."

They had arrived in front of Gritta's shabby house, and the children spread out about the dooryard. Efi sniffed the air. Instead of the familiar smell of the tanning pits, a rich, savory draught drifted on a spring breeze. It smelled unfamiliar to Les

Tanneurs, although it was familiar enough up the hill in the finer parts of the city.

"Appel, something smells delicious. Indeed, something smells like meat. Oh, I haven't tasted meat in a fortnight at least!"

Appel narrowed her eyes. The smell was coming from Gritta's house. Rosmunda ran inside and immediately began to scream.

"Oh my God," Appel said. "Margitte!" She ran through the door with Efi on her heels, expecting to see a sight even more horrible than what they had found in her ale cauldron.

Margitte hunched over the fire, her back turned as she hummed to herself. Rosmunda knelt on the floor and cried nearby.

"What..." Appel began, and then she saw it. Gritta's nanny goat, which she had purchased with the proceeds of her ale sales, was rotating on a spit over the fire, glistening with dripping fat that reflected the flickering light.

"That was our milk goat," Rosmunda sobbed, her tears dripping down her face and making small mud puddles on the dirt floor. "We were to sell the kid goat and have milk that Ma would make into cheese to eat in the winter."

Margitte shrugged. "I was hungry. And your brothers and sisters are, too, by the looks of them. Starvelings, all of you. Here now, I've saved the heart so you can bury it at the door of the man who you want to love you, and the kidneys, of course, for divinin'."

Appel stepped forward, drawing herself to her full height, which towered over the hunched old woman.

"Margitte, what have you done? The goat was not yours to take!"

"Times is hard," Margitte said. "Sometimes I must do things that don't sit well with others. Times is hard, Appel."

Appel could feel Efi's eyes boring into her, and she cleared her throat. "It was wicked, Margitte. What you did was wicked!"

Margitte threw her head back and laughed a shrill, high-pitched chortle that sounded almost like a scream.

"I don't care two teats if I am wicked. I am still alive, Appel. I survived the pestilence. When the mortality came for me, I swelled and fevered and grew deathly ill like my husband and my son. But I lived! If the pestilence could not touch me, neither can God and his angels. Wicked, indeed."

For the second time that day, Appel felt a chill. Margitte's deeply lined face was half-lit in the flickering fire, but her eyes were wide and earnest.

"I lived," Margitte whispered. She drew the spit from the fire and thumped the roasted goat onto the trestle table. "Come!" she shouted at the stunned children. "Eat! Eat now, for tomorrow may bring another pestilence!" Again, she laughed, and the hairs raised on Appel's arms.

What have I done? Appel thought to herself. *What have I brought into Colmar?*

The gate yard
In which Gritta witnesses a chilling display

THE SUN ROSE ON another day, and Gritta groaned, rolling over in her pile of straw. At home, she covered the mattresses of straw with blankets of soft wool, making a comfortable nest for herself and her children. The sweet smell and the crackle of the fodder beneath her was always an enticement to stay abed longer than she should in the morning after a night of sleep. But here, in her prison, she slept directly on the stuff, and it poked and bedeviled her limbs through the night. At least here she didn't have to spend the night being kicked and punched by her unconscious children.

Next to her, Jorges opened his eyes and blinked at the sun falling across his face through the window.

"Gritta." He yawned as he spoke. "Are we still in the tower?"

"Yes, my love." Gritta kissed his forehead. Jorges sighed deeply, smiling, and closed his eyes again.

"Well, there's not much else to do, so I shall sleep until I've had my fill."

He was asleep again instantly, and soon his snores were like a cat's purring. Gritta climbed to her feet and stretched. Other than the straw, there was no place to sit but the sill of the arrow-slit window, which was wider than the opening that faced the street. Every day, Gritta would lean into the deep well of this window, watching the commerce and bustle of the gate yard below her, sometimes dangling an arm out into the warm sun. Yesterday, she saw her children. Perhaps she would again today.

People came and went all day. Jorges rose to use the chamber pot, and they ate their meal of pottage on a trencher of stale bread. The pottage was thin and almost flavorless, but Gritta didn't have to cook it herself, and so she was willing to endure some bland, starchy meals in exchange for a respite from the cooking pot.

As the sun transited the sky and the heat of the day intensified on Gritta's outstretched arm through the arrow-slit, she noticed a new person making their way through the gate yard below. This person might not have caught Gritta's attention since many people came and went through the gate every day, and not all of them were her neighbors in Colmar, but this woman was memorable because instead of simply walking through the gate, she stopped, pulled her cowl down – revealing a head of stringy gray hair – and looked directly at Gritta.

For a moment, Gritta held her breath. The woman below the tower had Gritta's eyes in the grip of her gaze. Without looking away, the woman slowly raised a hand above her head and pulled the sleeve of her cotte up to her elbow, revealing a withered forearm. Then, as if she were moving slowly through water, she grasped the eating knife which hung from her girdle and drew it across her arm, leaving a thin trail of blood. The message was clear. The woman was demonstrating how to sever an arm from its body.

The true murderer was right there, about to leave Colmar, and Gritta could do nothing to stop her.

Appel paced the few steps from one end of Gritta and Jorges' tower cell to the other. It was a very short distance. From the street below, the gate towers looked intimidatingly large, but inside, they were quite small and loosely accounted for. The guard didn't bar the door after her, and gaps between the doorframe and the stones were large enough to put a hand through. She looked at Gritta, who was sitting quietly next to Jorges.

"And you are convinced, my dear, that this woman in the gate yard was signaling to you that she was responsible for the hand in our mash cauldron?"

Gritta nodded enthusiastically. "That woman demonstrated an effective way to remove a hand from a body better than any actor or king's fool could do it. Appel, I saw it as clearly as I see you. She took the hand from Gilbert of Sundhoffen, and she wanted me to know. She may have been the person who killed him, too."

"Which direction did she travel? Was she bound for Vogelgrun?"

"How should I know? I'm locked in a tower, not astride a mule that I could go chasing her down the road. Half the day has passed since she left, and there will be no finding her now."

"This gesture she showed you is very bold," Appel mused. "There must have been other people who saw her in the square. Did anyone else react?"

"Well, I didn't notice. I was so alarmed that I backed away from the window."

"Into my embrace, she did. I was there to comfort her," Jorges said, putting a protective arm around his wife and pulling her close. Appel was at a loss for words. On the other side of the small room, Efi stared, slack-jawed, at the unusual display of tenderness. For some reason that Appel couldn't quite understand, this affection between man and wife made her more uncomfortable than their constant bickering. She cleared her throat loudly.

"Gritta dear, do you think you could describe this woman? What did she look like? I can ask Sheriff Werner to put the guards at the gates on alert for her."

Gritta searched her memory, which seemed to be stored near the ceiling, for that is where she kept looking. "Well, she was a woman, that's for sure."

"How do you know?" Efi asked.

"Had a pair of tatties she did, though it looked as if they were practically dragging on the ground. She was old. Gray hair, too, but not all gray, sort of black and gray at the same time. And she wore a cowl, which she removed."

Appel scowled. "Was she not wearing a wimple or a bonnet? A cowl alone is odd for a woman, is it not?"

"Well," Gritta said with irritation. "So is slicing your own arm in the middle of the gate yard! I call that odd."

Before anyone could respond, the door to the room was dragged back, scraping loudly against the splintered wooden floor. The guard poked his head inside and grinned. "Alright, maidens, time to leave."

"Who are you calling maidens, young man? Efi and I are both widowed," Appel said, the tone of her voice arching almost as high as her eyebrows.

The guard nodded at Efi. "Tha' one still looks like a maid."

"I am Frau Efi Kleven, widow of Harald Kleven, and you had better put a respectful tongue in your mouth before I pull it out and cook it!" Efi snarled, pointing at her chest, her face red. The guard's impudent grin faded, and his eyes grew wide.

"It was you, wasn't it? I heard it with my own ears!" He turned, called to one of the sergeants in the tower, and stabbed a finger in Efi's direction.

"Heard her say it, I did! This dried-up wench threatened to remove my tongue. She could remove an arm, too!"

"Only a moment ago, you called her a maiden, and now she's a wench?" Gritta asked, her arms crossed. "I swear on the saints, everyone in this city has gone mad for accusing their neighbors. Appel, Efi dear, you had best not visit for a while. It seems these two are less intelligent than my nanny goat. Although," Gritta mused, smiling, "my goat has an excuse because she's swollen with her kid. Can't say that I can think straight when I am with child, either."

Appel and Efi exchanged a look of dread. In their amazement upon hearing Gritta's story, they had forgotten to tell her about her goat. Appel cleared her throat. "Gritta, there's something that...Efi needs to tell you."

Efi turned to Appel, her eyes wide. "How could you? You can't make me tell her this! You can't – wait, Appel, where are you going?!" she yelled, but Appel was already making her way through the door and into the dimly lit hall with the guards.

"I'll see you back at the house!" Appel called, and as she quickly walked away, she heard Gritta address Efi.

"Now, what is it that you need to tell me?"

A parcel tied with string
In which evidence and indignities mount

Appel frowned as she walked back to her house. It didn't take her long to stop feeling guilty for leaving Efi alone to tell Gritta that instead of caring for the goat, Margitte had cooked it and then used its entrails for divination. This was a task best left to a young person. But she could not let go of the feeling that Gritta's description of the woman who cut her arm in the gate yard could have been Margitte. It would be unsurprising to discover that her old friend had done something so strange and upsetting in public, disregarding how those around her would interpret the action.

"Nonsense," she said under her breath. "This town is full of strange old women. Could have been any one of 'em."

She was walking next to the trench, and Gritta's house was ahead. Anstett and Mattheus were coaxing a toad from the nearest canal, guiding it to hop under Anstett's hat, presumably so they could drop it down the back of Rosmunda's dress when she bent to stir the pot over the fire. Little Wina was outside, sitting on her bare, chubby bottom and clapping her hands each time the toad took another reluctant hop. Appel knew she needed to put her suspicions out of her mind. Now was the time to straighten her posture, don a smile, and care for these children.

Appel admonished the boys to toss the toad back into the canal, picked Wina up, brushed the dirt from the girl's face, and stepped into the house. It still smelled of rich, meaty broth, and Appel inhaled deeply. Despite herself, she felt her mouth water. Near the fire, Rosmunda sat on a stool, stirring a pot and staring miserably into the distance with an unfocused gaze, pondering her misfortunes.

"Rosmunda, why do you look so despondent, child?"

Rosmunda looked down into the pot. "I am boiling the bones of the goat for the third time, Frau Appel," she said quietly. "But there is nothing left in them. No meat, no marrow, no fat. They have been bleached as white and dry as the linens that my sister dries on the rocks near the river. Now we have no food and no promise of food for later. No cheese. No money from the sale of the goat kid. What are we going to do, grandmother?"

Appel felt her heart hurting for the girl. She wasn't sure how old Rosmunda was, but she had probably only had her first bleed very recently. The Great Pestilence would have happened during the critical time when this young woman was learning about life. Appel sat slowly on the bench next to the table, suddenly feeling all her years, however many those may be – she couldn't be entirely sure.

"You have lived through much worse, Rosmunda, and so has your mother. The goat is unfortunate, but there will be other goats and other meals. I, too, was disappointed to see what had happened, but I had to make a choice to cry and lament or enjoy the first meal of meat I've had since Michael's Mass. As for the rest, I spent all of yesterday afternoon praying to Saint Martin to bring your family another goat."

"You said extra prayers for us?" Rosmunda looked up at Appel, her eyes red and swollen from crying. She was a plain-looking young girl with an open, round face and dark blonde hair, like all of Gritta's children except Lisette, the eldest. Gritta always complained that chestnut-haired Lisette hoarded her beauty and didn't spread it to her brothers and sisters. But a pretty face was not enough to move anyone out of the poor situation into which she was born, as if such a thing were even possible.

"Yes, I said an extra prayer for each of you children, and one for your ma as well."

"And what about Pa? Did you say a prayer for him?"

Appel knew it was wicked to lie, so she evaded the question instead. "Well, you know that your ma and pa share everything, so they can share the prayer I said."

This seemed to satisfy Rosmunda. She rose from her place by the fire, dried her eyes, and began to wipe the dust from the table with a cloth. Most of Gritta's children fell into two categories: ill-tempered or wicked. Rosmunda, by contrast, was sweet and diligent and seemed to want only to be helpful. Appel's eyes misted. Maria, her daughter, had not been as compliant or gentle as this girl. Her only daughter had been fierce and strident, holding her head high even after she got with child by a traveler from another city.

How I hated the man who put the child in her. Until I met my grandson, of course. Dear sweet baby Charles. Appel didn't often allow herself to venture into this part of her memory. After her husband, daughter, and young grandson died in the pestilence, she retreated into her house and did not come out for days. She did not even have the energy to ask God why she'd been spared from the vile affliction. All around her, while her neighbors and family succumbed to the Great Mortality, she remained whole and healthy – in body, that is. Her spirit died along with her loved ones. There was a time that she considered taking a draught of poisonous hemlock so she could join her family, but of course, the consequences would be extreme. Her family, who died in innocence, would be in heaven, but Appel would go to hell for taking her fate into her own hands. And besides, she didn't have the coin to buy a bottle of a potion foul enough to bring about her death in a quick and painless way. She knew all the ways to end a life in a bottle, but those days were behind her.

"Are you well, Frau Appel?" Rosmunda's voice interrupted Appel's reverie. She blinked a few times and smiled.

"What did you say, my dear?"

"I asked what you want me to do with the old woman's things. To be sure, I think they would make good fodder for the fire, but knowing she's a friend of yours, I would not dare."

Rosmunda held up a few raggedy objects, and Appel squinted at them. "Her things? Where did she go?"

"Out of town." Efi's voice interrupted them from the doorway. Appel and Rosmunda turned to greet Efi, but the sight of her made them stop and stare. Her wimple was missing, her normally luscious blonde curls were disheveled, and bits of straw stuck out from her dress. In her hand, she held a parcel tied with string that occasionally dribbled onto the floor of the threshold. In the dim light, Appel couldn't make out what it was. Efi took a few steps forward. "Margitte has gone out of Colmar and not back to Vogelgrun, neither. But before she left, she did this."

Efi held up an arm, pulled her sleeve back, and pantomimed cutting the hand off with an imaginary knife. The parcel swung and dripped wildly with the motion.

Appel felt her heart sink. She knew the truth, but had been unwilling to face it. "It can't be," she whispered. "Efi, you truly suspect Margitte of putting the hand in our mash?"

"I do not suspect, Appel. I know." Efi dropped the parcel to the floor, and it thumped loudly.

"What is that?"

Efi stomped to the bench, sat, and raked her fingers through her hair. "That is something the city guards at the gate gave me. They found it on the road to Riquewihr."

Appel picked up the parcel. It was large and roughly round, wrapped in straw and tied with twine, but she felt something damp on her fingers. When she looked at her hands, she saw blood. "Oh Jesu, please tell me it isn't what I think it is..." Appel whispered, feeling her stomach lurch as the bile rose in her throat. She untied the string with shaking hands, and the straw fell away. Appel drew her apron to her mouth and tried to contain her disgust. The straw revealed a bloody mass of flesh, bone, and...a hoof. Appel looked up at Efi, confused.

"Part of Gritta's goat," Efi said, sitting stiffly on the bench. She massaged her neck for a moment and plucked a few bits of straw from her hair.

"Oh Jesu, Efi! I thought I was about to find another piece of a man's body in here!" She gave the younger woman a gentle shove.

"Margitte must have taken this hoof for her lunch on the road."

"Why would she leave it on the road, though?"

Efi shrugged. "There are wolves in those parts, and bands of vicious people who took to thieving and kidnapping after the pestilence. Perhaps she met her demise. We may never know."

"Efi, this is an ugly discovery, but it does not *prove* that Margitte killed Gilbert of Sundhoffen. It only shows that Margitte is a hungry old woman who cooked Gritta's goat and is most certainly a little mad."

Efi crossed her arms and pouted, while nearby, Rosmunda wrung her hands. Appel cleared her throat and finally began to notice Efi's state of disarray.

"Efi, what happened to you? Where is your wimple, and why is there straw in your dress?"

"Gritta was very displeased to learn of what befell her goat. She was in a mood to punish the nearest person to her."

Appel gently laid a hand on Efi's shoulder. "Did she beat you terribly, dear? Gritta has a mighty temper but usually uses an open hand, not a fist."

"I looked much better than Jorges did when I left. The sale of that kid goat was her hope for the future. Margitte has wronged her. Even if the old witch didn't kill Gilbert of Sundhoffen, she deserves punishment for what she took from Gritta."

Across the lane, they heard someone pounding a fist on a wooden door. Rosmunda stopped her conspicuous worrying and went to the window to peek through the shutters. "Why, it is Friar Wikerus!" she exclaimed. "He is pounding on your door across the lane, Frau Appel."

Appel went to the window and hailed the friar, who hopped over the trench and hurried toward Gritta's house.

"Thank the Lord in heaven I found you! I managed to leave Brother Tacitus behind, but only just. Alewives, where is your friend, Margitte? She must be detained at once!"

"Friar Wikerus, calm yourself and catch your breath," Appel said, leading him to the bench outside Gritta's door and ordering Rosmunda to draw some small ale from the jar in the cupboard.

"Friar Wikerus, I thought you would still be in Vogelgrun now with Sheriff Werner and Lord Frider."

"Indeed, but I learned some things that drew me back to Colmar immediately. Frau Appel, you must locate your friend

Margitte and bring her to the sheriff as quickly as possible. Otherwise, I fear that suspicion may fall upon you."

"Margitte has left Colmar. Why do you seek her, Friar?"

Friar Wikerus looked at Appel, Efi, and Rosmunda with serious, blue eyes. "I seek her because I believe she is the one who murdered Gilbert of Sundhoffen."

The suspect

In which Friar Wikerus presents his findings

G RITTA STOOD IN THE dark main room of her house and scowled at the half-wall that separated it from the stable where her nanny goat had been living. She sighed, and her shoulders slumped. "I did not kill and dismember Gilbert of Sundhoffen, but I would kill Margitte of Vogelgrun right now if I could. I never even met this woman, and yet I wish so much harm upon her."

She turned to face the room. Appel, Efi, Friar Wikerus, and three of her older children stood around looking uncomfortable. "I never met this woman," Gritta said again, louder this time. "And yet you brought her to Colmar and into my home. You let her near my children!"

"I am sorry, my friend," Appel said, her eyes downcast. "Margitte was alone in that large, empty house in Vogelgrun. I thought it would be a charity to bring her to the place of her birth and let her live out the rest of her days in the company of others."

"She would never have gone into your house at all, Frau Gritta, had she not burned down our privy," Efi chirped helpfully.

Appel elbowed the young woman in the ribs and cast her a scathing look.

"Burned down your...No, I do not wish to know why that happened, only to understand why you brought her here. What will my family eat? My children are so thin they could run between raindrops during a thunderstorm. We need food!"

Friar Wikerus stepped forward, holding up his hands as a gesture of peace. "Frau Gritta, the brothers at Saint Martin's will help you through this challenging time."

Tacitus, who sat with his arms crossed in the corner of the room, snorted loudly.

Gritta pulled the bench back from her trestle table and sat down, folding her hands in front of her. "Tell me again: what cleared my name, inspired Sheriff Werner to release Jorges and me from the tower, and implicated Margitte in this crime? I want to hear all of the details."

Wikerus sat across from her, and the other occupants of the room settled themselves at the table. Rosmunda poured mugs of small ale and passed them out as Wikerus cleared his throat.

"When I arrived in Vogelgrun and met with the sheriff there, he and his men spoke of 'Margitte the witch.' Of course, many will assume a woman of strange proclivities is a witch, yet it is a serious accusation and one that the church takes seriously. Sometimes, a woman will do things that make sense to her but not to those around her, and she is called a witch without just cause. Sometimes, the same happens to a man. In almost every case such as this, I favor the opinion that a person is not guilty of witchery without proof. But the more I learned about Margitte, the more I grew concerned."

"Friar Wikerus, I never met this woman, and I already hate her. But honesty and curiosity compels me to ask how you think Margitte could have killed Gilbert of Sundhoffen. Just because they were both from Vogelgrun doesn't mean they knew each other. Vogelgrun may be smaller than Colmar, but by all accounts, Gilbert did not live there long, nor did he spend much time away from the docks."

"But they did know each other, Frau Gritta. You see, Margitte rented the lower floor of her house to Gilbert. He had no wife and no people in Vogelgrun, so he lodged with her. The neighbors said they could hear Margitte and Gilbert arguing sometimes in the evenings after they had both drunk too much wine."

"Gritta and Jorges argue in the street when he has had too much wine, but it does not mean that she will murder him," Appel said, ignoring the look of disgust from Tacitus. "I will admit that Margitte is a strange woman who has probably lost her wits, but none of this makes her a murderer."

"Stop defending the woman who killed and boiled my nanny goat, Appel!" Gritta shouted, thumping her fist on the table.

"What she did was reprehensible, my dear Gritta, but a woman should not be put to death at the end of a rope just because she makes people uncomfortable."

Friar Wikerus held up a hand. "Please allow me to finish, Frau Appel, and you shall soon see why all signs point to her guilt.

Margitte and her husband, a prosperous warehouse owner, also used to take too much wine and yell at each other while he still lived. The fighting was so terrible that, a few times, the night watchman had to break them apart, and once, Margitte was tied to the pillory for a day as punishment for intoxication. And then her husband died."

"He died in the pestilence, Friar. And so did mine! So did most of the husbands on this street!" Appel rose to her feet, her eyes glistening with tears. Efi gently pulled Appel down to her seat on the bench and wrapped her arms around the older woman's shoulders. "I miss him," Appel whispered, tears falling down her cheeks now. "I miss my husband."

Efi quietly shushed her, as a mother calms a baby, and for a moment, everyone in the room found themselves remembering the ones they had also lost – friends and colleagues, merchants, and playmates. No one had been safe from death, and for those who were inexplicably spared, the feelings of guilt followed them like a shadow that dimmed a little more as each day passed.

"I know, Frau Appel. There are many widows in Les Tanneurs. There are widows, widowers, orphans, and mothers whose arms are empty. And so it seems inconceivable that someone would intentionally take a life during the pestilence, and yet that is what Margitte did."

"How do you know, Friar? How could anyone know what killed a man during the pestilence unless the knife was still buried in his chest?" Efi asked. Appel was still leaning on the younger woman, taking deep breaths to steady herself. Friar

Wikerus found the juxtaposition of the younger woman comforting the older touching.

"Margitte's husband had not only been arguing with his wife but also had found himself in want of companionship, and so he frequently visited a woman who lived in desperate poverty near the docks. Apparently, this was a well-known secret among the porters and warehouse owners in Vogelgrun."

"Aye," Jorges said, nodding his head slowly. "We knew that a fancy man would visit the girl who lived under the bridge at Vogelgrun, but I didn't know who he was. Must have been the husband of the witch."

"When Margitte found out, she grew enraged, and within a week, her husband was dead. He had died with foaming red froth coming from his mouth, but there was no evidence of pestilence on him. No darkened skin, no buboes, and his body did not burn with fever while he ailed."

"Poison," Gritta said grimly. She turned an accusing stare on Appel and Efi. "And you two harlots let this poisoner cook food for my children!"

Appel began to cry again, and Efi clucked her tongue. "We were only trying to do the charitable thing, Gritta."

"Indeed, Frau Gritta, please forgive your friend. It was a mistake to bring Margitte here, but now is the time to put your anger to rest."

"I am sorry – although not surprised – to hear about the fate of Margitte's husband," Jorges said. "But it still doesn't mean the woman murdered Gilbert." When he noticed his wife's incredulous stare, he lowered his gaze. "Well, it don't," he mumbled.

Wikerus nodded. "Indeed, yes, Jorges, you are correct. It is not wrong to ask difficult questions, even if we want in our heart for someone to be guilty so that we may punish them for a wrong they did to us."

At this, Gritta snorted and crossed her arms.

"However," Wikerus continued, "the timing does make sense. Gilbert moved in very shortly after Margitte's husband died, and soon afterward, he also fought with Margitte. Then Gilbert vanished, and no one saw Margitte outside her house for days. They assumed she was mourning, but she could have really been hiding."

"You left out a crucial and obvious detail, Friar," Appel said, sniffling and wiping her eyes on her sleeve. "How did Gilbert's hand get from Vogelgrun into my ale pot?"

"Margitte was known to vanish for days at a time. She would set out alone on the road to Colmar, saying she was looking for herbs. People who saw her leave the gate said she often carried a bundle wrapped in a wool blanket tied to her back. She could have taken Gilbert from her house in pieces, spreading them around so that suspicion would fall on others."

"That would be too heavy. Gilbert would have been a big man if he was a dockside porter, and Margitte was a hunched old woman."

"Not if she took him out in pieces, aye," Jorges said, rising to his feet. "I'll wager there are parts of Gilbert all over the countryside."

"I think I am going to be ill," Efi said, covering her mouth.

But Gritta was shaking her head. "You said she didn't leave her house after Gilbert disappeared. Vogelgrun is small. Even if she removed Gilbert in pieces at night, someone would notice."

"Right you are, Frau Gritta!" Wikerus was starting to pace the room now. "So, if she didn't take him out in pieces, how did she get rid of the body of a brawny porter?"

"Witchery, obviously," Brother Tacitus commented from his seat in the shadows. "This is why we need to seek out all those who do the Devil's work and put them to the question. Her sin will go far, I assure you. It shall corrupt other towns as the spirit of the Devil emanates from the limbs she scattered about the four corners of the land." He had risen to his feet, and in the darkness of the room, his tall, angular figure looked more menacing than usual.

"Yes, Brother Tacitus, thank you for that. And now, perhaps you would like to return to your work at the priory since your punishment of spending time with me is over?" Wikerus struggled to keep the irritation from his voice. Brother Tacitus was a fanatic whose conspiracies and suspicions frightened those around him. He did little to bring comfort to anyone.

Tacitus turned and stalked from the house without speaking another word, and Gritta released a large breath of air. "I, too, think that Margitte of Vogelgrun is guilty of murdering Gilbert, but I do not care to have anything else in common with Brother Tacitus. He is frightful."

"So, what should we do next, Friar? Margitte has fled Colmar, but she is still out there," Appel said. "And we still do not have all the answers. How did she kill Gilbert? How did she hide the body? Why would she put his hand into an alepot – especially with that recognizable spot upon the thumb? And why did she choose my alepot?!"

Wikerus pressed his lips into a thin, grim line. "Lord Frider alerted Sheriff Werner, and he is assembling a posse of city men to find her. He will also send riders ahead to alert the rulers in Riquewihr, since that was her last known destination. For now, there is nothing to do but wait and pray."

"Very good," Jorges said, grinning as he slammed a large clay pitcher on the table. "Shall we celebrate with a drink?"

Witch-hunters

In which the brave men of Colmar do a brave thing bravely

SHERIFF WERNER SQUINTED INTO the middle distance from atop his horse, sucked in his paunch, and placed a pudgy fist on his hip, hoping that the posture looked as noble as he imagined. This was how the young and fit knights sometimes rode, posing astride their mounts as if the world was a feast, and they were prepared to eat, drink, and make love to every person they saw.

He spared a backward glance for the patchwork of men who followed him, mustered in a hurry as he scrambled to find able and willing bodies to join a posse. Some of the wealthier ones sat in saddles at his eye level, but most stood afoot and leaning on their staffs and pikes, so he had a prime view of their bald spots and dusty shoulders. They weren't knights, but they would do. He had roused the bravest, brawniest men of Colmar in his quest to find the witch, Margitte. He just hoped that they felt prepared for the battle that would ensue. Knowing she was a witch, he had also enlisted the help of one of the brothers from Saint Martin's. None of the holy men were eager to hunt down the old crone except Friar Tacitus – and he was a little too keen.

Sheriff Werner glanced at the man as he sat on his donkey, his long, spindly legs sticking out on each side of the gentle beast, his skin white as milk against the animal's dun-colored coat. Seeing the brothers riding an animal was unusual, as their vow of poverty and humility usually meant walking. But humility didn't suit Friar Tacitus.

"Why did you stop?" Tacitus called out. His voice was ripe with patronizing annoyance, and Sheriff Werner bristled. He brought the man along to counteract the devilish tricks the old woman may be hiding, but he began to regret his decision as soon as they set out. Tacitus started to preach in a loud voice once they left the city gates, and he had not let up since. The townsmen already felt ill at ease with the thought of pursuing the witch of Vogelgrun, the widow who became famous for her unlikely survival of the pestilence. Having the gaunt friar yelling sermons at them did nothing to improve their mood.

"I see something ahead." Sheriff Werner deepened his voice, hoping it made him sound more authoritative. The men stopped, and a few of them readied their weapons. They squinted at the horizon, shielding their eyes against a sun that hid resolutely behind a thick layer of late spring clouds. It wasn't a necessary gesture, but it made them feel important. Ahead of them, the road curved sharply to the north. A dark shape hunched at the side of the road, partially concealed by the shadows of the trees, but wearing a hooded cloak that was dyed red.

"Why does she stand so still?" one of Sheriff Werner's men whispered.

"Can't say curses when you're moving around," another answered. Sheriff Werner didn't know if it was true or not, but the figure on the road was standing unnaturally still. It must be true, he decided.

"Weapons out," Sheriff Werner said to his men. "Friar Tacitus, you stay at the back. Pray for us, Friar. Pray for our souls."

A few of the men crossed themselves. Despite their bravery, their hands trembled, for what was more frightening than a woman who had relations with the king of hell himself? Having dismounted his donkey, Friar Tacitus stood at the back, hands raised in pleading supplication toward heaven. He prayed rather too loudly.

"Softly, Friar," Sheriff Werner said. "We must keep the element of surprise. See, her back is still turned."

He sent four men into the woods to cut off her escape, and they edged forward slowly, their prey still standing with her back to them. There was a moment of silence when the men, horses, and even the birds in the trees seemed to pause with expectation, and then a sharp scream split the air, followed by the sounds of men shouting. Sheriff Werner and his posse rushed forward. "Grab her, lads!" The sheriff grunted, pulling back on the reins of his horse to let the stronger, braver men go first. Friar Tacitus was no longer praying quietly behind them but at a full-throated bellow.

The men reached the figure in the shadows and stopped. The bravest among them jabbed at it with his rusted spear. They huddled around the hunched figure for a moment, whispering amongst themselves with a few backward glances. One of them snatched the red cloak and held it up. Sheriff Werner groaned.

"It was a waystone with a cloak draped over it?" Friar Tacitus shouted behind them. "Do you all have poor eyesight, or just insufficient brains?!"

Before the sheriff could respond, they heard more screams, and the four men whom he had sent to cut off the witch's escape tumbled from the thick hedge, one of them displaying a colossal black eye and another with a bloody gash on his forehead.

"Did you find her?" Friar Tacitus gushed. "Did you fight her?"

Before the men could answer, a large stone crashed through the verge and struck one of them on the foot. A woman followed, dressed only in her chemise, her hair dripping and eyes blazing.

"Oww! Wench!" the injured man shouted. "We told you we were here on official business of Colmar!"

"Is your business watching me while I bathe? Hand me my cloak!"

Seeing the cloak clutched in the hands of the confused sheriff, the woman snatched it and returned the way she had come through the leaves.

"Did she do that to you?" the sheriff asked, noting the wounds on his men's faces. They nodded miserably.

"Came upon her while she was bathing, we did. Hans said he thought she must be a succubus, here to lure us into the water.

Well, she didn't take it kindly when she saw us. Hans made it worse when he tried to pinch her bottom."

They walked on, their confidence significantly shaken. Two more times they thought they spied the witch of Vogelgrun on the road to Riquewihr and prepared to take her into custody. They apprehended a pilgrim traveling home from Besançon and a young heifer who had wandered from her herd along the road, and each time, the bumbling ineptitude of the sheriff and his men elicited louder and more eloquent grumbles from Tacitus.

The presence of this friar, along with the bungled apprehension of an empty cloak, made the sheriff feel vaguely insecure. Sheriff Werner had asked for a friar from the priory to attend and was delighted when solemn and holy Tacitus had volunteered to come. But his admiration soured quickly. Friar Tacitus practically excreted disdain from his pores. He glanced nervously at the man as they rode in silence toward Riquewihr. Tacitus stared straight ahead, his cheeks and nose turning purple with the cold.

Sheriff Werner reined his horse back. Ahead, a figure lay on the side of the road, sprawled and unconscious. It wasn't another waystone because a rag-wrapped foot was clearly visible. One by one, the rest of his men noticed the person on the road, but given their prior failures, no one wanted to call out the order to make an arrest.

"It's her," the sheriff said. "This time, I am sure of it. Now is the time for prayers in earnest, and all men should prepare their souls for this battle. I see a woman's long gray hair, and I recognize the walking stick lying beside her. Quickly now, where is the friar?"

Tacitus spoke to his donkey, and when it did not move, he gave it a sharp kick in the flanks with his heels. The beast slowly plodded to the sheriff, and Tacitus looked up.

"Dismount when you speak to me, Sheriff Werner. I am a member of a holy order."

Sheriff Werner reluctantly slid from his horse and held the beast by the bridle. Tacitus inclined his head slightly in acknowledgment.

"She is ahead, Friar Tacitus. While my men approach her, we will rely on you to say prayers of protection against the Devil."

"The Devil is no match for the name of Jesu Christi," Tacitus declared, and Sheriff Werner nodded, waiting for the rest, but it seemed that Tacitus had no more to say on the matter. The sheriff cleared his throat and turned to his men, motioning them to circle around him. He gestured to the road with his chin.

"She appears to be asleep."

"What if she's dead?" one of the men asked, and Sheriff Werner paused. This was also a possibility.

"Regardless of her state of life, we must approach with caution. I shall go first." But as he said it, Sheriff Werner instantly regretted his bravado. His knees trembled, and his heart thumped in his chest.

They walked forward slowly, and Sheriff Werner found himself hoping that she was indeed dead. They may never have all the answers to the mystery of the dismembered man from

Vogelgrun, but at least they would be safe from the woman's curses.

The closer they walked, the more certain Sheriff Werner grew that the woman was Margitte, the witch of Vogelgrun. He could hear the voice of Friar Tacitus intoning the words of prayer on his donkey behind them, and he expected to see her stir, but she lay motionless, snoring loudly, mouth wide open, arms and legs splayed in the new spring grass. The whole party approached and stared down at her. Not knowing what else to do, Sheriff Werner nudged her with the toe of his shoe. Margitte snorted and opened one thin, wrinkled eyelid. A bright blue eye looked around, taking them all in, then narrowed with malice.

"Jesu, protect us against the Devil and his mischief!" Tacitus shrieked behind them, and at that moment, Margitte sprang to her feet with a speed and agility that she had no right to possess at her age. With a wild scream, she launched herself at Tacitus, hands extended like talons. Tacitus, in turn, unleashed a high-pitched scream and fell from his donkey. In her fright, the beast bucked her hind legs, sending the friar further sprawling down the incline of the embankment at the side of the road, where the soft ground gave way beneath him, and he slipped and slid, arms windmilling, toward a small stream.

"God will save me!" he yelled. "My soul is prepared!"

"Nooooo!" Margitte wailed and ran after him, hands still outstretched. While Sheriff Werner and the rest of the men looked on, paralyzed by shock, Tacitus fell into the brook and began to thrash. "Help!" he yelled. "Help me, you fools! I do not know how to swim!"

Margitte pounced on him, tearing the leather sack from his shoulder. She clawed back up the embankment, holding the sack in her teeth by its straps, and squatted in the dirt, overturning the bag. A few of the more courageous young men crept down to the brook and dragged a dripping, furious Friar Tacitus from the water, which did not cover his shins. Margitte shouted when she found what she was looking for in the sack. It was a damp loaf of bread. She picked it up and began to tear into it like a wild animal.

Sheriff Werner watched for a moment. "You were hungry? Is that why you attacked the good friar?"

"Good? Ha!" Margitte spat crumbs as she spoke with a full mouth. "That one does not have a good bone in his body or a pious thought in his head."

"I must arrest you, Frau Margitte. But if you come willingly and keep your curses in your mouth, I shall make a note of it to the council when you appear before them for your trial." Sheriff Werner braced himself, expecting Margitte to resist, but instead, she shrugged her shoulders and continued to eat. Tacitus squelched in his dripping sandals to where she squatted on the ground and snatched the sack from her.

"Give me that! You must not rifle through the bag of a man of God, you foul woman!"

Margitte outstretched a skinny arm and held up a small stick. "Here. This is yours, I think."

"No, it is not," Tacitus said quickly.

"'Tis. It came from your scrip, not any tree growing in Colmar."

Tacitus snatched the twig, tucking it into the sleeve of his black wool robe, and stomped back to his errant donkey.

"Why should you give the man a stick, Margitte? It has no value to him," the sheriff said.

Margitte waved the heel of bread in the direction of the friar. "Weren't no ordinary stick, m'lord. 'Twas a stick of cinnamon. Very tasty." She squinted up at him and then winked. "What kind of food do you have in your prison?"

Honey cake treachery

In which a popular sweetmeat causes sour feelings

A PPEL DRAGGED HER FEET as she returned from the morning market down Trench Lane and back to her home. The bright and unseasonably warm spring weather had turned foul. Rain dripped from the eaves of every house, the tip of every green bud, and the tip of her nose as well. The water carved rivulets in the lane, which all led to the trench and thence to the canals that ran high and swift with filthy brown water.

She knew she should feel happy. After all, accusations of murder and dismemberment no longer haunted Gritta and Jorges, the recalcitrant stonemasons had agreed to return to her house and finish her hearth, and as soon as she rebuilt her privy, she and Efi could move back in. But she didn't feel relief; she felt shame. She had brought Margitte back to Colmar without thoroughly investigating the woman's character. Now Margitte had ruined Appel's good reputation with her neighbors, burned her privy to the ground, and turned Gritta's goat into soup and sausages. Appel wasn't prone to bouts of melancholy or self-pity, but this was one of the rare days that she let herself feel thoroughly miserable.

The exuberant cursing and gossip of the stonemasons quieted as soon as she entered the house. Casting suspicious glances in her direction, they lowered their voices and whispered amongst each other. Appel thunked her basket of turnips on the table and turned to them, hands on her hips.

"You might as well spread your slander about me with full voices. Honestly, you are worse than the idle merchant's wives who have nothing better to do!"

Seeing their heads droop in shame gave her a warm feeling of satisfaction. Let them ponder her comments for a while. She had work to do and she couldn't allow her gloomy mood to keep her from her tasks. She overturned her basket of turnips in a basin of water and scrubbed the grime from them with the roughest parts of her callused palms. For a while, only the splashing of water and the crack of stones as the masons set them into place made sounds in the house. Appel mused at how the stonemasons had somehow managed even to make the sandstone blocks of her hearth sound like they were guilty of sin.

Efi broke the silence when she breezed inside with her leather yoke and waterskins across her shoulders. Appel noted how the eyes of the stonemasons followed her across the room. One of the younger ones, a handsome – albeit not very tall lad – sprang forward.

"Let me help you with that, Fraulein Efi." He flashed her his most charming smile, and Efi smiled back under lowered lashes.

Appel cleared her throat and handed Efi an iron knife, blackened with age and use. First, she addressed the young man.

"Frau Efi is a widow, and you will address her with the gravitas of her station in life. She is no blushing maid." Turning to the young woman, who was, in fact, blushing as red as a sun-kissed apple, she continued. "Efi, we will start the pottage before brewing today, and then I need you to take the dough to the oven. And you —" she pointed a long finger at the young stonemason's apprentice "— if you must swoon over my young friend, at least make yourself useful and help with the supper."

The young man sat on the bench next to Efi as she picked up a slender turnip and began to scrape the peel into a bowl with her blade. "I'll wager my day's pay that you are a fine cook," he said. Efi bowed her head demurely, and Appel rolled her eyes.

Gritta strode into the house in a cloud of curses and chicken feathers. "Efi is the worst cook in Les Tanneurs and possibly the whole city – unless you prefer to eat your meat only after it has been turned to ash," she proclaimed. In her arms, she carried a basket of freshly malted grain. "But I'll admit that she looks very fine while ruining the meal. Very fine indeed." Gritta's eyes twinkled as she took in Efi's outraged glare.

The young stonemason shrugged. "Well, there's still time to learn. When I marry, I shall have my wife apprentice herself under my mother to make sure her cooking and house management are ready for a husband. She must be efficient, for I plan to become a master stonemason someday, and I will also need her to keep the books and mix mortar for my business."

"And what a lucky wife you will have, I am sure," Gritta said, her famous sarcasm infusing every word. "But Efi has already had a husband, and we were all surprised that it wasn't her cooking that killed him. Now, Efi, you had best get that dough off to the oven before you find yourself wed and washing another man's feet before today's sunset."

Efi dropped the denuded turnips into a pot and stood to go. In that pause, the stonemason's apprentice took a moment to admire her narrow waist and wide, round hips.

"Back to work, young man. I'm not paying you to make love to my friends," Appel said, handing Efi a tray with two small balls of dough shaped into boules and covered with a scrap of floured linen cloth.

"Always making me do all the unpleasant work," Efi grumbled, and Appel nodded sagely.

"It is appropriate, otherwise your opinion of yourself will grow larger than those bosoms of yours. Now, off with you!"

Friar Wikerus called a greeting from the dooryard and stood aside with an agreeable smile on his face as Efi left with her tray of dough.

"Well then," he said, sitting in his usual place on the bench near the window. "I have just been to visit poor old Margitte in the guard's tower. She seems well pleased with her situation there and says she's not in a hurry to leave any time soon."

"She is welcome to the guard's tower. Jorges and I have been free of it for three days, and I hope I never return."

"And where is Jorges now, Frau Gritta?"

"Off to work in Vogelgrun. My children brought in some coin from their small labors while Jorges and I were locked away, but we are poorer than ever. My man is off to earn his salt and keep us from starving, and I have taken in some mending to earn a bit extra while I wait for this next tun of ale to become mellow and sweet."

"I hope the guards won't hurt Margitte, Friar," Appel said. "What she did was beyond the comprehension of any good Christian, but she's not in her right mind, you see. And Gilbert of Sundhoffen had no family that requires compensation."

The stonemasons slowed their work, their ears straining to hear the gossip, and Friar Wikerus frowned in thought. "Ah, but to take a life is a grave sin, Frau Appel. It means that Margitte was trying to put herself in God's place. Only God is allowed to claim someone's life."

"But if she begged for forgiveness, would she not be granted some leniency? I have gone to Saint Martin's every day to say prayers for her and for the soul of Gilbert."

"Ha!" Gritta barked out a harsh laugh. "Gilbert's soul is right where it deserves to be. And Margitte didn't take one life; she took four." Noticing the perplexed looks in the room, she held up three fingers. "Gilbert, my goat, and my goat's unborn kid. And if she also killed her husband back in Vogelgrun that's four. Four lives, Appel. I hope she stays in the tower for many years."

"Perhaps she will, Frau Gritta, but I don't think it would be the punishment you hope she deserves, for she seems quite happy there. She said something about enjoying a bed of her own and plenty of food that she was not compelled to prepare."

Gritta wrinkled her nose. "There is food in the tower, to be sure, but nothing to get excited about. Just some plain barley pottage and water."

"She had a fresh honey cake and a pot of plum syrup when I saw her."

"Plum syrup? Where would she have gotten..." Gritta turned on Appel and pointed at her. "You are famous for your plum sweets. Have you been bringing Margitte fine foods?"

"Only a little. She's an old woman, you see."

Gritta ripped the wimple from her head and held up her braid, the mousy brown hair streaked with iron gray. "I am an old woman, too! When I was there, you brought nothing but self-righteous sermons and news of my dead goat!"

"Well, it was Efi who told you about the goat," Appel corrected her, and Gritta stomped her foot. "Oh honestly, Gritta! I thought you were enjoying the tower. Meals and no work seemed to suit you."

The stonemasons had now given up all pretense of working. One by one, they dipped their wooden cups into the pot of sweet, malty new ale that Appel had set out to rot and squatted near the hearth, watching and listening with rapt attention.

Gritta only flinched for an instant. "Aye, it was a good way for me to rest, and Jorges and I also had a time of it, getting to spend some days in each other's company with no distractions. But why, Appel? Why would you bring fine food to the very woman who committed the crime that Jorges and I were accused of?" Despite herself, Gritta felt the sting of tears rising to her eyes.

"It is as I said. Margitte was a friend of my youth —"

"And I am a friend of your life! Did Margitte bring meals when you were in your childbed with your daughter or assist in the tannery when your husband was overwhelmed with his work? Did Margitte pick up her spade and dig the holes to bury your family because you were out of your wits with grief?"

Appel shuddered at this and sank to her knees on the floor, burying her face in her hands. Friar Wikerus stood and put a gentle hand on Gritta's shoulder.

"That is enough, Frau Gritta. Your words are hurting your friend."

"Ain't no friend that treats my enemy so well." Gritta spat her words toward Appel.

"But Frau Gritta, it's only a bit of cake."

Gritta turned an icy stare on the friar. "No, it's not just cake. I never knew I had put so much of my trust and friendship in a traitor." She whirled and stalked across the lane to her house, slamming her door behind her. For a moment, no one moved. Then, Appel threw her arms over her head and wept. Friar Wikerus gently placed his hand upon her head and recited a prayer of comfort as, one by one, the stonemasons put down their half-empty cups and shuffled outside.

The sound of Efi singing confidently but off-key drifted down the lane as she returned from her errand at the oven. She skipped into the house with her empty tray under one arm and a small basket dangling from the other.

"Ah, back from the ovens, are you? And how is Herr Bäcker? I have not seen him in my confessional in several weeks," Friar Wikerus asked, but Efi wrinkled her nose.

"I no longer use the oven of Hans Bäcker because he is a rude, lecherous scoundrel. I use Frau Ghent's oven instead, and her cakes are finer. See, Appel, I had an extra penny, so I brought a few honey cakes home for our supper!"

"Honey cakes? Oh, Efi, how could you?!" Appel wailed, and she began crying in earnest.

"Dear Appel, what has happened?" Efi dropped to her knees, the cakes forgotten. Friar Wikerus recounted the details of Appel's argument with Gritta, and Efi clucked her tongue.

"You know that Gritta's temper will cool down, Appel."

"But she won't forgive, Efi," Appel said, sniffling into her sleeve. "She remembers every slight against her."

There was a tap at the door. Sheriff Werner stood there, his face grim. "I am looking for Frau Gritta, and since she spends more of her time in this house than her own, I came here first." He paused. "Is everything alright, Frau Appel?"

"Everything will be fine with a little time and prayer, Sheriff Werner," Friar Wikerus answered quickly. "Frau Gritta is at her own house this day."

The sheriff grunted and turned to go. "Best prepare yourselves, alewives. Frau Gritta will need the sympathy of her neighbors this night."

"Sheriff, why?" Friar Wikerus asked.

"Because, although Margitte, the witch of Vogelgrun, is still locked in the tower, we found a body on the road to Vogelgrun. The hands had been hewn off, and they were in the possession of Jorges Leporteur. He's our killer, and he will hang for murder before the week is done."

Return to Vogelgrun

In which Friar Wikerus realizes he's being followed

IN THE FINER PARTS of Colmar, the news that a dock laborer was responsible for the recent gruesome murders was a sensational story, told and retold in the weinstubes and the shops, but in Les Tanneurs it was a scandal that divided the neighborhood into two factions. Some felt gleeful vindication, knowing that Jorges Leporteur was a fool and a sloth whose drunkenness brought the watchful eye of Sheriff Werner and his men upon Les Tanneurs more often than necessary.

Others felt relieved that a deranged, hand-collecting killer no longer menaced the public. No one even considered that Jorges might be innocent of his accusations. How could he be? As the details of the crime emerged, there was simply no way to prove his innocence. And so, it was with complete incredulity that Father Konrad heard Friar Wikerus's petition to return to Vogelgrun to investigate the second murder in as many weeks.

"Say it to me one more time, Brother Wikerus, because my ears refuse to believe it. I need to hear you say it again," the prior practically shouted. Why was it, he thought to himself, that Wikerus was the only man of his priory who could elicit such strong and loud emotions? In a corner, Sheriff Werner sat on a stool that was much too small for his plump frame, hands clasped across his belly. He hadn't uttered a word.

Brother Wikerus assumed his usual posture of humility; his head bowed, arms tucked into the sleeves of his robe. "I believe Jorges Leporteur may have been falsely accused of this crime, Father."

"Brother Wikerus, do you know the circumstances in which the sheriff discovered Jorges? There is absolutely no way that man is innocent of another murder and dismemberment! He was found sleeping in a ditch with two bloody, severed hands in his sack. A short distance away, a handless man lay in the road, dead!"

"Someone else could have could have killed the man and then placed the hands in Jorges' sack."

"Without Jorges noticing?! Although I am not an expert in these matters, I do believe that it's difficult to slip a set of dripping and still-warm hands into someone's bag!"

Brother Wikerus turned to the sheriff, who cowered slightly out of habit, like a boy in school waiting for the sting of the headmaster's stick.

"Sheriff, you said Jorges Leporteur was asleep when you found him. Can I assume that he was asleep from too much drink?"

The sheriff shifted on his seat. "Well, it is true he had a powerful smell of wine about him."

"In such a deep state of sleep, it could be relatively easy to put anything in the man's sack, could it not?"

"Well, Jorges had stopped drinking, you know? In the tower, he didn't take a single sip of the water of Dionysis." The sheriff's eyes darted at Father Konrad. "Learned about that phrase when I was in my schooling, Father."

"Yes, Lord Sheriff, your education is very impressive," Father Konrad said with a dismissive flutter of his fingers, and Wikerus took his opportunity.

"Let us not forget that Jorges was sober because there was no drink available to him in the tower. And a man who has been off the drink for a long enough time will no longer have a stomach for it. It takes far less to get him drunk than when his stomach is warmed by wine every day."

"Brother Wikerus, your point?" Father Konrad asked.

"Father, I wish to travel again to Vogelgrun because I have some questions that I would like to ask about the town. I want to know who Jorges saw the day the body was found, and who gave him the wine."

"I am sure he must have acquired the wine himself."

"No, I do not think so. Jorges was out of work for a long time in the tower, and he wouldn't have had enough money for wine."

"He could have spent his earnings from the day's labor."

Wikerus paused, scratching his chin. "Perhaps the harbor masters in Vogelgrun do not pay at the end of each day."

"An absurd notion. Porters are paid at the end of their duties. Wikerus, I cannot spare you from your responsibilities as a minister to Les Tanneurs for you to take another trip to Vogelgrun. Let us send the sheriff instead."

At this, Sheriff Werner held up his hands. "I apologize, Father Konrad, but I consider this matter resolved with no doubt about the guilty man. Jorges committed both crimes, and he will hang for them after the feast of Saint Irene, which is in three days. I can't leave Colmar for another journey to Vogelgrun, and I doubt Lord Frider will, either."

For a moment, all three men were silent. Wikerus turned his pleading blue eyes on Father Konrad.

"Please, Father. Enough innocent lives have been lost already. Give me another opportunity to try and save one. I will only stay overnight; if I find nothing, then Jorges will hang, but please give me an opportunity to try."

Father Konrad considered the request, his fingers steepling and unsteepling on his table. "I consider the moral situation in Les Tanneurs to be dire, Brother Wikerus, and I know you are doing much good in that quarter of the city. I cannot spare you from your work, not even for a day. The eternal consequences are simply too steep."

Wikerus took a deep breath. Sacrifices must be made for the sake of preserving a life. "In that case, let Brother Tacitus take my place in Les Tanneurs. I am sure he will have just as much success with the tanners' widows as me."

Wikerus felt more than a slight pang of guilt as he walked through Colmar's gate toward Vogelgrun early the next morning. To leave anyone in the pastoral care of Brother Tacitus wasn't kind, but there was no other way he could obtain permission to leave for his investigation.

He was well outside of the walls of Colmar and descending toward the marshy lowlands of the Rhine River when he realized that someone had followed him. In an instant, Wikerus saw his mistake. Merchants, workers, and nobles traversed this road – all men who were either armed or had guards accompanying them. A solitary man walking on an empty highway was bait for the groups of bandits who had proliferated after the pestilence ravaged every city and town in Alsace. The last time he traveled to Vogelgrun was in the company of Lord Frider, who had a horse and a sword, and Tacitus, who would surely preach at his attackers until they dropped to sleep of boredom.

Wikerus stopped and bent to adjust the strap of his sandal, taking a moment to get a better look at his stalker: slight build, not very tall, body and head concealed by a tattered brown robe. Most alarmingly, the follower carried a gnarled wooden club in his hand, which he occasionally dragged in the dust as he walked. Wikerus straightened and quickened his pace, realizing with dread that it wouldn't matter. Vogelgrun was still a great distance away, and returning to Colmar was impossible since it would mean passing his assailant on the road. He felt beads of sweat dribbling down the back of his itchy wool robe.

"The Lord is my shepherd; I shall not want." Wikerus whispered the *Dominus regit me* between parched lips. "He leads me to sleep beside quiet waters."

The thought of quiet waters made him realize that he was powerfully thirsty. But he could not stop to drink, or his stalker would take advantage and attack. If I stop, I would be like the doe who drinks at the stream, only to be set upon by wolves! he thought to himself. He walked faster, and his follower also increased his pace.

As Wikerus considered all his options, including climbing into a nearby tree, he noticed a sound, quiet at first, coming from the direction of Colmar behind him – wagon wheels juddering and rattling over the rutted road.

Jesu, I am saved, he thought. No one will attack when there are witnesses about, and I can beg a ride on the wagon and evade this man who is following me! He kept walking, and so did his mysterious shadow.

Meanwhile, the sound of the wagon grew louder, and finally, to the great relief of the friar, an oxcart emerged from the trees, driven by a solitary man who transported a load of wooden wine barrels. Wikerus glanced back and noticed that the club-wielding would-be attacker pulled his cowl closer about his face and made an obvious attempt to look nonchalant – more indication that whoever was behind Wikerus on the road had intended to do violence.

The wagon rider, who walked next to his ox, reached out and yanked hard on the beast's halter, grunting a low command until the animal lumbered to a stop. Wikerus stepped off the road and ducked behind a hazel tree. The ox driver spoke quickly with the club-wielder and grabbed the man about the waist.

Wikerus rubbed his eyes. "Is that cart driver trying to kiss my stalker?" he asked aloud. Sure enough, the oxcart driver had the other man in an embrace and was leaning into the hood of the large, enveloping cloak, lips puckered.

The club swung up and clobbered the driver on the side of the head. The driver toppled backward into the tall grass next to the road. Then, the club-wielder began to run at full speed toward Wikerus, tripping occasionally on his long, flapping cloak. The friar decided he wasn't about to suffer the same fate as the ox driver. He grabbed his robes and trotted as fast as his sandal-clad feet would take him.

"Friar!" his pursuer shouted. "Friar, please wait! Friar Wikerus!"

Wikerus spared a glance behind him and then looked again. "Frau Appel?" His foot caught on a stone, and he soared off the road and into a nearby rosebush.

His pursuer caught up to him. The cowl had flown back, and Frau Appel Schneider's fraying, gray braid was clearly visible. "Oh, Friar, are you hurt?"

"Ow!"

Appel took one of his arms and dragged him from the rose bush.

"Frau...Frau Appel," Wikerus panted. "What are you doing on this road all alone?"

"I wasn't alone. I was with you. Always kept you in my sights, and I have a weapon." She looked around for a moment. Spying her discarded club lying in the road, she trotted back for it.

"It looks like you have damaged Herr Fuhrmann, the carter. You must return and see that he receives tending by a healer."

"He is not injured, Friar. Just embarrassed."

Sure enough, Herr Fuhrmann pulled himself up from the ditch, grasping at tufts of spring grass and clawing his way toward the road. He stood, dusted himself off, and quickly mounted his cart.

"I thought you meant to take your barrels to Vogelgrun, Herr Fuhrmann!" Appel called to him.

"Changed my mind!" Herr Fuhrmann called back. With a flick of his long willow switch, he motivated his ox to move with haste back toward Colmar.

"He knows that you saw him try to kiss me. He's probably returning to Colmar to tell his story before I can," Appel said grimly.

"And you must also return to Colmar, Frau Appel. This is a dangerous road for women, as we just saw!"

"It is also dangerous for solitary friars. I heard you are traveling to Vogelgrun to clear Jorges' name, and I intend to help you."

"Absolutely not. No, I insist that you return to Colmar immediately."

Appel planted her feet and crossed her arms. "Shall I walk back to Colmar alone, then? Or do you suggest I ride with Herr Fuhrmann? Which would be a safer option? Personally, I would rather take my chances walking home with a pack of starving wolves."

"I will walk back with you."

"And waste the precious time that you have to investigate Jorges? Friar Tacitus said that the prior only granted you one night."

She had him trapped.

"Very well, you can stay. But you will do exactly as I say. There are dangerous men about."

Appel didn't acknowledge him. Instead, she set her mouth in a firm line and threw the cowl over her head. "Shall we continue?"

"Yes," Wikerus said. "We have very little time and much to do."

The minstrels' tale

In which vital details emerge, but not in song or verse

BY THE TIME Appel and Wikerus arrived in Vogelgrun, it was mid-morning. They spoke little on the road, as neither of them had spent any actual amount of time alone in each other's company before, and they rarely traveled outside the walls of Colmar. The newness of their surroundings made them shy.

The road stretched ahead of them, unbroken by hills and curves, flanked on either side by black-brown furrows of freshly plowed earth and the occasional stand of trees just beginning to show their leaves. As usual, water collected everywhere. It stagnated in ponds, pooled in the natural hollows and depressions in the land, and trickled through trenches that the farmers dug to irrigate their crops. The sound of flowing water became as normal as the birdsong, and the streams grew more significant as they neared the Rhine River. Appel enjoyed the new surroundings, unaware that next to her, Wikerus felt growing dread, for Breisach, the town of his birth, was visible across the river.

So great was his distraction that he didn't notice the large, dark brown stain in the dusty road until Appel gasped, "Why, it's blood!" Wikerus looked down at his feet. He was standing in the center of a pool of dried blood as big as the wheel of a cart. Appel followed a trail of dribbles and gore to the side of the road and discovered another puddle of blood, still wet, on the side of the wagon track.

"This must have been where it happened," Wikerus said quietly.

"Mother Mary, preserve our souls," Appel whispered and crossed herself quickly. Wikerus squatted on his heels, his face close to the dirt.

"Many have come this way since the murder happened," he said with a scowl. "I see horse tracks, wagon ruts, and even a few footsteps through this blood."

"How can we ever determine Jorges' innocence with nothing but a dried puddle," Appel said. She sat heavily in the dirt.

Wikerus leaned forward and ran his finger along two deep divots in the dust.

"I think this is how," he said. "This is where the hands were removed."

"Oh! How do you know, Friar?"

Wikerus scraped at the dirt, held up something small and stained dark red, and favored her with a grim smile.

"It is a piece of bone. And see, the soil here is delved deep and narrow. No horse, wagon, or walking stick made this mark. It was a knife, sawing through flesh and bone. I only hope the poor wretch was dead before the murderer cut the hands from his body."

"Do you yet know his name, Friar? Who was it that lost life and limbs where we're standing?"

"If Sheriff Werner and his colleagues in Colmar knew the name of the dead man, they did not think it important enough to tell me. Come. All shall be revealed in Vogelgrun, I think." He bowed his head and said a silent prayer for the dead man. Then he rose and continued walking, with Appel scrambling to find her feet and catch up.

Vogelgrun was exactly as Appel had left it. Low-slung thatched huts and smithies on the outskirts of the town made way for tall warehouses and a market square as they moved close to the central courtyard. Friar Wikerus and Appel wandered around for a while, unsure of their destination. Appel wrung her hands as they walked, her eyes darting about.

"I don't know where to start, Friar Wikerus!"

"Aye. Let us start first by trying to determine the poor man's name." He nodded toward the house where he had met the sheriff of Vogelgrun on his last visit.

Appel hitched her stride, suddenly unsure.

"That house looks very fine, Friar Wikerus. Why, it's built of stone! Perhaps I should wait outside while you speak to the occupants."

Friar Wikerus took her firmly by the elbow. "You will not find the owner as fine as his house. And as a daughter of Colmar, you must speak." He turned to her and flashed one of his broad, luminescent smiles. "As you recall, I am only an immigrant. An interloper from Breisach. Your words hold more weight here than mine. These people revere citizens of Colmar."

Like his first visit, a roar of revelry emanated from inside. He pushed the door open without knocking, and the first thing they saw were two men dancing a lively jig together in the center of the single room, arms linked, cheeks rosy. A dog barked and jumped at the dancers, and several men were singing and slapping their thighs.

"Well!" Appel said from where she stood behind the friar. "I shan't complain about our own sheriff! Not after what I've seen here!"

Friar Wikerus scanned the room, a frown on his face.

"None of these men are Sheriff Vogel, although this is his house." He tapped a cheering man on the shoulder. "Friend, where can I find the sheriff?"

The man thumbed over his shoulder toward the animal partition. Friar Wikerus peeked around the wall. Sheriff Vogel was curled up, fast asleep in the straw. He turned back to the man, who had resumed his cheering, and tapped him on the shoulder again, this time more forcefully. "And what of the citizen of Vogelgrun who was found murdered on the road yesterday? Is there no one who cares?"

"Who?"

Wikerus threw up his hands and turned to Appel. "Let's go. These men are useless."

Appel followed meekly behind the much younger friar as he stomped from the house. "Well, I am sure the sheriff knows best," she mumbled. Friar Wikerus stopped in his tracks, then spun and faced her. He looked at her for a moment, then he looked over her shoulder, his blue eyes growing wide.

"Appel? Frau Appel? Where are you?"

Appel pulled a perplexed frown. "I am standing before you, Friar Wikerus."

Friar Wikerus took a few tentative steps past her, his eyes darting around like a man lost. "Frau Appel!" he shrieked. A regiment of the emperor's soldiers were marching past, as Vogelgrun was not a free city, and a few of the men turned their heads in alarm at the outburst.

"Ssshhhh!" Appel hissed, clutching at the friar's rough brown robe. "I am right here!"

Friar Wikerus staggered away from her and nearly stumbled upon a woman who walked along the road laden with a tray, supported by a hemp rope slung over her shoulders. She was selling small, white ingots of goat cheese. "Excuse me!" he panted, clutching at the woman. "I am looking for someone. Frau Appel Schneider of Colmar, have you seen her?"

Nearby, Appel gasped. What had gotten into him? The cheese seller's face softened when she realized the man who clutched at her was a friar. "There, there now," she said slowly and loudly. "You just rest yourself for a moment, Friar, and I will find someone from the church to give you aid."

"She was here. I knew her in Colmar," Friar Wikerus mumbled. "Fierce, brave. Frau Appel Schneider wouldn't let anyone intimidate her, not even a drunken sheriff of Vogelgrun and his stone house." He turned to Appel, and she thought she saw his eyelashes flutter into a furtive wink.

"Ah! I see what you are trying to do, Friar Wikerus." Appel laughed and handed the confused vendor a coin. "I would like one of those lovely cheeses, if you please."

Friar Wikerus produced a loaf of fine, white bread from his robe, and he and Appel made their way toward the river to find a place to eat their lunch. All shyness and misunderstanding between them was now only a memory.

The Rhine glowed green under the spring sun. Appel didn't see the river often, but every time she did, the largeness of it stole her breath away. At first glance, water appeared to flow slowly until one observed a boat or a piece of flotsam in the current, and then the river's power was easy to see. Because of the spring thaw, the reeds and grasses normally at the water's edge bowed under the current, and the water reached the roots of nearby trees that clung to the bank. Some of them, robbed of the clay under their roots, slumped over, dipping their bare branches into the river.

A little wooden dock, standing stalwart against the flow of the water, accepted ferries that took passengers across, and a small crowd had gathered there. "They are fewer than normal, you see, because the water flows fast, and it is a treacherous crossing. Those who cross during the high spring water are the people who have no choice but to cross. Many would choose instead to take lodging nearby and wait for things to dry out," Friar Wikerus said between bites.

The thought of the river rushing high brought back a painful memory of that terrible year not so long ago when it seemed the sun never shone and rain fell ceaselessly. With the memory came the unwelcome image of his brother being swept away into the current while the water was fast and brown with silt. That was the year the harvests failed, hunger tore at people's stomachs, and then came the pestilence. It was sometimes overwhelming to consider all that had happened in such a short time – the people who had died, the towns and villages abandoned, and the terrifying increase in crime. He felt his knees buckle and caught himself just before he stumbled. Appel reached out to steady him.

"Are you well, Friar Wikerus?"

"I am well. I just wasn't paying attention. Here, let us sit upon this large stone to watch the excitement." No, he couldn't talk about it. Those memories stabbed him.

They sat in silence, munching their bread and cheese and sharing a skin of small ale, watching as a ferry struggled against the current and nearly missed the dock, its oarsmen working madly. As soon as it disgorged its load of terrified passengers, the captain stepped onto the dock and called out.

"No more crossings for today! The river is angry, and we'd best let her have some peace until the water is calmer. Come back again tomorrow."

The people waiting to cross groaned, and a few of them tried to argue with the captain, including a man traveling with a party of minstrels. While his comrades held his lute, the minstrel yelled at the captain, waving his arms and using his well-practiced singing voice to shout his displeasure. It was a useless effort. The minstrel stomped back to the two other men of his traveling party. From where they sat, Appel and Friar Wikerus could easily overhear their conversation.

"He said no."

"Aye, we heard. And so did the whole town," replied a man in a deep blue tunic with a matching blue cowl, patting the lutist on the shoulder. "Let us try to find lodging before the other passengers rent all the beds in this place and we are left to sleep under a wagon."

The angry minstrel paced, snapping his fingers and huffing. "I want to leave here. I want to get as far away from this side of the river as possible. Did you know the body we found on the road yesterday wasn't the first? It was the second body discovered in as many weeks! I heard it from not one but two people in the market today. A murderer is lurking around here, and I want to leave before we're next."

Appel and Friar Wikerus, overhearing this conversation, exchanged a look of understanding, and then Friar Wikerus jumped to his feet.

"Excuse me, friends, but did you say that you discovered a body lying in the road yesterday?"

The angry minstrel narrowed his eyes. "Who's asking? I don't trust anyone in this place."

Friar Wikerus grinned and gave a slight bow. "I am Friar Wikerus of Breisach, currently in residence with the Dominicans in Colmar. And I have been tasked with learning what I can about these murders that have shocked and terrorized our community. I would be grateful if you could tell me if a drunk man was nearby, possibly asleep?"

"Here now, yes, there was! The poor man was terrified when he awoke from his wine-sleep."

Wikerus took a step closer, and Appel joined him. "And can you tell me, were there two severed hands in his sack?"

The minstrel shuddered. "There were. It was a terrible sight that will haunt my dreams."

Friar Wikerus nodded. "Friends, can I buy you a drink while you wait for the ferryman to allow you to cross? We have some questions we'd like to ask you."

Falling out and falling back in

In which an argument is put aside

WHEN APPEL AND WIKERUS set off for Colmar the next morning, the sun had barely crested the horizon's edge. The light was gray as they walked in the dawn shadows, their eyes and ears as attuned to the sounds of the morning as rabbits in a vegetable patch. Before they left Vogelgrun, the widow and the friar had agreed that the information they had found was compelling, puzzling, and definitely worth a stay of execution while they attempted to confirm the details. Neither Appel nor Wikerus, however, were so naive to think that the council would wait for more proof of guilt before hanging a penniless porter from Les Tanneurs. Such mercies were rarely extended to men like Jorges Leporteur. For the rest of their walk, they didn't speak. There was nothing to say.

On their return to Colmar, Friar Wikerus made his way up the gentle slope toward Saint Martin's, ready for his bed and the healing voices of his Dominican brothers, raised in worshipful supplication during Prime. Appel walked alongside the trench into Les Tanneurs, tiptoed up the stairs to the second level of her house, and slipped into bed next to Efi, whose snoring rattled the floorboards. She sank into the straw next to the warm body of the younger woman, her muscles aching from the long walk, her mind exhausted from what she had learned in Vogelgrun, and promptly drifted to sleep.

She remained in a dreamless slumber until the sun was nearly at its zenith. When she finally trudged down the stairs and into the house's lower floor, Efi was already scooping up bowls of steaming barley pottage and slicing in some fresh asparagus for the midday meal.

"I thought it best to let you sleep," Efi said, not meeting Appel's eyes. "Don't know what you were doing, but I hope you received some money from it because we're nearly out of grain – for eating and the brewing."

"Just what are you insinuating that I've been doing all night, Efi?" Appel's voice was ice.

"Only what everyone else in this town appears to know already. That you take lovers, including the married men of the town. I shall be moving out as soon as I can find a husband."

"Well, I would certainly hope so. I don't need another one of your brilliant husbands here to burn my house down or drown himself."

"Oh, Appel!" Efi whispered. "How could you!" She covered her face and ran outside.

Appel watched through a crack in her crumbling walls as Efi knocked on Gritta's door across the lane, and someone welcomed her inside. Then, she turned and surveyed the main room of her house. Efi had swept the packed earth floor until it was as smooth and polished as stone. The walls, which had once been plastered and painted, were dingy and chipped. In some places, the woven willow branches showed through, but Appel noticed that Efi had begun to patch some of the holes with daubs of mud and straw. A large table dominated one side of the room, and Efi had set it for a meal with two green-glazed clay bowls, spoons, and a few sprigs of woodruff in a wooden cup. At the nearly finished hearth, a small iron pot bubbled on its trivet over some well-tended coals.

"She really is learning how to keep house," Appel mumbled to herself. When she had first met the girl, Efi was lost, helpless, and empty-headed – a heartbroken and terrified new widow. Almost a year later, the girl had become as dear to her as a daughter. Appel tore off her apron and marched outside, hopping the trench in the middle of the lane, and knocked loudly on Gritta's door. A small boy, one of Gritta's identical twins, opened it.

"Ma!" he yelled. "Frau Appel has come visiting. Shall I let her in, or do you still hate her?"

Gritta shooed the child away and crossed her arms.

"Well then, what is it? Come to take another stab at young Efi here?"

In the house behind Gritta, Efi sat at the large trestle table, sniffling over a steaming cup of broth.

Appel cleared her throat. She knew she should apologize but couldn't bring herself to do it. Instead, she said, "Jorges didn't do it. I have proof that he didn't."

Gritta pulled the door shut behind her and stepped outside with Appel.

"You have a way to change the sheriff's mind, do you?"

"Yes. I went out yesterday with Friar Wikerus to the place on the road to Vogelgrun where the sheriff arrested Jorges. We found —"

"It doesn't matter what you found," Gritta interrupted her. "No one cares what you found. No one cares about Jorges or me and my children. If Jorges hangs for this crime, there is one less reason for Sheriff Werner and the rest of the city council to leave Herr Schlock's weinstube every evening to drag my husband home. You hear them, Appel. They want me to have fewer children. They want Jorges to drink less. Well, I ask you, why would I have fewer children when every city, town, and village has empty houses and markets, filled with mothers who weep for lost babes from the pestilence? Why would Jorges stay away from the drink when it is the only thing that offers him solace? What other way can he make those memories of death and sickness quiet enough that he can sleep at night?"

"My friend, you mustn't think your life and Jorges' are unimportant."

"Why? Give me a reason not to think it."

"Well, Friar Wikerus —"

"Father Konrad commanded Friar Wikerus to care about this community. Do you think he would come here if his prior hadn't ordered it?"

"Probably not, and as a result, my days would be dull, devoid of joy, and deprived of fine ale," Friar Wikerus interrupted the two women as he walked around the corner of the house in the dooryard. "You may have observed that many in this city think your lives don't matter, and you are right: to those who have more money and more power, the fate of Jorges Leporteur is not important to them. But if we allow people like Jorges to take punishment for crimes they didn't commit, this will continue long past the time of our death." He took Gritta's hands in his own. "And I know that Jorges is innocent."

Gritta released a deep, heavy sigh at his words, and Appel saw the battle go out of her.

"Appel knows it, too. She was with me on the road to Vogelgrun, and she is a witness to what we discovered."

Appel nodded, and Gritta's face hardened again. "And I suppose that when the true murderer is locked up and awaiting hanging, Appel will show up with spiced wine and sweet cakes to cheer them as she did for that witch, Margitte."

Friar Wikerus stepped forward. "Frau Gritta, it is time to put this behind you. We all make mistakes. Maintaining your feud is not worth the destruction of a lifelong friendship."

Gritta crossed her arms again and sulked while Appel did her best to appear aloof. Efi, having dried her eyes, pulled the door open and stepped outside.

"Appel also did say disparaging remarks about my dear deceased Harald! And I have heard that she deals illicitly in Les Tanneurs. With married men!"

Gritta stepped in front of Appel. "You painted whore! How dare you spread slander about Appel! Why, I have heard it said that you go out in the moonlight and bed the Devil to bring your empty-headed husband back!"

"And I have heard," Efi screamed, shoving Friar Wikerus aside, "that you put pig shit in the ale when Appel and I aren't looking, and the men in Karl Gastwirt's inn can taste it!"

"Alewives, who has been saying these things?" Wikerus narrowed his eyes and was not surprised when Gritta and Efi replied, "Friar Tacitus!" in unison.

"Jesu, forgive me. I never should have allowed Tacitus to minister here, but it was the only way to convince Father Konrad to release me to Vogelgrun. Now listen while I tell you what we learned. Jorges was discovered between Colmar and Vogelgrun, sleeping with his head in the tall grass at the side of the road and his feet still in the wheel tracks. He slept where he had fallen."

Gritta's shoulders slumped. "And now I suppose you are going to tell me that Jorges fell to sleep because he was drunk."

"Well, yes, but —"

"But it was not Jorges' fault. Not really," Appel cut in. With a knowing smile and a twinkle in his eye, Friar Wikerus took a step back and let Appel continue.

"We looked at the place where he fell. There was a dreadfully large brown stain of blood on the road and then more that dripped and spilled over to where Jorges lay in the ditch.

Certainly, he would have looked guilty to the men who found him."

"And who did find him? A crofter? The sheriff of Vogelgrun?"

Appel shook her head. "No, it was a group of minstrels on their way to Vogelgrun. Friar Wikerus and I managed to find them as they waited for a ferry across the river. They were terrified when they saw Jorges lying in the ditch and the handless body in the road, so they turned back for Colmar, but on their way, they encountered Sheriff Werner and a small cadre of his men on their way to the river. It seems the sheriff was on his way to Sundhoffen to collect rents owed from a few wayward tenants. The minstrels swore upon the earlobes of the Virgin that Jorges did not have any blood on his own hands or tunic when they discovered him. They even pointed it out to the sheriff, but he told them it was unimportant and sent them on their way."

"Unimportant?" Gritta squeaked. "Why, that seems like a pretty important detail to me! Surely the man could not ignore something so obvious. If Jorges' hands and clothes were clean, then he didn't do it."

"He could have willfully ignored the detail because he is impatient to put a rope around someone's throat and make himself look like a hero to Lord Frider and the burghers, or he could just be incompetent," Friar Wikerus mused.

Gritta began to pace, her ire at Appel forgotten. "Or the sheriff murdered the man himself or knew who did it and is trying to protect someone."

"Also possible." Wikerus nodded slowly. "But the minstrels also passed someone else on the road before they discovered the body. They met a single rider heading in the opposite direction on a dappled gelding. The minstrels told us that this man looked pale, distracted, and seemed to be in a great hurry. When they asked him where he was going, he acted defensive and suspicious. He eventually told them that he was a merchant bound for Mulhouse. Also, he carried a sword at his side."

Gritta's face was grim. "A sword would be adequate to cut the hands from a man's body. Jorges doesn't own anything sharper than his eating knife. Did they learn the man's name?"

"Heinrik. It was Heinrik of Strassburg," Appel responded. "I met him when I went to Vogelgrun weeks ago and brought Margitte back to Colmar with me. He was very charming. Too charming, I now think. He could have befriended anyone and convinced them to cut off their own hands if he wished."

"And what did Sheriff Werner say to that, eh? Is the presence of a nervous man with a blade on the road also an unimportant detail?"

"We do not know. The minstrels didn't think to tell the sheriff they had encountered anyone else. Perhaps they were too frightened."

"Imbeciles! This 'Heinrik' must be found, and soon! Jorges will hang in just two days!" Gritta cried.

"I know, my friend," Appel said quietly.

"I spoke with Father Konrad this morning. He agreed that I could take this information about the man on the road to the sheriff, but not until after I had done my day's chores and worship at the priory. I fear we will lose precious time. I was only able to slip away right now because the brothers are all fishing in the grand canal. I pretended to catch a hook in my finger and begged their leave to visit the barber to have it removed, then came straight here. I must return before I am missed, but I came to say that you, alewives, must go to the sheriff immediately. Convince him to look for Heinrik of Strassburg and to halt Jorges' execution until the man can be apprehended."

"Us, Friar?" Gritta said. "What makes you think he will listen to us?"

"You three can be very convincing; if you make him think it is his idea, he will likely go along with it. Now, hurry!"

"I'll get my bonnet!" Efi chirped.

An interview with an entourage

In which a pretty face and a few white lies prove useful

Everyone knew that the city council held official meetings in the market building, then met afterward at Herr Schlock's weinstube to drink and gossip. This is where the real work happened, lubricated by cups of crisp white wine and seasoned with the satisfaction of knowing how lucky Colmar was to be a free imperial city that was allowed to make and enforce its own laws. The weinstube also served as a refuge for the men of Colmar – a refuge, that is, from the women. There was no rule against women in the weinstube; it just wasn't done. Herr Schlock's was a place for the men to recline near the fire, play dice, and have their Very Important Conversations in the company of each other without the inconvenience of women, which is why Appel, Gritta, and Efi simply stood outside the door and called in when they sought the sheriff.

On this evening, Sheriff Werner was not in a favorable mood to speak with them, and after ignoring their cries for some time, Gritta finally growled and stomped over the threshold. All conversation in the great, dim room stopped as she planted her feet in front of the table where the sheriff sat, affixed her hands to her hips, and glared silently at him. She jabbed a finger toward the door.

"Well then? Are you going to leave those widows outside to cry for your help, or are you going to do right by us and listen to what we have to say?"

Sheriff Werner glanced out the door at Efi and Appel, who were doing their best to look forsaken and put-upon. "I think letting the three of you resolve your quarrels is the best thing to do." He reached into his tunic and withdrew a small leather bag that held his day's money. Tipping a small pile of copper coins into his palm, he smiled at Gritta. "Here now. Take this coin and buy your friends a few trifles in the market or some cakes from Herr Bäcker. That will stop the disagreement quickly enough."

"Disagreement? What on earth are you talking about, Sheriff? I am here because you have my husband locked in your tower once again, and the day after tomorrow you plan to kill him!"

Sheriff Werner looked down into his cup. His cheeks, already rosy with wine and good company, now burned scarlet. "Oh. I had heard some talk that you and Frau Appel were not speaking to each other. Some women's quarrel over a lover or a chemise. Something like that."

Appel stepped over the threshold, slipping an arm around Gritta's waist, and Efi trotted in after her.

"We are friends, Sheriff Werner, and sometimes that means we may argue, but it will take the hand of God to make us turn our backs on each other," Appel said. "Now, will you help us find the real killer, or will we have to do your work for you?"

Appel, Gritta, and Efi stood outside the weinstube, pondering their misfortune. Twice, they had explained to the sheriff what Friar Wikerus and Appel learned from their trip to Vogelgrun: that the minstrels swore upon the blessed Virgin's earlobes that they saw no blood on Jorges' hands and clothes, that someone in Vogelgrun had been buying Jorges many drinks that day, and a mounted, agitated man with a sword was seen on the road, hurrying away from where they later discovered a handless body.

As they spoke, the other patrons in the weinstube abandoned the pretense of playing their games and gathered to watch, which outraged Herr Schlock, who grumbled about wanting to commit a murder of his own if the three women didn't leave his premises.

Sheriff Werner listened in silence, waggling a finger to Herr Schlock to bring another pitcher of wine, and when the alewives finished with their tale, he smiled with exaggerated patience.

"Good women, go back to your homes. Gritta, I saw Jorges myself when my men discovered him on the road with the unfortunate man's hands in his sack, and of course, there was blood on him. Would you trust the word of those minstrels in Vogelgrun over the sheriff of your own town? I am insulted."

"Jens Töpfer."

"I beg your pardon?"

"That's the name of the 'unfortunate man' who lost his hands. Everyone knows he was a potter who had lived all his life in Vogelgrun – the only member of his family to survive the pestilence. And if you couldn't be bothered to learn the dead man's name, you certainly can't be bothered to find the truth. Jorges is always the first one you blame because it's convenient for you!" Gritta was fuming, her voice rising with each word she spoke.

One of the assembled men, a council member, stood. "Be quiet, woman! You speak to one of your betters!" he barked at her.

After that, the sheriff would hear no more, and the women removed themselves from the weinstube only after Herr Schlock threatened to have them thrown out.

"What will we do?" Efi said, her voice full of despair. "There is not time enough for us to find Heinrik of Strassburg before Jorges hangs."

Gritta sniffled loudly and swiped a few tears from her cheeks. "Well, I won't give up until they have my husband swinging from a rope, and after that, I shall stand outside the sheriff's house and yell insults at him every morning until after the brothers of Saint Martin's sing their prayers at Prime. Come with me." She walked resolutely from the weinstube, where the sounds of the men's talk and laughter had resumed.

"But where are we going, Gritta?" Appel asked.

"To talk to the other men who were with the sheriff when my Jorges was found."

"But I already did. The minstrels were there."

"And so was the posse of simpletons that always surrounds the sheriff whenever he leaves the walls of Colmar. That pompous old coward never travels without his entourage."

They walked through the gloom to the sheriff's large house, perched on the pinnacle of the gentle slope that rose near Saint Martin's. Unlike the wood and daub houses in Les Tanneurs, which made them easy to pull apart and rebuild when the canals flooded, Sheriff Werner's home had mortared stone walls on its first level and housed a courtyard with a stable holding three bays of horses. Gritta's step quickened, but just before her fist could land on the gate, Appel pulled her back by the scruff of her threadbare dress.

"You must stay in the shadows, Gritta. Efi and I will handle this. Because Jorges is the one locked away, they'll be expecting you, but not us."

Gritta nodded and slipped around the corner as Appel knocked on the postern, a small door in the heavy wooden gate. A man wrenched it open.

"The sheriff ain't here, so – oh...hello, Frau Efi." Even in the rapidly growing darkness, the man's face flushed visibly. Appel looked at him for a moment, then turned to Efi, who was standing and smiling coyly behind her.

"Ahem." Appel cleared her throat and swallowed her annoyance. "Good evening to you. I know the sheriff isn't here. I just saw him at Herr Schlock's, and he asked us to come straight to his residence to talk with the men who found Jorges Leporteur on the road to Vogelgrun. As you may have heard, I also accompanied Friar Wikerus on a journey of inquiry, and I have authority in this matter."

"Well," the guard said. "I don't know. 'Tis late, and the lamps aren't lit tonight because the sheriff is not at home, and his lady is traveling to Kaysersberg to take the waters."

Appel reached behind her and pulled Efi closer to the door. "We both have many questions to ask."

Efi giggled and ran a finger along the edge of her crisp cotton wimple, edged with stitches in red thread. One golden lock of hair slipped from the chaste head-covering and revealed itself.

"If the sheriff says so, then who am I to disobey?" The guard grinned. "Say, Frau Efi, are you courtin' yet? Harald has been dead for a season now."

"Efi is doing no such thing." Appel pulled Efi behind her protectively.

But Efi fluttered her eyelashes and laughed. "I am courting Peter, the stonemason's apprentice. And Herr Tisch, the carpenter, has also been very attentive lately."

Appel scowled at her friend. Efi continued.

"And there is also the meat pie vendor who sells in the market. He did offer me a fine prospect."

"Efi, how did you find time to court so many men? You rarely leave my house!"

Efi giggled. "It is such a funny coincidence! I keep meeting them in the mornings when I fetch water from the stream at Saint Martin's for our ale. Just yesterday, Peter, the stonemason's apprentice, was there, and I have no idea why, for his workshop is on the other side of town. We had the loveliest talk as he carried my waterskins for me."

"I wonder, indeed. He must take a very roundabout way to walk from his bed in the stonemason's stables to his work in the stonemason's workshop, which is right next to the very stables that he sleeps in." Appel rolled her eyes. She would have to keep a closer eye on the girl lest something untoward happened. After all, a woman of childbearing years like Efi couldn't afford any mishaps.

The guard pulled the door open wider and ushered them through. Just inside, a few other men shared a bowl of wine and warmed themselves against the evening's chill at a small fire in the courtyard. The guard swaggered to his companions.

"Lads, you have all met Appel and Efi of Les Tanneurs, have you not?"

One of the men, the youngest, stared up from where he sat near the fire with wide eyes, and the other two leered. The gate guard gestured at Appel with his thumb. "Seems the good sheriff sent them here to…" In the flickering firelight, his confidence turned to confusion.

"To ask a few questions of you all," Appel finished his sentence before the guard could think too hard about why he had let them through the gates. "There seems to be some bafflement about the day you found Jorges Leporteur on the road, and since the lord sheriff is very busy and doesn't wish to be disturbed while he discusses this murder with the city council, he asked us to come gather a few answers and report back to him."

The men looked at her blankly for a moment, so Appel continued.

"I, er...the sheriff wishes for you good men to recall whether or not Jorges Leporteur had blood on his hands and clothes when you found him. His memory of the day is clouded by his extreme distress at the gruesomeness of the crime, which I am sure you also feel keenly."

The men glanced at each other and shook their heads.

"Weren't no blood on his hands, Frau Appel. Not till he woke from his wine-sleep."

Appel leaned closer to the man. "Why? Why was there blood on his hands after he woke up but not before?"

The man sat back on the log he used for his seat and wrinkled his brow. "Well, now, Jorges was upset when he woke, wasn't he? Fast asleep he was, in the grass by the side o' the road, probably dreaming of making another baby with Frau Gritta, when Tomas here shook him awake."

"Why did Tomas, not the sheriff, wake Jorges?" Appel asked.

Beside him, the man named Tomas shrugged. "Sheriff Werner didn't wish to dismount his horse. It's quite a chore to get him back on his mount, and besides, you never know what will happen when you try to rouse a sleeping man on the side of the road."

"And what did happen?" Efi asked him.

"Well, Jorges rubbed his eyes and smiled up at us. Said good morning like it was the finest day he'd ever seen. The sheriff from atop his horse tells Jorges to turn out his bag, and that's when we find the hands."

Appel could feel her pulse quicken. "So, the hands were not visible to you yet? They were hidden in the bag?"

"Not visible, but the blood on the ground was there. A trail of it leading from the body in the road to where Jorges lay."

"But his hands were clean?"

Upon the additional questioning, Tomas looked at his companions around the fire, who nodded solemnly. "No blood on his hands. Not until he tipped his bag upside-down, and we all saw what was there. Then Jorges picked up those bloody things and began to wave them about, screaming and crying."

"What was he saying?"

"What was he saying? Who knows. The man was still drunk. Sounded like he was just scared."

"And then what happened?" Appel was leaning in closer, and Efi clutched at her arm.

"Then the sheriff commanded us to take Jorges and bind him tightly. We put the handless body over the back of the sheriff's horse and walked back to Colmar. Left a dribbling mess of blood almost all the way back to the city gate."

"And you recognized the dead man?"

"Aye indeed," the guard scratched at his armpit as he spoke. "Old Jens. He made those blue clay wine flagons that all the goodwives are always clamoring for. A nice old man, was Jen Töpfer. It's a shame, what happened to him."

"Where is the body now?" Efi asked.

"In the ground. Friar Tacitus was the only man about the priory when we returned, as the rest of the brothers were in their beds, so he said a prayer, and we buried the poor soul before midnight."

"And did you see anyone else on the road that day?"

"Only a group of minstrels. It was they who alerted us to the murder."

"No one else?"

The men looked at each other for a moment, then shook their heads no.

Tomas squinted at Appel. "Sounds like you know something you ain't telling us." The other guards, all seated upon their rough-cut logs, leaned forward.

"There was another man upon the road that day," Appel said, the light of the fire flickering on her creased face. "By all accounts, he was agitated and in a hurry."

"And he wore a sword at his hip," Efi said. "Sharper than anything that Jorges Leporteur owns."

Tomas scratched his roughly shorn chin. "Where did this man go?"

Efi fluttered her hands and allowed her large, blue eyes to fill with tears. "That is just the problem. We do not know. He was in a great hurry. He told the minstrels he was bound for Mulhouse, but that could have been a ruse to lead people away from his true destination."

Tomas glanced at the other men. "There must be a reason we could think of for the sheriff to travel to Mulhouse tomorrow. Ain't there a Jew living there who works in gold to make baubles for the sheriff's mistress?"

The old guard from the gate put a hand on Tomas's shoulder. "I know you wish to please the fair young widow Efi, Tomas, but there is no reason for us to travel to Mulhouse. And besides, 'tis two days' walk there. We would never return before Jorges hangs." He turned to Efi and Appel and smiled sadly. "You are a good woman, trying to free your friend's husband. But I am afraid it is impossible. He will hang after tomorrow night."

The witch of Vogelgrun
In which Margitte returns

It took some time for Appel and Efi to extricate themselves from the sheriff's home. Worried that he would stagger back from the weinstube and discover them questioning his men, they made a few polite excuses and stood to leave, but the men begged them to stay. They finally left when Efi offered to sing them a song. As the tuneless noise began, the men's expectant expressions quickly faded to confusion and then discomfort. Appel crossed her arms, smirking as the men squirmed with every missed note. When she had finished, the men had a change of heart, and the guard escorted them to the gates.

When they reported to Gritta that the guards had no new or helpful information to share, she didn't take the news well.

"Where is my hoe?!" she screamed as she marched back to Les Tanneurs. "I shall beat that fat sheriff with it until his own hands fall off!"

"Hush, my dear!" Appel hissed. "If someone were to hear you making threats against the sheriff in such a way, you would hang alongside your husband."

"But I would die beside my Jorges!" Gritta wailed.

"Honestly, Gritta. I never thought you had such high regard for him." Appel crossed her arms.

"Oh, it is love – like in the courtly tales!" Efi breathed.

"Shut up, Efi," Appel snapped. "The courtly tales deal chiefly in lust, not love." She squinted at her friend. "What has gotten into you, Gritta? Only a few months ago, you spat on the floor whenever someone mentioned your husband's name. And now you claim to be ready to die with him?"

"I cannot deny it, Appel. Being thrown into the tower with Jorges was the best thing for us. When he is not raving with drink, he is quite sweet."

"Oh, such a pity," Efi breathed, clasping her hands at her breast. "It is a tragic tale."

"The tragedy is that your Jorges could not ignore the drink when he was in Vogelgrun, and he became involved in this mess almost immediately after the sheriff released him from the tower," Appel said. She was annoyed that Gritta felt such affection for her husband. When Gritta was angry at Jorges, she would stalk across the lane, surmount the trench, and spend her evenings in Appel's house, sipping wine and telling jokes. Of course, Appel had Efi living with her now, but it wasn't the same. Gritta's sharp tongue was more than adequate to keep up with her sparking wit, and Appel felt – without acknowledging it aloud – that she looked forward to Gritta and Jorges' arguments. At least when they fought, Appel usually had some fine company afterward.

"So it must have been Heinrik who fed Jorges so much wine in Vogelgrun. Who else could afford such a thing?" Appel continued. "And then he waited on the road for his victim. Jorges fell asleep on the side of the road from too much drink, and then Heinrik was at liberty to stab poor Herr Töpfer, remove his hands, and place them in Jorges' bag. He must have been unpleasantly shocked to meet with the minstrels upon the road that day."

Gritta nodded, but Efi wrinkled her brow. "No...at first sight, it seems to make sense, but when I turn it in my mind, it doesn't make any sense at all."

"You are the one who doesn't make sense, Efi," Gritta growled.

"Stop it, both of you," Appel said. She was tired. She felt every bone in her body and hair on her head weighed down with sadness for the situation. "Off to bed with you both. Tomorrow, the Lord will give us a new day and fresh eyes with which to see."

It was not the crowing of the cocks that woke Appel and Efi the following morning as they slept beneath the quilt that Appel had stitched from scraps of old dresses and cowls. It was the cries of men echoing through the streets. The sound bounced along the city walls and whispered through the narrow lanes in Les Tanneurs.

"Murder!" the voices yelled. "A dead woman was found on the road! Hands. Someone has taken her hands!"

Appel sat up straight, feeling the straw shift and crackle beneath her. Where Efi should have slept, there was a rapidly cooling hollow of blankets and straw. Efi stood at the small window and peeked through a shutter into the pre-dawn light, her nightcap threatening to fall from her blonde head.

"There is a great commotion, Frau Appel," Efi whispered loudly.

Appel pulled the quilt from the bed, wrapping it around her shoulders, and stood at the window. Below them, a young boy ran, dirt kicking up from the wooden heels of his shoes. A short time later, he returned with a sleepy and disgruntled Sheriff Werner waddling behind him. The sheriff had been roused so quickly from his bed that he wore only his long, woolen tunic, a sleeping cap embroidered with delicate flowers, and a pair of long-toed embroidered slippers.

"Pompous ass," Gritta snarled behind them, and Appel jumped.

"How did you get here, Gritta?! Where are your children?"

"Sleeping soundly. Where do you s'pose they are? Rosmunda is at home still abed, and my Wina is in her fourth year now – old enough to take care of herself."

Appel knew it was the truth, so she didn't question her friend further. The three women all crowded close, and Appel shared the quilt, spreading it out around their shoulders like the wings of an enormous, mottled bird. They pushed their faces together and watched through the small window as men and boys ran about in the street and animals brayed from inside their stables. Things quieted for a while, and the sky began to turn pink. More townsfolk emerged from their houses. Servants and children staggered into the morning light to empty the night-soil into the communal privies, and the goodwives made their sleep-heavy trek toward the wells, carrying yokes and waterskins for the day's cooking and washing.

The loud clatter of an oxcart rose above the increasing din of voices, and Herr Fuhrmann's shaggy beasts lumbered down the lane. Instead of hay, there was nothing in the cart but a single, dark shape. Appel leaned further out the window, dropping her grip on the quilt.

"Ow, Appel! You're taking all of the view for yourself!"

"Dear blessed Mother in heaven," Appel swore quietly.

"What?" Efi hissed. "What do you see?"

"It's Herr Fuhrmann. He has a body in his cart with no hands." Appel's voice was grim as she looked at her two friends. "It's Margitte."

The visitor

In which Appel and Efi are roused at a most impolite hour

T HE PRESSURE BETWEEN SHERIFF Werner's eyes had been growing steadily for days now, but the appearance of another handless body was the final drop that made the pot spill over. He had a whole, throbbing egg of pain growing in his skull, and the voices of the three alewives did absolutely nothing to make it go away. He sat on his customary bench at Herr Schlock's weinstube, balancing a cup of sweet wine on the top of his belly. To him, this was a sacred space where he could freely speak his mind and take his ease without the meddlesome ears of the less fortunate townsfolk around him. But Appel, Gritta, and Efi – the three most meddlesome of all, no longer respected the sanctity of the weinstube. They marched inside without hesitation, ignoring the great impropriety of their presence.

"Tomas," he grumbled to his servant, pinching the bridge of his nose between his fingers. "Can you not take them away? Their shrill voices cause my brains to hurt."

Tomas dipped his head quickly and took Efi by the elbow. "Now, fair Efi, let us walk while you tell me about the fine ale that you brew with Frau Appel..."

But Efi shook him away and stood her ground. Next to her, Gritta seethed.

"For the second time now, my Jorges languishes in the tower because you locked him up, and for the second time, another body has appeared without hands. A woman's body, no less! How do you suppose my husband managed to kill Margitte of Vogelgrun and steal her hands while imprisoned in the guard tower?!"

"I shall release Jorges in good time, Frau Gritta. For now, the people feel safe having a man of suspicion locked up."

Gritta's expression took on an apoplectic hue. So angry was she that she could only sputter out her response. "But he didn't...he couldn't have done it from the tower! And do you think the townsfolk of Colmar are stupid enough to believe him guilty when another handless body turned up last night? It is only the merchants and burghers you try to please. Good, honest people who live near the lower canals know that Jorges is innocent."

Near the door, a few stools scraped loudly against the wood-planked floor, and men stood unsteadily at attention. Sheriff Werner turned and saw Lord Frider stride into the room in his usual way, looking for the world like he found the place odious. Behind him, Friar Wikerus walked softly, his head bowed, hands tucked into his sleeves. Lord Frider stopped before the sheriff and cleared his throat.

"What's this I heard, Werner, about keeping a man locked up for a murder committed while he was imprisoned?"

"Merely a precaution, my lord. Why, you became well acquainted with the lazy and foolish ways of Jorges Leporteur at the trial some weeks ago. He's a lackwit who often spends days in Vogelgrun, working as a porter at the docks on the Rhine. Highly suspicious, given that he owed money to Gilbert of Sundhoffen, also a porter in Vogelgrun, whose hand Efi Kleven discovered in a pot of ale – that his own wife brewed, I might add. And then he was found alongside the road with a pair of bloody hands in his sack." Sheriff Werner knew his case against Jorges was weak now. He slurped deeply from his cup, stalling for time to think of a better tactic.

"And his feelings toward this poor, murdered widow we discovered?"

"He had no thoughts or feelings toward Margitte of Vogelgrun, m'lord," Gritta said. "Because he has not been outside the guard tower long enough to make up his mind about her. Though she did slaughter and cook my goat, it is my grievance against her, not my husband's. I don't believe Jorges even knew we owned a goat."

Sheriff Werner squinted at her. "So, you might have killed the old witch, then? You certainly had the motivation."

"But not the strength, m'lord, for I heard that the murderer strangled her. And besides, my children and neighbors can attest that I was at my home the night Margitte was killed."

Lord Frider snapped his fingers at Herr Schlock, who scurried across the room and returned with a dish filled to the brim with wine. The nobleman took a long drink and then squinted at the sheriff.

"Oh, surely you can just let the fellow go free, Werner. Whatever your petty grudge against the man, put it aside. Can you not see his wife is in distress?"

Sheriff Werner shot Gritta a withering look.

Friar Wikerus stepped forward. "Perhaps it would be wise to release Jorges but to keep him close and watched within the walls, Sheriff. Let the poor man go free. Since he is a porter, he can work here in Colmar instead of Vogelgrun. He could make himself useful at the poissonnerie. And I know you both have fields and vineyards that require workers during the growing season. Jorges may look wispy, but he's as strong as eel leather from lifting baskets and crates every day."

"No one in Colmar will hire him – certainly not me," Sheriff Werner scoffed. "I wouldn't let Jorges near my crops and fields for all the gold in Strassburg cathedral. And there is no way that Elise, the guildsman's wife, will allow Jorges to handle the baskets of fish at the poissonnerie."

"I shall speak with Frau Elise." Friar Wikerus bowed his head, then flashed them one of his brilliant, easy smiles. "In the meantime, I suggest he starts in the fields immediately. If he's kept busy, he has less time to drink."

"But Friar Wikerus, I just finished telling you why Jorges is not allowed near —"

"Think of letting Jorges work in your fields as atonement for the trouble he's caused you," Friar Wikerus interrupted.

The two lords blinked at the young friar for a moment. "And he would do this work...for pay?" Lord Frider asked. "How would that be an atonement for his bad behavior? Keeping Jorges here at all times would be a collective punishment on the whole city."

Friar Wikerus nodded as sagely as he could. "Yes, Lord Frider, for he would be doing you honest work, and so he deserves fair payment. But if you keep him here, the sheriff and the townspeople can keep an eye on him. And I think he and Gritta would do well to spend more time together, since he is oft away for days at a time." The friar's eyes sparkled.

Gritta crossed her arms over her bosom. "Now wait, Friar. I ain't wasting my tears wishing for Jorges to rush home from Vogelgrun each Lord's day. I think the arrangement we have works quite well for us."

Sheriff Werner brightened. "And why, Frau Gritta, do you not wish for your husband to be in Colmar with you?"

"He causes problems for me too, m'lord. Snores something terrible, eats all the pottage before midday, his singing is an assault on my ears, and his stench is an attack on my nostrils. Working at the poissonnerie all day with fish won't make him smell any better."

Sheriff Werner smirked. If there was one person in Colmar he despised more than Jorges Leporteur, it was Gritta. "Well then, I think that the good friar speaks sense. Let the man work in Colmar with his own people." He slammed his cup on the bench beside him, feeling satisfied that this would bring her some measure of suffering.

"But...but..." Gritta sputtered. "Jorges earns far more coin working in Vogelgrun than in Colmar! And me, with so many mouths to feed, we need every copper!"

"A punishment you shall have to bear," the sheriff said, and he turned to Lord Frider. "Will you join me for another dish of wine, my lord?"

The discussion was over.

Gritta hung her head and retreated from the weinstube with Appel and Efi shuffling after her. They stepped down into the street and walked in silence toward Les Tanneurs. After a few streets, Gritta spoke.

"A fine lot you are, staying silent while the friar, the lord, and the sheriff conspired against me."

"I think more may have just happened than we know," Appel said. "Friar Wikerus has never done ill by us in the past. Let us wait and see what he has to say about it." Indeed, it was the quick wits and deft scheming of Friar Wikerus that had saved them from the pillory and possibly from murder only a few months back when the city council accused the alewives of killing penniless widows in Les Tanneurs.

They spent the day filtering their new ale by straining it through a linen cloth. Then, they carefully poured it into three watertight barrels bound for Karl Gastwirt's tavern. It was the most significant quantity of ale that they had brewed in a single sitting, and it pleased Appel that her new hearth had managed to accommodate the days of boiling water and drying grain so well. Gritta was sullen and chose to take her evening meal at her own house, so Appel and Efi ate simply – a few leeks, a heel of bread, and some hard sheep's cheese – before they crawled into bed, bodies aching from the day's heavy labor. It felt like they had just closed their eyes when they both jolted awake at a sharp pounding on the ground-level door. They sat upright in the pre-dawn light, shaking and clutching each other. Appel groaned, feeling every bone and muscle complaining.

"Why must there always be a commotion at my door before the sun is up?"

"I shall go see who it is, Appel dear," Efi whispered, slipping from under the quilt.

"No, Efi, please do not! Wait until Josse the night watchman comes round! He will chase the scoundrel off."

But Efi was already pulling her cotte over her head. "It could be Gritta or another goodwife of the lane."

Appel looked askance. The pounding on the door was masculine; she could tell by the forcefulness. "Appel! Frau Appel!" a man's voice called out from the street, and Efi pulled back.

"Oh, Appel! How could you allow a man to visit you when I share your bed every night? Can you not take your lovers to a stable or a field instead?" she hissed.

Appel rose quickly and tied her sleeping cap tightly underneath her chin. Her long, gray braid was twisted and fuzzy from her sleep, and she wore a red chemise down to her ankles that she had fastened chastely at her throat.

"Get dressed, Efi," Appel whispered. "I did not invite a man to my house. Dress yourself and hide beneath the bedstead until I return. Hurry now."

Appel pulled a shawl over her shoulders and opened the door a crack to peek out. Then she pulled it open wider and walked down the stairs, which clung to an exterior wall of the house.

Efi searched in the dark for her frock, which hung on a peg, but gave up when she heard Appel walking down the steps. She scrambled to the small window and peered into the darkness just as Appel spoke.

"Whatever do you mean by knocking upon my door before the first cock has crowed, Heinrik of Strassburg?"

The accomplice
In which Friar Wikerus presents his suspicions

Appel drank from her wooden cup of strong ale with a shaking hand while Gritta and Efi paced the floor of her house. Although the sun was well up by now, no one had lit a fire in the new hearth, and she still wore her shift and nightcap. Her shawl, given to her by her daughter, had been lost in the scuffle.

"So, you opened the door to a strange man before the sky was not yet light, and then you walked out from the safety of your sleeping chamber to speak with him in the street? And then what?" Gritta asked. "I suppose after that, you offered him a bowl of pottage and welcomed him to take his ease!"

"He wasn't a strange man. He was Heinrik of Strassburg, who, as you know, I have met before. I approached and asked him why he had been so rude as to knock my door before anyone in the city was awake."

"And how did he appear, Appel?" Efi asked.

"He appeared...handsome," Appel said, and even she was stunned by the stupidity of it all. He looked disarmingly beautiful, even in the darkness.

Gritta stomped over to Appel and slapped her cup of ale away. "The man could have killed you, Appel! He's a murderer!" She grabbed Appel's hands in her own. "And these! He could have cleaved these from your body and tossed your corpse aside like all the others. What were you thinking?"

"I was only thinking I saw a familiar face."

"A handsome one," Efi offered.

"Aye, yes. He also seemed tired. Riding all night, I assume."

"But why did he come to your door, Appel? Surely a merchant would have many colleagues and friends in Colmar to beg for a bed. He could have stayed at Karl Gastwirt's inn. What wares does he sell that he must travel at such a strange hour, and doesn't seek lodging where the other merchants stay?"

Appel's brow scrunched. "I never asked him what he sells, and he never told me."

"Ha!" Gritta's laugh was like the bark of a dog. "Show me a merchant who does not brag incessantly about his goods. This 'Heinrik,' as he calls himself, is no merchant, Appel. He is something else entirely."

"I know," Appel said, breathless with the thought of the risk she had exposed herself and Efi to by opening the door to a man she suspected of murder. "And now that he has taken Margitte's hands, we know that he will not discriminate between killing men or women. Opening my door to him was unwise, and I am not too proud to admit it."

Gritta began to pace. "Of course, I was fast asleep when he came, or I would have run over to help you. Didn't rouse myself until Jorges came crashing through my door with the news that he was free from the tower, and that's when I heard a terrible scuffle happening outside. By then, it seemed like every man in the city had been summoned to the scene."

"I climbed through the window and fetched the sheriff's men," Efi said proudly. "That scuffle you heard was all my doin'."

"And wearing nothing but her chemise after I instructed her to dress herself and stay hidden beneath the bed. You are a disobedient girl, Efi." Appel wagged a finger at the young woman, but her face was beaming. "And your disobedience probably saved me my life."

"I would have expected more resistance from the sheriff and his men, considering the last time we spoke to him about the matter," Gritta mused, but Appel just chuckled.

"To have a fair young woman show up at his gate with her hair uncovered, only wearing her chemise, and begging for help? She met no resistance at all from the sheriff or his lackeys."

"Well, I wish they had managed to catch the scoundrel so I could personally lock him in the guard tower, but I'll wager my day's salt that he won't come near Colmar again – not now that he knows we've discovered his wicked secret. Surely it is him who has been murdering and stealing hands all along."

Efi jumped to her feet. "I almost forgot! I took this from his saddle when no one was looking! If he returns, we can skewer him!" She reached underneath the bench where she sat and grunted, pulling up a long, iron sword. Appel and Gritta both gasped in unison.

"Efi! If Sheriff Werner catches you with that weapon, the consequences will be extreme!" Appel shouted. "Get rid of it at once!"

"But how?" Efi wailed, jumping to her feet.

Appel tried to grab the sword, but it was heavy and fell with a dull metallic clang on the earthen floor. "Throw it in the canal!"

"And what good will that do? We are going into the hot season, and you know the canals will soon be shallow. Not enough water to conceal this," Gritta said. She circled the sword slowly where it rested on the ground, then hefted it with both hands and laid it across the table. The three women hovered over it for a moment, their mouths open in awe. The blade was long and blackened with use and age. The tips of the guard, which stood out at right angles, were unadorned. Worn brown leather encased the grip, which ended in a pommel shaped into a flat, round disk of hammered iron.

"It ain't the sword of a highborn knight," Gritta said, scowling at it. "Those pompous killers like more flash on their kit."

"This sword has taken at least three lives and six hands," Appel said, her voice husky with emotion. "I want it out of my home. Now!"

Gritta picked it up. "I shall take it to my house and dispose of it when the time is right." She paused for a moment. "And that time will not come until Heinrik of Strassburg hangs for his crimes."

"Should we not give it to the sheriff to examine?" Efi asked timidly. She leaned her face close to the blade and shuddered. "Perhaps he can find some blood upon it. Or maybe Father Konrad can sense the Devil's presence in its metals?"

"No indeed. It's clear to me that Sheriff Werner is looking for any excuse he can find to have my husband and me arrested, so I would rather keep this secret from him. I shall place it atop one of the wooden beams on my ceiling. That is where I hide my spare coins from Jorges. No one will look there."

It was almost midday by now. Outside, a young boy herded a small flock of goats down the lane, and their high-pitched cries drowned the splashing of the tanners as they washed the half-finished hides in the canal. As soon as the herd passed, the sound of sandals slapping against the ground in a hurry stopped outside Appel's open door, and Friar Wikerus peeked inside, panting from his exertion.

"I am sorry I didn't come sooner," he gasped. "Was anyone hurt? I heard that the scoundrel got away. Climbed to the rooftop of the glover's house and scuttled over the walls like a crab."

"Heinrik leapt the walls?" Appel raised an eyebrow. "Has anyone looked for his broken body yet? How could a man run away after such a fall?"

Wikerus paused and then smiled. "I suppose you are correct. I heard that news from Brother Evart, who heard it from Brother Tacitus, who heard it from Brother Marcellus."

"Which means the killer may still be in the city," Gritta said grimly.

"Aye, and it worries me that he knows where you live, Frau Appel, and came right to your door. It was brazen, and moreover, his reasons were unclear," Friar Wikerus said, having recovered his breath.

Appel could feel Gritta's eyes boring into her. She squirmed. Wikerus took notice of the look that passed between the two women and coughed politely into his sleeve.

"Goodwives, could you give me a few moments alone with Frau Appel?"

Gritta looked at Appel harder, and the older woman's shoulders slumped slightly. "No need for secrecy, Friar. These two gossips know all there is to know about me. But before you ask, I assure you that although I have met Heinrik of Strassburg before, I never met him alone, coyly or otherwise. After all, he is far too young a man for me." Her voice took on a dignified tone. "It would be unseemly."

"Never stopped you before," Gritta mumbled.

"Well, it did this time. The man is too smooth, too cocksure. I like a humble man with a bit of padding around the middle."

"And very little hair," Efi volunteered.

"Jesu, give me patience..." Friar Wikerus raised his eyes heavenward for a moment. "Frau Appel, you know what people say about you around the town. Your reputation for enjoying the pleasures of a man's bed has implicated you in this crime. Sheriff Werner is already considering adding you as the associate of Heinrik of Strassburg. To all who don't know you, it seems that the evidence points to you as complicit."

"To me? Why, that is a preposterous notion! I am too old for murder."

"Not if you had a strong younger man to do the work for you."

Gritta put a hand on Appel's arm to stop her friend from speaking. "Hold on a moment. Friar Wikerus has a point. Appel, the hand was discovered in your house in the first place. Then you brought the wretched Margitte back to Colmar from Vogelgrun —"

"Which irritated everyone," Efi interrupted, "although the goat stew was delicious."

At the mention of her goat, Gritta growled low in her throat. "Indeed, it vexed us all," she said. "And none of us, you included, made it a secret that Margitte had worn out her welcome. Then Margitte died while Heinrik of Strassburg was in Colmar, and he came straight to your house."

Appel turned to Gritta, her face flushed with outrage. "Are you really suggesting that I did this? That I killed people and removed their hands?"

"No, but I can see how others, like Sheriff Werner, would think you were involved. There are too many coincidences." Friar Wikerus held up his index finger. "There's the fact that Heinrik is frequently in Vogelgrun, and that is where all the victims lived." He held up another finger. "There's the matter of him owning a sword, which means he had a weapon sufficient to quickly and efficiently cut through bone and flesh. Yes, Efi, I know you took it. Brother Evart saw you and told me," he said as Efi's mouth dropped open in surprise. "Then there's poor Jens Töpfer, the potter found murdered on the road to Vogelgrun with his hands stuffed in Jorges' bag. As far as anyone knows, Appel has no connection to Herr Töpfer. But Heinrik of Strassburg does. The minstrels described seeing an identical man on the road just before they discovered the body, and if the sheriff thinks the two of you were working together, it will not matter that Appel never saw Herr Töpfer in her life."

"Then we must find Heinrik," Gritta said. "He is probably still in Colmar and should be caught and locked up in the tower before anyone else can fall victim to his depravities."

"Yes, but it is not up to the three of you to search for him. Leave that to the sheriff and his men," said Friar Wikerus. Appel, Gritta, and Efi all exchanged glances with each other, and the friar knew they had no intention of leaving the capture of Heinrik up to the sheriff. This fact annoyed him, but he accepted it with the resignation of a man who had spent many years of his life being ordered about.

"At the very least, Appel and Efi, it would be best if you slept elsewhere until the sheriff's men catch Heinrik. He came to your house once, and he could do it again."

For a moment, Appel and Efi stared at him. Then they hung their heads.

"Friar, I don't think anyone would take us in. Might we stay with the Dominicans?"

"Well, I...I am not entirely sure, to be honest." Friar Wikerus frowned. The friars occasionally took lodgers into the priory, but the Dominican order in Colmar also had a nearby abbey that housed rooms for well-heeled guests, in addition to cloistered monks.

"Stay with me. Don't know where you'll sleep, but I'll make some space for you," Gritta grunted. It was a clever attempt on her part to sound ambivalent, but Wikerus knew better. He knew that Gritta loved Appel and Efi as much as her twelve children.

"You live across the lane, Gritta. It's hardly a clever hiding place," Appel said.

Friar Wikerus brightened. "Or it might be a brilliant place to hide! Just stay out of the street and instruct the neighbors to tell anyone who asks that Appel and Efi have gone on pilgrimage."

"Well then, it's settled." Efi leapt to her feet and walked to the cold fireplace. Snatching up a stick from the woodpile, she began to scrape around in the ashes, probing with her fingers and pulling things out one by one.

"What are you doing, you daft girl?" Gritta asked.

"What does it look like I'm doing? I'm digging up my dowry coins. Don't want them alone in the house without me."

"You have been keeping your dowry in the ashes?!" Appel and Gritta both said at once.

"But how did you retrieve them from the privy? I thought they were lost when Margitte burned it to the ground," Appel said.

Efi blushed. "Peter, the stonemason's apprentice, dug into the ruins of the privy and retrieved them for me. He wasn't able to find them all, but most of them came back to me. I offered him a coin for his troubles, but he refused. He is so gallant." She erupted into a fit of giggles while Appel, Gritta, and Friar Wikerus stood dumbfounded.

"So now that so-called gallant young man knows exactly how many coins you have saved and that you hide them in odd places."

"And he probably helped himself to a few and then told you they were lost in the wreckage of my privy!" Appel shouted.

"Dear Efi, I think you would be wise to practice a little more caution with your money." Friar Wikerus shook his head. "Now, alewives, you must make for Gritta's house and for safety. I hope you will heed my warning and not try to find Heinrik of Strassburg alone. He is dangerous, and he is desperate."

A splash in the dark

In which Jorges meets his hero

Jorges Leporteur stumbled along the wagon-rutted Grand Rue, his arm draped lazily across the strong young shoulders of his son Lonel. Darkness had long since fallen, and in the windows of the houses and shops the oil lamps and rushlights flickered to life as people took their supper and prepared for sleep. A few townsfolk still walked about, as it was not yet late in the evening, and a mild spring breeze lifted the hair from his shoulders. He breathed deeply.

"Ah! Lonel, you're a good lad, no matter what your mother says. A good lad indeed, who takes care of his pa."

Lonel gave his father a sidelong look. Only last winter, the boy had surpassed Jorges' height. Lonel wasn't exactly sure how old he was, but he knew he wasn't finished growing. Still, although he may have overtaken Jorges in stature, his father's wiry frame was deceptively heavy.

"Only came to bring you home because Ma thinks you'll get murdered by that merchant from Strassburg." He grunted and pulled Jorges up a little higher. "Maybe if the man cut off your hands, it would make you lighter to carry home."

"Indeed, it would." Jorges nodded sagely. "Smart lad you are."

Lonel rolled his eyes and kept walking.

"Don't know why you take so much drink, Pa. Ma sure seemed happy that you were not always soaked in wine while the two of you were locked in the gaol. And here you are, only out again for one day and already as pickled as a cabbage."

"A great beauty she was, your ma," Jorges declared. His expression turned wistful. "The drink helps me appreciate her more. I see with new eyes and ears when I've had wine or some of her fine ale."

"You can't see with your ears, dummkopf," Lonel muttered. His nose told him they were only a few streets from Les Tanneurs, and he glanced around to get his bearings. They were near the poissonnerie, the great market where the fishermen took their shallow-keeled boats to sell their catch of shad and lampreys. Traders also brought barrels of slippery, scaly wares from the Rhine – larger and more exotic fish such as salmon and perch that the burghers and wealthy merchants preferred at their tables.

They navigated the uneven ground in the dark for a while, Lonel struggling to keep Jorges upright, when ahead of them, they heard a splash, and then the unmistakable rhythmic sound of someone walking through water near the shallower shoreline.

"Now there, who would be in the canals at this time of night, eh?" Jorges slurred.

"Who would be in the waters near the poissonnerie at all, since it is foul with fish guts?" Lonel asked, squinting into the darkness.

But Jorges gave him a jocular clap on the back. In the darkness, he didn't notice the puff of whitish dust that rose from his son's shoulders. "Well, son, do you fancy a dip? Shall we cool our bits in yon canal?"

"Absolutely not. My bits feel fine, and I don't fancy the thought of spending the rest of my night hovering over the privy pit with the shits. That water is foul, it is."

"Well, it's been nigh on two days since I moved my bowels, so I think I shall go for a swim," Jorges said, and with a whoop, he was in the water. For a moment, he thrashed, and then Lonel heard a gurgle in the dark.

"Deep! It's deep! Son, I cannot swim! I can't —" Jorges' cry was cut short as his head slipped beneath the filthy water.

Lonel leapt into the canal. Usually, he would be able to feel the rocky floor beneath his feet, but the warm spring weather had melted the snow in the nearby Vosges mountains, and the clear alpine water had torn through the foothills and into the valley, taking the fine clay silt with it until it grew into a soupy brown torrent. He clawed his way back to the bank in the dark. He could still hear his father splashing further downstream but could see nothing.

"Pa?"

Lonel heard more sputtering and gurgling in the darkness. Heedless of the fact that he wasn't a strong swimmer, Lonel plunged into the middle of the canal once more, trying to hear his father over the sound of his own splashing.

"Father?! Pa! Call out so I can find you!"

A few tendrils of a willow tree brushed his face, and he grasped the thin, flexible branches, holding tight as the water tried to drag him downstream. The sounds of Jorges splashing had stopped, and Lonel felt his heart drop. Jorges was drowning. The drunken fool had gone and killed himself.

"Pa!" Lonel screamed. "Someone, please bring a lamp! Help!"

By this time it was very late, and all who lived near the poissonnerie had donned their sleeping caps and put out their lights. Overwhelmed with panic, Lonel lost his grip on the willow branches. Struggling to keep his head above water, he thrashed his way to the canal's edge and dragged himself halfway out of the water, which had burst its bank and swamped an abandoned stable. His eyes filled with tears. His whole family had survived the Great Pestilence – even when it ravaged the world, taking kings and paupers, priests and babes with it. A family who could all live through such a horror seemed incapable of dying. How could Jorges drown? After surviving the pestilence, how could his father be anything but immortal?

"Mother Mary," Lonel groaned as he lay on the soggy hay in the flooded stable. "Blessed Mary, no, please no." On the streets above the canal, he heard a shout and saw the distant wobble of torchlight bouncing off the walls of the nearby buildings. Hands grabbed him by the collar of his tunic, pulling him away from the filthy stable yard and onto the soggy ground near the water's edge. Voices whispered.

"Who is this?"

"Just some boy from Les Tanneurs. A pauper."

"What possessed the boy to swim in such darkness with the water all a'raging?"

"Young man! Why did you call for help?"

"My father," Lonel wept. "My father fell in. He sank to the bottom of the canal like a stone."

A few of the men ventured into the water, holding torches and oil lamps aloft, scanning the foamy surface of the raging water.

"Ah well, he will be on his way to the mill by now, and hope he don't get caught up in the wheel, else the miller will be in a full rage in the morning," someone said.

"What is happening? Why are all of you men gathered here and not in your beds?" a voice boomed above the rest. It was Sheriff Werner, his face flushed with wine and the tunic over his belly stained with grease from the sausages he had eaten at supper. He looked down at Lonel, lying on his back in the mud. "Ah, I know this boy. Go on then, what mischief has he been up to? He was the night watchman until Josse replaced him. Gone back to your thieving ways, have you, Lonel?" The sheriff turned to the other men standing around, waiting for them to laugh with him, but they all looked silently at their feet.

"Come now, Sheriff. The boy's just seen his father drown in the canal. Use some of Christ's compassion," a man said, and

Sheriff Werner's face grew serious. He squatted down next to Lonel.

"Is it true, boy? Did Jorges go under the water?"

Lonel nodded.

"Well then, let us search the canal bank. Jorges isn't a big man, but he could break the millwheel nonetheless if he were to get caught up in it."

Several of the men hauled Lonel to his feet and handed him a sputtering oil lamp. The small group of men and Sheriff Werner slowly walked along the canal, calling out and sweeping the water with long branches. As they approached the mill, they heard a shout.

"I see something!"

The men all raised their lanterns in unison. Two wet, disheveled men sat on the side of the canal, panting heavily. One of them turned toward the light and flashed a gap-toothed grin.

"Pa!" Lonel cried, dropping his lamp and running ahead. The lamp shattered, and the oil caught fire. The men shouted, some of them falling to their knees to scoop leaping into the canal and scooping hatfuls of water to stifle the flames.

The man sitting next to Jorges assisted, splashing water onto the flames with his hands and stomping on them with his sodden boots. Sheriff Werner squinted at him.

"And who might you be? I don't recognize you, stranger."

"This man is my savior!" Jorges cried. "Found me beneath the water and pulled me to safety. Swims as strong as an otter, he does!" Jorges looked adoringly up at his rescuer, who was shaking muddy water from his gray-flecked beard.

"Heinrik," the man answered. "Heinrik of Strassburg. And by your look and smell, I guess you are Sheriff Werner, whom I have heard much about."

"I am." Sheriff Werner stood a little higher on his toes. "And your name is known to me."

"But not my face, because when your men were busy chasing me yesterday morning, you had not even risen from your bed," Heinrik answered. His expression registered disgust.

Sheriff Werner gestured sharply to the confused townsmen standing about in their dripping tunics and nightcaps. They glanced at each other.

"Well, Sheriff?" one man asked. "What do you need us to do?"

"Take hold of this man," the sheriff snarled.

Jorges hopped to his feet and squelched over to them, linking his arm with Heinrik's and grinning. "I have him, Sheriff. Don't think he's leaving town without me buying him a drink and a meal first. The finest that Herr Schlock has to offer for my hero!"

"No, you fool, he isn't leaving town at all except through purgatory!" the sheriff roared, and Jorges slunk back, cowering behind Heinrik's taller frame. Sheriff Werner threw a rope at the group of stunned men.

"Bind his arms tight behind his back, and then I will require two stout men to help me assist him to the tower for questioning tomorrow."

After the men tied Heinrik's hands, the sheriff led the posse through the city. They made a strange parade, the line of them all in their sleeping clothes, with bare legs and feet shuffling, some of them wet. One by one, the men peeled off and retreated to their homes, leaving Jorges and Lonel on their own to make the longer trek into Les Tanneurs.

Jorges shivered. It was nearly dawn – the coldest, darkest part of the day. "Well, wait until your mother hears that I nearly went to meet Saint Peter! She'll greet me with weeping and professions of love, my boy. Just wait and see."

Lonel withheld his opinions regarding his mother's reaction, which was more likely to be explosive than affectionate.

"But, Pa, what do you think the sheriff will do to the man who saved you?"

"Like as not, the same as they did to me, I think – feed me two meals a day of stale bread and turnips and leave me to my peace. Although I would have enjoyed a sip of wine now and then." Jorges winked. "Say, let us go back to the weinstube this very moment. If the steward is still awake, I will use my last coin to celebrate my resurrection!"

"You mean your rescue, Pa, not resurrection," Lonel corrected him absently. His mind was spinning. He had seen the sheriff casually arrest both of his parents and others in Colmar with relative ambivalence, but Heinrik's cool head and biting comments embarrassed the sheriff and enraged him. Lonel, who had often run into the sheriff's bad humor, had never seen the man shake with anger before. "I don't think Herr Heinrik will receive meals and time to repose. I think your hero may be in danger of being put to the question."

"Nonsense. Sheriff Werner never asked a question in his life."

"Aye, he only gives orders…" Lonel tapped his chin. He knew he shouldn't care what the bumbling sheriff did with any suspect in a crime so long as he turned a blind eye to Lonel's pickpocketing. But lately, the man rankled him. And besides, Heinrik of Strassburg had just saved his father's life. Lonel glanced sideways at Jorges, whose steps dragged and head drooped as his wine energy waned.

"Pa, your hero needs help. We'd better let Ma handle this."

A most unwanted helper
In which Wikerus is requested but Tacitus is given

A PPEL BLINKED, RUBBED HER eyes, and then blinked again. She looked up at the sky. The sun shone, and the breeze was fresh and cool, tinting her cheeks red as rose hips. She looked back at the man scowling before her and cleared her throat.

"God is great," she mumbled.

Friar Tacitus continued to stare at her. "God is great," he said flatly.

She turned and looked at Lonel, standing behind her with Efi and Gritta. The boy's shoulders were pale with dust, and so was his hair. He shrugged. Appel cleared her throat again.

"You see, Friar Tacitus, we wanted to visit Heinrik, er...that is, the prisoner, to thank him for saving Gritta's husband and to ask for Friar Wikerus to offer him confession. We would never dream of troubling you while you do...the holy things. Your rituals and tasks. Um..."

They were standing in the gate yard near the tower where Sheriff Werner and the rest of the city council kept their prisoners. They had asked for Friar Wikerus but instead faced the disapproving glare of Friar Tacitus.

"I copy the holy texts, Frau Appel. Not that I expect a woman from Les Tanneurs to understand what that means."

Behind her, Appel heard Gritta gasp and stomp her foot.

"Of course," Appel said before Gritta had a chance to work herself up into a proper rage. "We did not want to disturb such important and time-consuming work. If you wish to return to the priory and continue to copy the texts, please ask Friar Wikerus to come to the gate tower in your stead."

"Friar Wikerus has chosen to take the day for solitude and silent contemplation of the scriptures and God's grace. Alas, it is I who must attend to this matter, and I wish you would allow me to get on with it."

Before she could answer, the door to the gate tower slammed open, and a horse-faced guard looked out at them from under heavy eyelids. "Well then? Sheriff wants to get this over with so as he can get the orders of execution ready before his midday meal."

"Sure seems slower than the hasty manner that he signed orders of execution for my Jorges," Gritta growled.

"'Tis not. Sheriff Werner didn't sign any orders at all for Jorges. Waste of parchment," the guard said as he turned back to the gate tower. Tacitus, Appel, Gritta, Efi, and Lonel followed until the guard spun around. "Only the friar may enter. The rest of you lot can wait or go and make yourselves useful elsewhere!"

"Well, I —" Appel started, but Tacitus walked into the dark room, and the guard slammed the door shut. Appel turned and faced the others.

"What shall we do?"

"Why do you even want this Heinrik to receive his confession, Appel?" Gritta asked. "If he's locked up, then Jorges and I will no longer be under the sheriff's suspicious eyes."

"Even if Heinrik murdered those three people, he deserves absolution from God. And if he didn't, and if the murderer strikes again, you and Jorges will be implicated regardless of the truth because the sheriff wills it."

Gritta's expression hardened. "And what did you do to defend Jorges' eternal soul when he was in the gaol, Appel? Once again, some usurper from Vogelgrun has received more attention from you than me, your neighbor and oldest friend!"

"Heinrik is of Strassburg, not Vogelgrun," Efi said. Gritta spun and swiped at her with a weather-worn hand.

"I was just trying to be helpful," Efi muttered, but she backed out of Gritta's reach.

"Not this old argument again," Appel pleaded with Gritta. "Friar Wikerus and I traveled to Vogelgrun and spoke with the minstrels to prove Jorges' innocence. It is well, my friend. Do not be upset."

Gritta huffed loudly and then shrugged. It was as good of an admission of wrongdoing as anyone would get from her. The three women leaned their backs against the scratchy sandstone of the tower wall. Efi opened her bag and produced a small meat pie with a rich, flaky crust, which she broke into pieces and shared amongst her friends.

"Efi, you mustn't be saving all of your coins for a dowry if you can afford fine food like this," Gritta said, her mouth full. "This is a rich, delicious morsel."

Efi tittered behind her hand, and Gritta's eyes narrowed.

"What?"

"Well, it's just that I didn't buy this pie. Arlo, the man who sells pies in the Saturday market, gave it to me."

"I have never known a market stall owner to be generous. Is he another of your suitors? I do not approve of him."

"Why not?" Efi pouted.

"I just don't. A girl who is still as pretty as you should either marry a handsome man or a rich one, and since you have already buried a handsome first husband, you should see to it that the second one is rich. Arlo is neither."

For a moment, Efi chewed her pie in thoughtful silence. "What if I marry handsome again? Peter the stonemason's apprentice is well to look upon, and he will have his own stoneworks someday."

Appel and Gritta exchanged a glance over Efi's head. Peter the stonemason had only slightly more sense than Efi's first husband, Harald Kleven, who drowned when he attempted – and failed – to leap across one of Colmar's many canals with a sack of iron hammers strapped to his back.

"Give this time, my dear," Appel said, patting Efi's arm. "There is no need to rush back into a marriage – not when you have your own means to support you."

"But I wish to have children someday," Efi sighed.

"I'll give you a few of mine," Gritta said. "You can have Lonel. Say, where is Lonel?"

The boy had disappeared.

"Oh, he is up to no good thing. I can feel it in my knees when that nuisance of a son is off finding trouble." Gritta pushed the sleeves of her thin wool frock up to her elbows, preparing for domestic battle just as the door to the tower slammed open. Friar Tacitus emerged from the dark recesses like a bear from its cave.

"Was it a good confession, Friar Tacitus?" Efi asked.

"He did not admit to being a killer, if that is what you mean. God hates a liar, Widow Efi. I have told Sheriff Werner as much."

"But Lonel says that Heinrik saved Jorges from drowning! Shouldn't that count for something?" Appel demanded, blocking his path. "What did the sheriff and Lord Frider think? Did you tell them exactly what Lonel relayed to Father Konrad?"

"I told them what I knew – and to be true to the law, lest a guilty man not receive his punishment, I did not embellish the truth with the facts like young Lonel Leporteur." Tacitus sniffed, then tried to move past her.

"What do you mean, Friar Tacitus?"

"I merely said that the man called Heinrik of Strassburg saved Jorges Leporteur from the canal, which we all know is not deep enough to drown him, and that it happened near the mill. They told me they already knew this since Sheriff Werner had to leave his bed to arrest Heinrik."

"But it was very deep that night. Jorges fell into the water far from the mill, and the current took him," Gritta shouted. "The waters are swollen with snowmelt from the Vosges."

Tacitus's already downturned mouth deepened into a haughty frown. "And when Sheriff Werner suggested to Lord Frider that Jorges may have been Heinrik's accomplice in the murder and hand-removal of citizens of Vogelgrun, it seemed like a reasonable proposal to me."

Gritta's mouth opened in wordless shock. Tacitus favored her with a thin-lipped smile, turned, and retreated toward the church.

"Not again. Oh, my dears, I cannot continue to worry that they will hang my husband." She slowly sank to her knees. "Not again."

No one noticed as Lonel slunk away from the guard tower and followed Friar Tacitus back to Saint Martin's.

Tacitus crossed Saint Martin's square, marched past the beggars and the pilgrims preparing for their journey to pay homage to the tomb of Saint Odile, and headed for the steps to the main door of the church. The stonework to complete the new narthex was still unfinished, and Tacitus glared balefully at the scaffolds of sticks and hemp rope that clung to the church's exterior like cobwebs.

Every morning, the shouts and clatter of the stonemasons rang out across the square and the city, even penetrating the thick walls of the chapel where they prayed. The crude language of the ditch diggers and the men who carried the stones up to the heights of the flimsy scaffolding echoed across the courtyard. Beneath them, the fledgling plants in the gardens wilted, choked with yellow-orange sandstone dust from the masonry. Though it would behoove Brother Tacitus to have some compassion on the men who sacrificed their time and bodies to build the edifice of Saint Martin's church for a far smaller sum than they deserved, he displayed no sympathy. Their existence was a scourge upon him.

He heard a loud crash as several planks slipped from their rope fastenings and fell to the stone steps. Tacitus shuddered. Had he not hesitated on the bottom stair, the scaffolding would have killed him. He cast a withering glance at the workers, pausing to ensure they noticed, and decided to enter through the back gate. Wisps of tall grass and a few thistles grew alongside the walls. A small cluster of sheep tethered nearby cropped the grasses and weeds short with their yellowing teeth next to a dusty footpath leading to the large courtyard of the Dominicans. The sound of men's laughter rose from the garden. He frowned harder. Who could possibly feel joyful when there was the Lord's work to be done?

In the rose garden, where the friars liked to stroll and contemplate God's grace – or share a particularly juicy bit of gossip

– several brothers gathered around a large stoneware pitcher, tipping back clay cups of ale and telling jokes.

"What is the meaning of this?" Tacitus called out, his robes flapping around his ankles as he stomped through the small door in the wall.

"Ah, join us, Brother Tacitus! We are enjoying the blessing of this beautiful day and this fine ale," a friar called out.

Someone handed Tacitus a cup, and he sipped. Immediately, his mouth flooded with sensations – tangy but sweet, herbal, rich with the scent of honey, and just a hint of bitterness. He drank again and then narrowed his eyes.

"This is not the small ale that we brew here for our consumption. Where did you get this?"

"It was a gift from the community," Brother Evart said. "As a thankful tribute for our good works."

"A gift from whom?"

"Surely I do not know, Brother Tacitus," Brother Evart replied. "Here, allow me to refill your cup."

Already, Tacitus could feel a lightness in his brain. He wanted his cup refilled, but instead, he clutched it to his chest.

"No! This is quite enough. It is too strong for me and for you as well."

One of the friars nudged Brother Evart with his elbow, and he smiled. "Here then, partake of some small ale. We have it here. The day is warm, and you look thirsty."

Tacitus was thirsty, for the guard tower where Heinrik of Strassburg said his confession had been hot and stuffy, and his wool robes did nothing to ease his discomfort. He accepted the cup and slunk a short distance away to drink it by himself. As soon as he had finished, Brother Evart filled the cup again.

"Drink in good health, Brother Tacitus!"

Tacitus finished a third one, and when Brother Evart approached to refill his cup a fourth time, Tacitus held up his hand.

"No more, please. I have had enough, and so have all of you. Return to your duties."

The brothers gathered their things, a few of them giggling softly, and shuffled back to the kitchens. Brother Tacitus made his way toward the privy to relieve himself.

"By God's yellowed toenails, that ale is going through me like water through a sieve," he mumbled to himself as he stumbled into the dark, pungent recess of the privy and arranged himself on the carved wooden seat. The corner of the courtyard that housed the privy was quiet enough that he heard the sound of a man's shoes swishing through the spring grass outside.

"Be gone! Leave a man to empty his bowels in peace!" Tacitus yelled.

The footsteps stopped. Because all had left the courtyard and gone their own way, no one was around to hear Brother Tacitus's screams.

The ale must flow

In which murder is no excuse to stop brewing

Gritta's fear that Jorges would be tossed into prison once again did not come to pass. Although she felt herself quake with terror whenever she saw the sheriff walking about town in the days following Heinrik's arrest, he and his men never appeared at her door, and eventually, she began to relax. Until she realized that, with Jorges working for less money in Colmar and with the ale not flowing, she was in desperate need of coin yet again. On an overcast morning, as the weather finally cooled to something resembling a typical spring day, she strode into Appel's house with a basket of sprouted barley in her arms and planted her feet.

"Stoke the fire, strumpets. It's time to brew!"

Appel looked up from her sewing. "The only strumpet I see here is you, Gritta Leporteur."

Gritta picked up a stick, poked at the glowing coals in the hearth, and added another piece of wood to the fire. She set the empty iron pot over the flames on a tall, metal trivet to heat up, then poured the grain into a shallow wooden box lined with cloth and inspected it, picking out kernels that had sprouted too much or rotted and tossing them on the ground.

"Have a care! Efi just swept!" Appel said.

"The hens will like this grain. Let them inside to forage. Say, where is Efi?" Gritta looked around. "I have hardly seen that girl. Since she decided it was time to get herself married again, she is off and courting any man under seventy winters with two legs and two coins to rub together."

"Aye, but she has no plan. Her finest prospect was Hans the baker, and what did she do? Get herself caught kissing Peter the stonemason's apprentice, that's what! And now Hans refuses to let me use his oven, even when I offered to pay him twice what he normally charges!" Appel opened the door, and the hens scrambled inside to feast upon the bounty of sprouted barley on the ground.

"Why don't you just walk a little further to the oven run by Frau Ghent?" Gritta asked. "It's where Efi goes."

Appel sniffed and settled back into her chair, squinting at her stitches. "Frau Ghent is a gossiping cow. Take your bread to her oven, and she'll tell you the whole neighborhood's story."

"And what is wrong with that? Don't you like to hear the latest news?"

"Not the way she tells it."

"You only say that because Frau Ghent noticed that Herr Yodle visited you more often than his own mother. And then she told his wife."

Over the fire, the pot was beginning to smell like hot metal. With Appel's help, Gritta removed it and set it on the floor, then carefully poured in the damp, sprouted grain while Appel stirred, keeping it in constant motion. Neither woman spoke, and for a while, the only sounds were the popping of the barley as it toasted, the scrape of Appel's paddle, and the sloshing of water as Gritta filled a second pot and set it to boil. When the room filled with the rich, nutty scent of the hot grains, they scooped them onto a willow sieve constructed to fit over the shallow box. Here, the grains would dry until it was time to toast them again. They would repeat the process for two days until the barley took on a reddish-brown color to match its many-layered flavor and was ready to be stored away or brewed.

When Efi arrived, the light of the still-short spring day was fading. "Look what I have brought!" She reached into her basket and pulled out the limp body of a chicken with a flourish. "We shall eat well tonight!"

"And where did you get that?" Gritta asked, hands on her hips. She circled Efi and inspected the carcass. "Why, this is a nice, fat cockerel! I thought you were saving your coins for your dowry, not tossing them away on expensive foods."

"I did not pay a single coin for this bird. Charles the butcher gave him to me. He said the goodwife who purchased it refused to pay him, so he took the bird back."

"And gave it to you? For no payment?" Gritta narrowed her eyes and snatched the dead rooster from Efi, slamming it on the table in a puff of feathers. "Charles the butcher is married, and I am sure I can discern what kind of payment he expects! Efi, you must stop this relentless courting."

"I thought he was just being nice," Efi sputtered, and Appel stood up, clearing her throat.

"Charles is not happily married. You would do well to remember what it looks like when you flirt with so many different men, Efi. Set your desire on only one, or else you will have a slew of heart-sore lovers and no reputation left to stake a bet upon."

"You are hardly fit to talk about flirting with men!" Efi shot back. "Why, you are known all about town for —"

"Hush!" Gritta silenced them. Through the open door, they could see the stout form of Friar Wikerus approaching in the lane.

"Greetings, alewives! I have come for some company and refreshment to cheer my soul on this dreary day. And I see you have your branch out to welcome customers, although the leaves do look wilted. Did you leave it up by accident again?"

"No, Friar, you are just in time for the last of the brew. Gritta and I have been perfecting it by toasting the barley and adding more heather to the gruit."

"And young Efi has not been helping you with this new ale?" Friar Wikerus asked, his eyes dancing.

"No. She's traipsing about town like a heifer in heat is what she's doing," Gritta grumbled. She sloshed a stream of amber ale into a wooden cup and handed it to the friar.

"Ah, well, if Efi marries again, then Father Konrad will have one less widow in Les Tanneurs to hold up as my failure to convert you all to respectable women," Wikerus said and tipped his cup back. "And while we are on the subject of unmarried women, Frau Appel, the murderer – Heinrik of Strassburg – has asked to speak with you. I believe he wishes to have you attest to his spotless character."

"Me, attest to his character? I will have nothing to do with that man. If I am seen anywhere near the gatehouse, the sheriff will surely toss me in there with his other prisoners. No, I would rather stay here."

"Suit yourself," Friar Wikerus said, and finished the contents of his cup with a smack of his lips. "I think you added too much heather. Perhaps you can balance the sweetness with a little more bitter hop flower?"

Appel wrinkled her nose. "I cannot abide the taste or smell of hop flower in my ale!"

Friar Wikerus shrugged and turned to go. At the door, he paused. "Oh, one more thing…Frau Gritta, have you seen your son Lonel today? I need to speak with him."

Gritta was pulling the feathers from Efi's cockerel, preparing it for the soup pot, but when she heard Lonel's name, she growled.

"What has he done?"

"Perhaps nothing. It's just that something strange has been happening to Brother Tacitus these past three days."

"What do you mean, 'strange,' Friar Wikerus?" Gritta lowered the bald bird into the pot and added a few shriveled onions and a scoop of barley.

Friar Wikerus cleared his throat. "Well, it seems that every time Brother Tacitus uses the privy, someone places a bar across the outside of the door or uses other means to trap him inside. No one noticed his absence or heard his screams the first few times because we were singing in the small chapel. Now he has asked some of the other brothers to keep watch for him, yet it continues to happen. Tacitus insists that someone is bribing our brothers to keep quiet. But, of course, it would be impossible to bribe the brothers to harm one of their own." His eyes twinkled. "Tacitus says that the brothers often have a strong smell of ale on their breath when they are near the privy."

Gritta and Appel exchanged a knowing look. Without a word, they both went to the locked door to a small lean-to where they stored the strong ales and pried one of the kegs open. Sure enough, it was nearly empty.

Gritta nodded. "That's my Lonel, alright. I'll tell him that if he does that again, I'll lock him in the common privy near the canals, which is far less pleasant than yours."

"Oh," Friar Wikerus said airily as he walked out the door. "There's no need to hurry."

Alewives and fishwives
In which the docks yield satisfying answers

"I THINK I HAVE reduced my suitors to two men who are a good match," Efi declared one day as she withdrew a generous ladle full of a previous brew and drizzled it into a cooling tun of yarrow ale. "Ingo and Peter both have good prospects. Ingo will inherit his father's gloving business, and Herr Otbert, the stonemason, has no heirs, so Peter is most likely to take over his business."

Gritta nodded absently as she worked a tangle from Anstett's hair with a wooden comb. "By Jesu's foggy breath, how did you manage to put so much barley pottage in your hair, child?" she grumbled. "Surely you know how to use a spoon by now. Did you pour the pottage on your head so your brother could lick it from you?"

Anstett nodded enthusiastically. "How did you guess so quickly, Ma?"

"You mean to tell me...Mattheus!" Gritta screeched, and Anstett's twin brother, Mattheus, made a mad scramble for the door. Gritta dropped her comb and gave chase. "It is not seemly to eat your meals from your brother's head!" Her voice echoed down the lane as she ran after them.

Appel chuckled from where she sat, still at her sewing. "Had more of my babies survived, I am sure I would have been scraping pottage from their heads too." She let her work drop in her lap for a moment, and her eyes misted.

"How many babes did you lose, Appel?" Efi asked.

"Four." Appel's voice was husky, and she swiped at her eyes. "Weren't really babes though, being unbaptized as they were when they died, and some still in my womb, too. But sometimes I wonder what it would have been like had they lived, at least for a few years." She snatched up her sewing and busied herself as if her survival depended on straight stitches. For a moment, there was a silence, thick with introspection and longing. Appel spoke again, this time in a whisper. "You and Gritta are a blessing in my gray years, Efi. You're the daughters that I never bore."

Efi planted a kiss on the top of the pale blue wimple that covered Appel's head, wrapping her arms around the older woman.

"And you are the mother I need. The pestilence took my mother, but even before her death she was sickly and angry. She never had much time for me."

"You don't often speak of your family, Efi. Surely you have some people still living back in Kleve?"

"No indeed. That is why my poor dear Harald and I moved here to Colmar. Nothing pegged us down in Kleve. There was no reason to stay."

"But didn't Harald…"

"Burn down the house of a lord? Yes, that was another reason not to stay in Kleve." Efi grinned as she spoke, and the two women laughed. Harald, Efi's husband, had been dead for a year now, and Efi was coming around to the idea that, although he was handsome, he was not the cleverest of men. Appel held her tongue instead of mentioning Efi's ill-conceived hiding places for her dowry.

"Well, now, let's taste this new ale, shall we?" Appel hoisted herself to her feet and tapped on one of the tuns that fermented in the cool, dark corner of the house.

"Without Gritta?"

"She'll be along presently, I am sure, once she catches and thrashes Anstett and Mattheus." Appel poured two small cups of the cloudy, golden liquid, and just as she and Efi had sat to taste, the door slammed open, and Gritta marched inside. As usual, a small flock of hens followed close at her ankles.

"It's happened again! And girls, Heinrik of Strassburg couldn't be the murderer because he's still locked away in the tower."

"There's been another death? Where is Jorges?" Efi asked, her voice trembling slightly.

Gritta smiled. "Sorting fish at the poissonnerie, Jesu be praised. Many can attest that he never left the quay."

"Who was killed?" Appel asked. "And where?"

Gritta sat on a bench and leaned forward, batting away a chicken as it tried to peck at her leather slippers. "Another from Vogelgrun, we think, because he was found on the road like Jens Töpfer. He is not someone from Colmar; we know that much."

"His name?"

"Dieuwert Moune," Gritta replied, her mouth contorting across the syllables. "At least, that's what the sheriff thinks. The name was carved into his walking stick."

"What kind of a name is that?"

"It's Frisian."

"And how would you know it's a Frisian name? You've never traveled more than three days from these walls."

"Well, what else could it be? It's certainly not Alsatian."

"I think I would remember the name Dieuwert Moune if he were a citizen of Colmar," Appel mused. "Do we know for certain that the man was of Vogelgrun?"

Gritta shook her head. "I only overheard the sheriff as he was trying to calm the poor soul who found the body. It was a leper traveling from Vogelgrun to Colmar to beg in the Dominicans' square." Gritta glanced over her shoulder and leaned forward. Appel and Efi drew closer to her as if pulled by strings. From Gritta's posture, she had a morsel of delicious news to share. "The body had hands. Still affixed to their wrists."

Appel stepped back and sat heavily upon her bench. "Well, now! It can't be the same killer!"

"Can't it?"

"Gritta, are you sure Jorges never left the poissonnerie?" Efi asked.

"Of course I'm sure! Jorges says he never left, and I believe him." Gritta planted her feet and readied herself for battle.

"That won't stop Sheriff Werner from trying to pin the blame on Jorges again. Come," Appel said, straightening her bonnet.

"We must go to the poissonnerie at once and speak to the fishermen."

Efi poured some of the new ale into a pitcher, and they set out.

The poissonnerie was only a few streets away from Les Tanneurs, located on one of the widest canals that ran through the city. Here, the water flowed slower and deeper, allowing more boats to crowd along the quays and the muddy shoreline. The sound of gently flowing water competed with the less harmonious melody of the fishermen as they sang, swore, and argued with each other.

The fish, caught upstream or imported from the Rhine, were sold near the water's edge and kept in tightly woven willow traps that stayed in the current to keep the catch from spoiling. Some of them, mostly eels and lampreys, would be salted, dried, and packed into barrels to be used as currency as well as food. Others would hang on frames to dry in the sun, sometimes with a smoldering fire beneath to impart some flavor and speed up the process. In the trees, carrion birds vied for space with the town cats; all watched closely for the telltale silver flicker of a dropped or discarded fish. Boys and girls prowled among the drying racks with long twigs to swat at the unfortunate bird or stray dog who ventured too close.

The fishwives moved amongst the men, cleaning and selecting the fish that they would sell, and ordering Jorges around as he lifted baskets of squirming bounty from the boats and onto the muddy shore. Jorges was carrying one such basket on his shoulder, tiptoeing on a plank set between the boat's gunnels and the rocky edge of the canal, and as soon as he saw the three alewives, his craggy face lit up with a gap-toothed smile.

"Gritta, my dove – come to watch your man at work, have you? See here; I am faithfully earning coin to feed our littles." He glanced at the pitcher Efi held in her hands. "And you brought some nourishing refreshment, I see!" He reached for the pitcher, and Efi snatched it back, hugging it close to her chest.

"No, you don't, Jorges Leporteur," Gritta snapped. "This is for the fishermen, for I need answers from them. Keep your hands off."

Before Jorges could protest, one of the more well-seasoned fishwives stomped to the quay and pushed Gritta back. "What do you mean by distracting my workers?" she snarled through wrinkled lips.

Gritta drew herself up. She was not tall, but the ancient fishwife, with her dingy wimple and her skirt tied up around her thick ankles, was as small as a child.

"Careful, Gritta," Efi whispered. "We came to speak to fishermen, not to anger their wives."

With a terse nod, Gritta stepped aside. The little fishwife shook her finger at Jorges. "Back to work with ye! Or you'll have one less onion with your afternoon meal today!"

"Wouldn't mind if that were the case, actually," Gritta muttered. "Every day I tell him to rub his teeth with a little salt for all our sakes, but he refuses, and his breath is foul enough to wilt the leaves from the trees."

Appel cleared her throat and flashed her most winning smile. "Frau Tisserand, we do not mean to stop your men from their work. But since it is time for the noon meal, might we speak with them? We brought some fine wheat ale for their refreshment."

Frau Tisserand's face relaxed into a gummy, toothless grin. She patted Appel on the elbow, which was about all she could reach. "Anything for you, young 'un!"

The alewives hurried past Frau Tisserand and the suspicious glares of the other fishwives at the dock. As soon as Efi offered to fill their cups with ale, the mood lightened. With the fishwives placated, the three alewives approached the semicircle of crates and baskets where the fishermen and merchants sat, taking their dinner and exchanging increasingly improbable stories of their exploits in their flat-bottomed canal boats. The three women held back for a moment, unsure how to proceed. Then Gritta growled in her throat, snatched the pitcher of ale from Efi's hands, and marched into the center of the semicircle. She held the pitcher aloft and waited for the men's conversation to fall silent.

"Alright, lads, we have a few questions, and once you answer them to our satisfaction, here's a free portion of ale to share amongst yourselves." She glanced back to the quay where the fishwives worked, their faces rosy from the drink. Frau Tisserand stood off to the side, arms crossed, watching them.

Gritta leaned forward. "And this ain't the small ale, friends. This here brew is a bit stronger," she said in a loud whisper with a wink. The men grinned, and Herr Fisker, the guild leader, stepped forward.

"What do you need to know?"

"I need to know where my husband has been today, and yesterday, too."

"You'll have to ask my wife. I pay little attention to the whereabouts of the porters. It's my wife, Elise, who keeps them on their tasks and pays them their wages." Herr Fisker reached for the pitcher, but Gritta pulled it away and handed it to Appel.

"I need someone to attest to Sheriff Werner, Lord Frider, and the sheriff of Vogelgrun that Jorges was here all day carrying loads at the poissonnerie." She took a moment to breathe deeply and swallow her pride. "And, Herr Fisker, although I know Elise to be a strong, capable woman, I need the testimony of a man in this case. You're the guild leader. If Elise will swear that Jorges was at the docks, will you trust her and also swear to it in front of witnesses?"

Herr Fisker narrowed his eyes, and a sly smile spread across his face.

"Well, it sounds like our Jorges is in a bit of trouble."

"Only because Sheriff Werner decides it. He has been trying to find reasons to put Jorges in the tower all season."

"And it makes sense. Jorges is a drunk and a layabout. You would do well to find another man, Gritta. With all those sons of yours, a tradesman who is childless might be happy to marry you and apprentice your children. Can Jorges offer you this much? Let the sheriff serve Jorges the punishment he deserves, and we will all be better for it. You included."

Gritta's face flushed to the color of a boiled beet, and she balled her fists. Appel quickly thrust the pitcher of strong ale into Efi's arms and stepped in front of her friend.

"Herr Fisker! Although I know your intentions are, er...noble, Gritta would like to keep the husband she has. Will you swear to Sheriff Werner and Sheriff Vogel that Jorges was at the docks?"

"Well, that all depends." Herr Fisker scratched his chin in an exaggerated manner, as if considering weighty problems. Appel's heart sank. She knew when a man was about to press his advantage. His cooperation would come with a price.

"Franz Fisker!" a voice screeched from the dock, and a woman stomped toward the semicircle of men. She had rolled up the sleeves of her dress, showing her muscled forearms, and she marched forward with a long, furious stride. She clutched her now empty cup of ale in one hand and a nice fat trout in the other. Elise Fisker was taller than most of the men who worked at the quay, including her husband. She argued the loudest, was the harshest employer, and tracked every copper coin and morsel of bread given to the dockworkers. As she approached, Herr Fisker's face paled, and the other men retreated.

"So, my word ain't good enough, eh? Jorges Leporteur was at the docks for the whole day, I say. Will you not testify on my behalf?" Frau Fisker jabbed the limp trout in her husband's direction.

Efi clucked her tongue with admiration. "Frau Fisker would be formidable in a knife fight," she whispered to Appel. "Look at the skill she uses to wield that fish!"

"Hush, girl!" Appel whispered back.

"Calm now, Elise. There are many men working on the boats and docks all day. All I am sayin' is you might not remember correctly. I am sure there is a way that Gritta can help you remember," Herr Fisker said, holding up both hands as if to show his wife that he was unarmed.

The alewives looked at each other. It was obvious that Herr Fisker intended to extort money or more ale from them for his cooperation. Elise caught their shared look of dismay, turned, and slapped her husband on the side of his head with her fish. It made contact with a loud splat.

"Elise! I told you to stop doing that in front of my men!" Herr Fisker raged, but Elise only laughed.

"I won't dirty my own hands on you, Franz. Not when I see you tryin' to cheat a desperate woman out of her hard-saved coin! You'll talk with the sheriff, or the next time you find a trout, it will be in bed with you instead of me!"

Gritta's face broke into a grin for the first time all day, and her eyes danced with humor. She bowed deeply to Elise. Efi handed the ale pitcher to the fishwife. Elise dropped her cup and her trout to the ground, raised the pitcher to her mouth, and drank deeply until it was empty. Then she tossed the pitcher into the canal, wiped her mouth with her sleeve, and leveled Herr Fisker and the merchants with a stare, cold and dark.

"Alright! Back to work. All of you!"

"Well, my Jorges is safe," Gritta said with some satisfaction. She, Appel, and Efi walked arm-in-arm, with Efi in the middle, back toward Les Tanneurs at a leisurely pace. Above them, spears of pink and orange clouds pierced the early evening sky.

"When he insisted that he never left the quay, I thought at least he would visit the privy," Efi commented. "And now I do not think I shall ever bathe in the waters of the grand canal again."

"Aye, aye, he should use the privy instead of the canal to relieve himself, but the point is, friends, he is innocent! Let that bloated sheriff try to put the blame on him now and see what comes of it. We have many voices to attest to his innocence."

"And Herr Fisker will think twice before making suggestions about the accuracy of his wife's memory," Appel said. "We now know it was not Heinrik of Strassburg because he is locked in the tower. It was not Margitte because she was a victim of the killer. It was not Jorges, or Gritta, or me. All of this is good news, but the reality remains that there is still a killer on the loose in Colmar, and until he is found, no one is safe."

Banished

In which Brother Tacitus plays his hand

When they were in their meager chambers, which was rare, the brothers of Saint Martin's priory were expected to spend their time kneeling in humble prayer. The dormitories were not quiet. Although the halls always had fresh straw to dampen sound and insulate against the cold, the sleeping room had bare stone floors and walls of rough planking. Father Konrad considered himself generous by allowing them two woolen blankets instead of just one. Keeping the friars' rooms as uncomfortable as possible proved an effective way to discourage them from spending inordinate amounts of time alone and out of sight. Discreet contemplation of God's wonders was fine – as long as it could be observed in an open place, such as the gardens or the cloister.

Brother Wikerus pondered these things as he lay on his back in bed. The beds were supposed to be simple wooden planks with a thin layer of fodder and a blanket. Most uncomfortable, indeed! Wikerus had learned to conceal small bundles of hay under his robes whenever he made his way back to his quarters, padding the bed until he had a nice mattress of wheat grass, barley straw, rosemary and lavender sprigs, and dried puffs of green moss.

All evening after prayers, he had been pondering the murders, idly playing cat's cradle with a length of twine. When the light from his narrow window faded, he continued in the dark, staring blankly at the ceiling, manipulating the string without sight. Gilbert of Sundhoffen. Jens Töpfer. Margitte of Vogelgrun. And now Dieuwert Moune. What did they all have in common? He worked the string faster and faster. As his thoughts accelerated, so did his fingers until he could no longer keep pace with the steps to the game, and he became hopelessly tangled.

The door to his chamber slammed open, and the intruder stepped inside without knocking. Startled, Wikerus sat straight up, but his fingers were still tied together. It took a moment for his eyes to adjust to the brightness of the oil lamp. The gaunt face of Brother Tacitus materialized from the darkness.

"Well, I shouldn't be surprised, and yet, even I find this shocking, Brother. Playing games while you are supposed to be contemplating God?" He strode forward, pulling a small, sharp knife from his belt. For a moment Wikerus shrank back. The knife couldn't kill a man if stabbed, but in that instant, all Wikerus could think about was that small, dirty blade plunging into his throat.

Tacitus quickly severed the twine around Wikerus's fingers. "When given the chance, you always revert to your hedonistic ways, Brother Wikerus. The Franciscans are weak and undisciplined."

"Here now, playing with a piece of string is not an act of hedonism!" Wikerus stood, feeling the heat rise to his cheeks. But Tacitus looked past him at the mattress, which was as plush and padded as a sheep's coat before the spring shearing. Stepping past Wikerus, he whipped the wool blanket from the bed and gasped.

"You have been stealing hay to make your bed opulent. What next, Brother? Will you steal the feathers from the priory geese to make yourself a pillow?!"

Wikerus took the blanket back and spread it over his rosemary-scented mattress. "Brother Tacitus, why are you here? Why did you enter my room so suddenly and without knocking? It is almost as if you wish to catch me in some misdeed."

"That wasn't my intention. I am here to call you to the evening meal."

"The bell calls me to the evening meal, as it does for you and the rest of the brethren."

Tacitus set the oil lamp on the wooden bench that served as seating and table in the sparse room. "Very well. I am here to ask if you have noticed the likes of Lonel Leporteur lurking about the church grounds. I suspect him of mischief."

"That is a safe suspicion," Wikerus said with a chuckle. He lay back on his mattress and pillowed his head with his arms. "Lonel has caused trouble in the past, but he is a boy with a good heart."

"His behavior wants correcting before he turns to crime."

Wikerus raised an eyebrow. "Beyond his pickpocketing?"

Tacitus huffed. He looked at Wikerus straight in the eye. "Your work in Les Tanneurs has been ineffective. You should know I have formally requested that you be returned to Breisach."

Wikerus sat straight up on his bed. "What?!"

"You do not belong here, Brother Wikerus. You must go home to your own people."

Wikerus jumped to his feet and searched for his sandals beneath his bed. "I shall go straight to Father Konrad. You cannot simply decide for yourself when I will leave. Father Konrad won't allow it."

Brother Tacitus put a hand on Wikerus's arm. "It is out of his hands. Your old abbot in Breisach, Father Guillaume, wrote to Father Konrad and requested that you return. As a member of authority in your Franciscan Order, if he wants you back, you must go. Although you seem to have no respect for authority in Colmar, I hope you will obey your Order and remember to humble yourself before God."

"I hate you."

The words slipped from his mouth before he could stop himself.

"And I hate Franciscans," Tacitus hissed in response. Wikerus had finally managed to get his feet into his sandals, and he tried to stand chin-to-chin with Tacitus, which was impossible because there was a handspan of height difference between them.

"We shall see what Father Konrad has to say about this."

"But, Father Konrad, can you not write back to Father Guillaume in Breisach and tell him this is not a good time for me to return? I feel I am very close to understanding who has been killing and mutilating people from Vogelgrun. I've identified some common traits that tie the victims together." Wikerus held up a finger. "First, they were all from Vogelgrun, and second —"

"Father Konrad, if I may," Tacitus interrupted. "Surely Breisach has its own quandaries for Brother Wikerus to resolve."

The sneer in his voice was impossible to misunderstand. Tacitus always doubted that Wikerus had any skills at finding killers and thieves, just as he did not believe Wikerus was capable of doing any good in Les Tanneurs. Wikerus balled his fists at his sides, thankful that the sleeves of his secondhand robe were slightly too long.

Father Konrad shook his head slowly. "I am sorry, Brother Wikerus. I am as mystified as you that Father Guillaume wants you back in Breisach so suddenly. Especially after he was so eager to get rid of you last year."

Eager to be rid of me? Wikerus's thoughts spun. Why would Father Guillaume be in such a hurry to get rid of me that he would toss me into a group of Dominicans across the river like refuse? The realization that he should have questioned Father Guillaume's motives mixed with his shame.

"What will you tell him, Father Konrad?"

"Well, I must tell him that you will come immediately. I cannot refuse his request. Although I do find something interesting..." Father Konrad tapped his chin while Wikerus and Tacitus waited, leaning forward on their toes in anticipation.

"What do you find interesting, Father Konrad?" Tacitus finally asked. His effort to restrain his voice caused him to quiver slightly.

Father Konrad smiled and assembled his fingers into a steeple, a gesture that he was known for. "I find it interesting that Father Guillaume knew so much about the doings of Saint Martin's priory in his letter. For example, although it is very distressing to us here that Brother Tacitus finds himself so often locked in the privy, I didn't expect Father Guillaume to have heard of it."

Tacitus blushed violently.

"Ah well," Father Konrad continued. "It is a great shame, Brother Wikerus. You are troublesome, my lad. But I am fond of you. Very fond indeed. Now pack your things. You will leave after the prayers at Prime, tomorrow morning."

A bounty of suspects

In which the alewives find themselves in need of counsel

Appel was trying for the third time to explain to the ancient gatekeeper standing watch outside Saint Martin's priory that she needed to speak to Friar Wikerus, when Brother Tacitus floated by as if blown on an icy wind. His face was haggard, his normally clean-shaven chin a stubble of black speckled with gray. As soon as he spied the alewives, he reached out with a bony hand and drew the gatekeeper back.

"Thank you, Herr Lucien," he said, malice glittering in his eyes as he beheld the alewives. "I shall manage these three." He turned his gaze on them and scoffed loudly. "And I suppose you are here to seek rescue from your hero, Brother Wikerus, who always keeps you from suffering the consequences of your actions?"

"And what actions of ours require consequences?" Gritta asked, her voice taking on a dangerous edge.

"Drunkenness, licentiousness, spreading rumors, and encouraging that foul son of yours to...to..." But although he suspected Lonel Leporteur was behind the vicious antics of his fellow intoxicated brethren and the privy pranks, Tacitus couldn't bring himself to say aloud that he had spent hours of panic and contemplation inside the malodorous outhouse of God.

"Convinced him to lock you in the privy, do you mean, so you have to smell your stench like the rest of us do when you come to call? I did no such thing. Move aside. We seek Wikerus." Gritta attempted to push past him, but Tacitus barred her way through the postern with his arms.

"You may not come inside, for this priory houses pious men, and your presence befouls it."

"The order provides beds to women all the time in the guest halls. You would let us inside if we were noblewomen with full purses. You would let us inside if we were the wives of traveling merchants!" Efi shot back.

"But you are not those things, are you?" Tacitus pulled his mouth up into a thin-lipped smile.

"Shame on you!" Efi pushed up the sleeves of her dress, readying herself for battle.

"Wikerus is not here. He no longer lives at this priory. I am afraid your friend has been sent back to his own community in Breisach. It seems his skills at failing to catch thieves and murderers are needed elsewhere."

All three women recoiled. "Father Konrad can't just *give him* back!" Gritta yelled. "You are lying."

Tacitus met the eyes of the old gatekeeper as he turned to go. "Herr Lucien, do not let these women inside. If they continue to carry on at our gates, please escort them back to their homes or call one of the sheriff's men."

"Wait..." Appel said, but Tacitus had gone, and the door shut behind him.

"Well!" Gritta said. "He has what he wanted. He is rid of Friar Wikerus, and he is rid of us."

"It is clear that Friar Tacitus is the one of the murder suspects," Efi declared.

"No, it ain't," Gritta sighed. "But if it wasn't obvious before, we can now prove that he is a horse's arse."

Appel bit her lip in thought. "We do not need Wikerus to help us determine who is killing these people," she said, and she linked arms with Efi on one side and Gritta on the other. "Come now, I have an idea."

Back at Appel's house, they stoked the coals in the hearth and set a pot of water to boil with the bones of Efi's gift chicken from Charles, the lovesick butcher. The chicken had already been boiled for broth once, which fed all of them, including Jorges and eight of Gritta's children. The bones wouldn't yield much the second time around, but they would add a bit of fat and flavor to their pottage. Appel tossed in a few wilted turnip greens and some dried mushrooms while Efi set the table, and Gritta drew some fresh ale from the tun in the lean-to. Appel rummaged in her little cupboard and withdrew a half-burned tallow candle, and the other two women gasped.

"Surely you are not planning to burn that candle, Appel? A rushlight or the glow of the fire will do just fine. Candles are for weddings, christenings, and funerals!"

Appel marched to the hearth and touched the candle's wick to a red coal. It flashed to life, casting a strong, warm light.

"I can't think in the dark," Appel said, pushing the base of the candle into a knothole in the table. "Now, let us eat, and then we shall discuss what we know."

"Well, we know we're safe from this killer anyway." Gritta snorted and shoveled a scoop of steaming pottage into her mouth.

"Why is that?" Efi asked.

"Because he only kills people from Vogelgrun."

Appel was nodding. "'Tis true. And he has his stamp. He takes the hands of his prey. He may as well have a king's seal to announce his presence."

"He travels. He is on the road. Several of those killed were on the road. And he's been to Colmar because he placed Gilbert's hand into our ale pot."

They were quiet.

"It does appear that the most likely person is Heinrik of Strassburg," Appel said quietly. "I don't want it to be true."

"Aye, but what about the latest murder – Dieuwert Moune, the Frisian man. Heinrik was locked up."

"And Dieuwert Moune's hands were still attached. Perhaps – oh, I can hardly even say it. Perhaps there are two murderers in Colmar." Appel shuddered as she spoke.

"Or perhaps he didn't have time to take the hands? Maybe someone came upon the body lying in all its horror and scared the murderer away," Efi said.

"But, my dears, there is something else. These poor souls may have all been from Vogelgrun, but none of them were killed in Vogelgrun. All were in proximity to Colmar. They were all closer to Colmar than their hometown."

They sat and thought for a moment while Gritta ladled more pottage into her bowl. "Efi, your prancing about to seek a husband is unseemly and shameless, but I cannot deny that I enjoy it when you share your suitors' gifts with us. This pottage with a little chicken water in it tastes as if it were prepared by Saint Martha herself."

Appel clapped her hands loudly. "Back to the task at hand!"

At this, Efi snorted with laughter, and a bit of pottage landed on the table.

"Whatever is the matter with you, girl?" Appel demanded.

"You said the task at hand! It was a good joke, though in poor taste."

Appel rolled her eyes. "We cannot rule Heinrik out completely. Although I hate to agree with Sheriff Werner, it does appear that two murderers could be working together, which is why Jorges is a suspect again. We know Jorges is innocent, but perhaps someone else in town is working with Heinrik. Someone who would seem above reproach. There is another man we haven't considered."

Efi and Gritta leaned in closer.

"Friar Tacitus."

Efi and Gritta both pulled back as if hit by a gust of wind.

"Mother Mary's breath!" Gritta said. "That is a strong accusation, Appel! And you, the most pious of us all!"

"It was I who already suggested Friar Tacitus," Efi said, sticking out her lower lip. "Well, he doesn't like us, that is clear, but why would he turn to murder?"

"I'll tell you why." Appel waited until the other two had leaned forward, their breath stopped, their attention fully on her. "Because he wishes to make it look as if Jorges did it. He wants to accuse Jorges. And if Jorges hangs, then Gritta and her children will be cast out onto the streets."

"No, they won't! We shall take them in," Efi said.

"Indeed Efi. We will not let them starve."

Gritta exhaled loudly. "Appel, you do me proud. Even I could not imagine such a thing. But although Friar Tacitus may dislike Jorges and me, and especially Lonel, I cannot believe he would murder four people just to send Jorges to the gallows. There are far easier ways to get rid of us."

"Such as?" Appel asked.

"Show Jorges a better opportunity elsewhere. He would move, and we would move with him."

"But that would mean more success and prosperity for you and your family, Gritta, and a man like Friar Tacitus cannot bear to see good fortune befall anyone, especially not someone he feels is so far beneath him. That kind of envy eats a man – holy or not."

"There is one more man we have not discussed," Efi said quietly. "Hans Bäcker."

Appel and Gritta looked at Efi, confused. Gritta spoke.

"Hans Bäcker, that crook who runs the crumbling old bread oven on the edge of the green? Why is he suspicious? He hardly ever leaves his oven because he's so busy pulling the hard-earned coins out of the poorest of us all in Les Tanneurs."

Appel's brow knit. "Is not Hans one of your suitors?"

"No indeed! I appreciated the honey cakes he gave me, but I would never marry the man. He smells like yeast and evil intentions."

"What causes your suspicion, Efi?" Gritta asked.

"Well, he tried to kiss me one day behind his oven, and that is when I told him that if he did not leave me alone, I would tell the sheriff about his secret enterprise. The next time I visited his oven to bake our loaves, he charged me three times what is normally owed and burned the bread. When I demanded he return my money for the bread, he ordered me out of his shop."

"What secret enterprise, Efi? What do you know about Hans?"

Efi bit her lip. "I don't want to say," she whispered. "I don't know for sure; I only suspect. He is a dishonest man, and he frightens me."

"Cheating people is not unusual for a baker, Efi, and to kill and cut up travelers from Vogelgrun would be a huge risk for a baker with an established trade. It is a grave matter to accuse someone," Gritta said. "Let us wait until we know for certain."

"I wish Friar Wikerus were here." Efi's voice sounded small. "He can see things that we cannot."

"Aye, and there is another mystery. Why was the good friar sent away, and how do we get him back?" Appel said. "We have too many people that we suspect of these crimes, not enough information to connect them to the murders, and no wise friar to listen and offer his counsel. We are alone."

Loaves of mystery

In which the cost to bake bread unexpectedly doubles

Ever since Hans Bäcker had thrown her out of his shop, Efi walked the raw balls of bread dough across the city to a separate quarter for the baking. After she exited Les Tanneurs and crossed the busy quays near the poissonnerie, she made her way to the street of bakers, so named because it housed a busy communal oven and several shops with private ovens for baking pies and sweets.

The street of bakers always smelled of steaming, nutty boules of brown bread and kugelhopf studded with dried plums as the bakers pulled yeasty delights from the coals with long, wooden paddles. Along the nearby canal, a grist wheel churned away, crushing wheat and barley between the stones and milling them into flours ranging from smooth powders for fine holiday or church breads down to the grittier stuff that the poor could afford, which often had to be run through a sieve before baking or being used as a thickener in stews.

Colmar was a moderately flat city, with a low rise at its west end, and this incline seemed minor until one was saddled with a tray of heavy dough. Even though she could see her breath rising as white puffs in the cool morning air, Efi sweated under her wool dress and wimple, and by the time she reached the oven, she was sweaty and cross. She handed her dough to sour-faced Frau Ghent, who had been running her husband's business since he died in the pestilence.

"That will be two pennies," Frau Ghent said without looking up from her embroidery.

"But it was only one penny yesterday!" Efi said, nearly dropping her tray of dough in surprise.

"Well, it's two today. Pay it or find another oven."

"But...but..."

"Move on then!"

The goodwives in line behind Efi tittered amongst themselves. Most of the women in this part of town were married to merchants and tradesmen who made a comfortable living; they could afford fur trim on their frocks and honey with their bread. Her face burning with embarrassment, Efi ran from the building and back down the slope toward Les Tanneurs, fretting over how she would explain the unbaked dough to Appel.

"I suppose we can attempt to bake it ourselves on the coals of the new hearth," she said aloud.

"What was that?" Lonel's voice spoke from the branches of a tree, and Efi startled so quickly that she stumbled and dropped her tray into the dirt. The dough rolled into the lane, past two shepherds, and into the flock of sheep they were herding to the butcher. The churning forest of bony sheep legs and hooves ground the unbaked bread into the mud.

"Oh! And I thought my day couldn't get worse!" Efi wailed. "That's the last of our wheat flour until next week!"

Lonel swung down and dropped silently from the tree. He helped Efi pick up the dough, which was stuck with twigs, leaves, and sheep dung. "I am sorry, Frau Efi," he mumbled. "I'll get your bread back, I promise."

"Promise yourself, Lonel Leporteur! Two of those balls of dough were your mother's, and now you shall also have nothing to eat, nor will your brothers and sisters!"

Lonel paled. His hair was so coated in dust that it was nearly as white as his skin. Efi thought that he looked like a lanky, man-sized turnip.

"Please say nothing of this to my mother." He tapped the dirt from her woven tray as he spoke.

"I think she will notice that she has no bread to feed her children," Efi snarled.

"Wait behind Frau Appel's house when the sun is midway in the sky. I will replace this bread. I will!" He turned and set off with his usual loping pace, arms swinging at his sides. "Just wait, you shall see!" he called back.

Efi tied the soiled dough up in her apron and made her way home with slow, heavy steps, taking care not to be seen. As she slipped into the dooryard, she could hear Appel and Gritta inside the house, exchanging gossip and slinging good-natured insults at each other. She dropped the dough at her feet and shooed the chickens toward it. "At least it will fill their bellies," she thought. Then, her heart filled with dread, she strode into the house with her empty tray.

No one asked her any questions about the dough.

The sun rose to the top of the sky, but Lonel did not appear as he had promised. Efi paced the house until Gritta ordered her outside to pull weeds from the garden.

"Oh, and you had best get to the ovens soon, Efi. 'Tis nearly time for the midday meal," Gritta called after her.

Efi dragged her feet as she walked around the house to the garden, her sharpened digging stick in hand. She might as well just tell them what happened. They would go hungry today and pay two pennies instead of one from now on to use Frau Ghent's oven. She squatted on her heels in front of a weedy patch of asparagus that was not yet ready to produce any of the slim, sweet shoots and stabbed her stick into the soil, yanking up a thistle and tossing it aside. While she worked, she rehearsed how to break the news to Gritta without being verbally lambasted or struck with a soup spoon, but after a few moments, she stopped and breathed deeply. A rich, heady smell drifted on the wind into the garden.

Bread.

She ran to the low stone wall that protected the garden from neighboring pigs. Lonel stood on the other side holding a basket bulging with loaves, a lopsided grin splattered across his face and his straw-straight dusty hair hanging into his eyes.

"Lonel!" Efi gasped. "You didn't steal these from the street of bakers, did you? If anyone finds out – and they will eventually – you shall be tied to the pillory or worse!"

"I did not steal these from the street of bakers," Lonel laughed. "Go on, take them!"

Efi opened the little drawstring money bag she kept tied to her girdle. Although she still managed to set aside a penny on Sundays for the church and another for her dowry, the prices for food and fuel continued to rise, just like the cost of using the ovens. Her purse was growing too light.

"Nothing. This will cost you nothing. Take it, with my apologies for startling you," Lonel said, and before Efi could question him further, he had disappeared around the side of Appel's house and down Trench Lane.

She examined the loaves. There was something odd about them. Instead of being a uniform color and texture, they were oddly mottled, as if someone had swirled two kinds of flour into the dough and then failed to knead it until it was perfectly smooth. Hearing the scrape of a sandal, she looked up and saw Friar Tacitus marching toward her. It was too late for her to escape, so she curtseyed quickly, called out a greeting, and pushed on the door to hurry inside.

"Not so fast, young woman!" Tacitus called out, and Efi's shoulders slumped. "I would like to speak with you about some alarming things I have heard in the confessional from several of the least sensible bachelors and widowers in town."

"Friar Tacitus, I have never touched or tempted any of the bachelors and widowers in Colmar, I am sure," Efi said, keeping her eyes downcast.

"But it's what you do to their minds, you harlot! It's what happens in their imaginations! You have put visions in their heads!" His gray eyes rested on the basket of bread. "Where did you get that much bread? Are you not poor? Did one of those foolish suitors give it to you?"

"No indeed! Now, I really must bring this into the house. Gritta's children are hungry."

Friar Tacitus snatched a loaf from the basket before Efi could protest and broke it in half. He squinted at the two sides, sniffed it carefully, and handed it back to her.

"I knew it," he muttered, sniffing at the loaf deeply. "Treachery! Treachery, I say!"

"Friar Tacitus, are you feeling well?" Efi asked. His behavior was alarming. Perhaps, she thought, *he has spent too much time locked in the privy.*

"Young woman, tell me where you came by this bread, and if you lie to me or withhold the baker's name, only a hell of burned loaves shall await you."

Efi was stunned. "I truly don't know, Friar Tacitus! The bread was given to me – not by a suitor, but by Lonel Leporteur."

Tacitus set his already thin lips into a hard line. "Right then. I know where this came from and what I must do." Without another word, he turned and stomped back in the direction from which he had come.

For a moment, Efi hesitated. Everyone knew that Lonel couldn't be trusted, and Friar Tacitus did seem angry about the bread. But then she shrugged and brought the loaves into the house. After all, when good things come unexpectedly, only a fool pauses to question why or from where.

Rising suspicions

In which some loaves are baked with flour and others with lies

APPEL WAS JUST ABOUT to cover the coals for the evening, and Efi was wiping the last of the freshly washed cups with a cloth when there came a pounding on the door. Both women froze. Heinrik of Strassburg was not out of the gate tower yet, and if it were any member of Gritta's family, they simply would have called out. Appel approached the door, walking slow and stately. Behind her, Efi took up the mash paddle and held it like a club over her shoulder. She stood in front of the door and checked to ensure the bar was secure.

"Who hammers on my door at such a time of night?" Appel shouted.

"Open up, in God's name! It is Brother Evart and Brother Stephen from the priory," came the muffled reply from outside. Appel wrenched the bar up and pulled the door open. Two black-robed Dominican friars stood on the threshold, their faces pale and scared in the flickering light of a long torch.

"Brothers, what brings you out so late?"

"We seek Brother Tacitus, Frau Appel. He was sent to Les Tanneurs by Father Konrad to minister here since Brother Wikerus returned to Breisach. But Tacitus didn't show up for the evening meal, nor for prayers, nor did he seek his bed in the dormitory," Friar Evart answered.

"Did you check the privy?" Efi asked, trying to keep a straight face.

"Well, yes, we did, and he wasn't there, either. We fear..."

"You fear he has been murdered and liberated of his hands," Appel finished for them, her face grim. The two friars nodded, their eyes wide.

"In that case, I am sorry to tell you he is not here."

"Wait," Efi said, dropping the mash paddle. "I spoke with him this evening. I saw him here in Les Tanneurs."

"Do you know where he went, Frau Efi?"

"I do not," Efi stuttered. "He was furious about some loaves of bread that I carried. He demanded to know where I had gotten them, but I told him they were a gift and that I didn't know the baker. He then left, saying he knew what he must do. But I do not know where he went or what he set out to do."

Appel was scowling at her, and the two friars seemed bewildered.

"I suppose he thought the loaves were stolen and went to confront the thief," Appel said.

Friars Evart and Stephen only hesitated a moment before they decided to return to the priory to report what they had heard to Father Konrad. As soon as they had left, Appel turned on Efi.

"I thought there was something unusual about that bread! It looked strange, and I sent you to the baker with four balls of dough, but you presented me with eight loaves this afternoon. Efi, you need to tell me exactly what happened!"

Efi recounted the whole tale – how Frau Ghent had tried to overcharge her, how Lonel caused her to drop the dough, how he promised to replace it, then would not tell her where the bread was from or allow her to pay for it. When Efi finished, Appel took her cloak from its peg by the side of the door and lit an oil lamp.

"Come, Efi," she said as she fastened the cloak under her chin. "We must find Lonel."

When Appel and Efi entered Gritta's house, she was standing in the center of the room, hands on hips, scolding her twins, who sat sheepishly together on the room's single footstool.

"Has the Devil stolen your senses? Are you trying to put me in my grave before my time?!"

"What have they done, Gritta?" Appel asked.

"Used every cup, bowl, and pot in my house as boats. Sent them all down the grand canal in an armada, and now I have nothing left but spoons and knives! How, Appel? How could this happen? Truly, I could not have spat two such menaces from my womb! Three, if you count Lonel."

"And it is Lonel that we are here to talk to you about," Appel said.

Gritta narrowed her eyes. Seeing their chance, Anstett and Mattheus jumped up from the stool and dove into a pile of straw near the animal partition, burrowing to safety from their mother's wrath. They knew that whatever they did would always pale compared to Lonel's mischief.

"What has he done?"

"We're not entirely sure yet," Appel said slowly. "Do you know where he is now?"

"Out carousing with his useless friends, no doubt."

Efi stepped forward, hanging her head. "Gritta, the bread we ate today was not from the dough you and Appel provided. Lonel gave it to me. He may have stolen it."

Gritta shrugged. "Yes, the lad has sticky fingers, especially when we're hungry. I can hardly fault him for it because he always shares what he finds."

"Well, this time, his stealing may have gotten Friar Tacitus killed."

Gritta's eyes grew wide, and Efi spoke quickly.

"Friar Tacitus didn't return to the priory after his duties today, but I encountered him on the street on my return from meeting Lonel to get the bread. When he saw the loaves in my basket, he became angry and said he knew what to do. That was the last anyone saw or spoke to him. We fear that the murderer may be about town. The only person who can tell us more about those loaves is Lonel, and we must find him. Your son may be in danger as well as Friar Tacitus."

"Or," Appel said, her voice barely louder than a low growl. "Or Friar Tacitus is the killer, and he has Lonel with him."

Gritta paled, and her hands started to shake. Ordering Rosmunda to put the children to bed, she draped her shawl around her shoulders, and the three women set out into the dark.

Lonel wasn't sitting under any of the bridges with his friends, nor was he with any of the milkmaids or the washerwomen behind the stables. They eventually found Jorges in a low-reputation weinstube, his face rosy with drink, but Lonel wasn't with his father either. Gritta considered bringing Jorges with them to search for their son, but given his loud state of drunkenness, he seemed like more of a liability.

"That boy will get a thrashing from me when I find him!" Gritta raged, but her voice shook, and Appel knew that Gritta was terrified for her child. After all, with a murderer still on the loose in Colmar, Lonel could be a victim – or a suspect.

They circled the city walls but still did not find him. The last door they knocked on belonged to Herr Gluck, a barber-surgeon whose daughter Lonel was sweet on. Upon hearing Lonel's name, Herr Gluck's expression grew stormy.

"Tell that young lackwit to stay away from my daughter!" He wagged a finger at Gritta's face. "He is always loitering about, picking his teeth and nose, making rude comments to my customers, and looking disheveled, with flour in his hair!"

"Did you say flour in his hair?" Gritta asked, incredulous.

"Indeed. Lately, when Lonel Leporteur shows up, he is a mess, with baking flour on his head and shoulders. I am a barber! He puts the flour on his hair to insult me, I am sure of it!" Herr Gluck slammed the door, and the three alewives stood in silent shock.

"And all this time I just thought the lad was dirty," Gritta mused.

"Why would Lonel have flour on his head?" Appel asked.

"Oh no," Efi said quietly. "I think I know where Lonel has been going. And I think I know who has been killing people from Vogelgrun."

Bloodstains

In which you can't spell "hands" without "Hans"

"Slow down, girl! Where are you leading us?" Appel panted as she trotted to keep up with Efi, who walked quickly in the dark. The moon was full enough that they could see the trenches, stones, and piles of dung in the streets, but being out at night with a murderer roaming about was unsettling.

Efi didn't answer. She walked to a door on the darkened street and hesitated. Light flickered from the cracks in the building's shutters, but they heard no sounds of voices from within. The rich, nutty scent of bread hung in the air. She put her finger to her lips. "The murderer is in there," she whispered.

"But this is the oven of Hans Bäcker!" Gritta said, and Efi quickly shushed her. They heard a sudden patter of feet from inside, and someone smothered the candles.

"We must go for help," Efi whispered. "He is dangerous. We must fetch the sheriff."

"If Lonel is here and that baker intends to kill him, it will be too late by the time we fetch the sheriff!" Gritta hissed.

Suddenly, the door flung open, and the stocky form of Hans the baker stood before them, enveloped in shadow. "What do you mean by standing outside my door and yelling while good Christian men are trying to sleep? Off with you!" he bellowed.

The three alewives froze with terror. Hans wore his usual clothes – a white wool tunic with yellowing sweat stains under the arms, dark brown hose, and a flour-dusted apron. The apron had spatters of red across the front. Hans looked down, noticed the apparent bloodstains, and dropped his pretense. Before any of the women could react, he had grabbed Efi by a fistful of her thick blonde hair, wrenched her inside his house, and slammed the door shut. Appel screamed, and Gritta pounded on the door until her fists bled. Nearby, a stray dog began to bark. A few neighbors threw their shutters open and looked out into the street.

"Help!" Appel shouted. "Someone fetch the sheriff! Hans Bäcker has taken Efi!"

There was a scramble in the street, and two boys took off running through the dark toward Sheriff Werner's house. Several bleary-eyed men staggered from darkened doorways in their nightcaps to determine why two women were yelling and crying outside the communal oven.

Appel and Gritta quickly explained their suspicions that Hans the baker was the murderer of Colmar, and he had taken Efi into his house against her will. While they spoke, the smell of smoke filled the air. Everyone looked up. Sparks spiraled upward into the darkness from the massive chimney that sprouted from the clay-tile roof. Hans had rekindled the coals in his baking oven.

More people arrived, including Friar Evart and Friar Stephen, who had come searching for Tacitus earlier in the day. Sheriff Werner eventually materialized from the darkness of the street, flanked by several of his men who still maintained a state of moderate sobriety.

"Why is that oven burning at this time of night?" the sheriff barked. "Where is Josse, the night watchman!"

"Here, m'lord!" Josse called from the crowd.

"I pay you to ensure that all the hearths are dark come nightfall. That chimney could set the whole city ablaze!" Sheriff Werner stabbed his finger angrily at the sky as he spoke.

"Sheriff, Efi is locked inside with Hans Bäcker, and I fear that Friar Tacitus is also there, possibly dead!" Gritta tugged on the sheriff's sleeve as she spoke. "And my son Lonel!"

"You accuse the good baker of being a killer? Nonsense! The man is an upstanding citizen of Colmar! Has been ever since he moved here from Vogelgrun five years back."

Appel and Gritta looked at each other. "He used to live in Vogelgrun?!" they both shouted at once.

"Indeed. He came here to start a new life after his wife died. I have shared many a cup of wine with Hans Bäcker at Herr Schlock's —"

But before Sheriff Werner could finish, there came a piercing scream from the crowd. A spark from the baker's chimney had landed on the thatched roof of a nearby stable, and flames quickly ate at the dry fodder.

"Buckets!" the sheriff shouted, and chaos erupted. Women ran into their homes and stables to find as many pots and waterskins as they could, while the men formed a line to the nearest canal and began handing filled pitchers and barrels toward the stable. But it was no use. The unseasonably dry weather had created the perfect tinder, and the flaming straw roof burned like a fiery portal to the underworld, eventually falling into the stable and igniting the fodder inside. A man managed to wrench the bar away from the stalls inside, and two terrified mules and one young pig shot into the street, their tails smoking slightly.

"Ma!"

Gritta spun around. Lonel ran to her, pushing through the throng of terrified people. "Ma, what are you doing here?"

"What are you doing here, you lumbering dalcop!" Gritta pulled her son into an embrace, holding him and crying. "I thought you were in there. With him!"

Lonel, still in Gritta's grip, looked over his mother's shoulder at Appel.

"Hans is the one who has been killing people from Vogelgrun, and now he has Efi and probably Friar Tacitus, too. We must get inside!" Appel told him.

Lonel disentangled himself from his mother's arms. "Hans? He can't be the murderer. I've never seen him murder anyone."

A gentle spring wind danced through the street, picking up more sparks, and soon, the building next to the stable also caught fire. The flames then licked across the dry grass that had died from the lack of normal spring rains and began to climb the wooden beams on Hans Bäcker's house.

"It's burning..." Appel said.

"And they are inside!" Gritta shouted. She turned to her son, but he was gone.

Appel and Gritta ran to the bakehouse door, pounding it with their fists and kicking it with their feet.

"The neighborhood is in flames, Hans!" Gritta screamed to the baker within. "Open up, or you will all die!"

But Hans did not respond. Inside, it was dark, except for the dim glow from the lit oven.

True love burns
In which fire burns overhead and all around

When Hans Bäcker pulled Efi through his door and into the wattle and daub building that housed his enormous stone oven, her heart sank. For a moment, she convinced herself that she could wriggle free. But although he had a portly figure from a diet rich in bread and cakes, his fleshy hands kept her arm in an unbreakable grip. He shoved her with such violence that she stumbled and fell against the side of the oven, gashing her head. Steadying herself with her hands, she felt the oven's warmth from its day's work. Warm, but not wrinkling the air with waves of heat. He had covered the coals for the night.

She reached up and felt her forehead in the dark. Warm blood trickled between her fingers. She could feel air moving through a rip underneath the arm of her frock. Her first feeling was anger, not because he held her hostage but because it was her favorite frock, and she was terrible at mending. Then she realized with chilling clarity that this was just the beginning. There were far worse things that Hans the baker could do to her than split a seam in her garment.

As her eyes adjusted to the dark room, Hans shoved a bar across the door and then moved about clumsily, checking the security of the shutters on the windows. Her fear grew until she couldn't breathe, and she backed up against the oven, pressing into it for support – for something solid to cling to.

"Your meddlesome friends called for the sheriff," Hans growled at her. "It will do no good. My house is so secure that the only way to open the door is to set it on fire."

She could make out his white teeth in the darkness as he grinned. "Well, I have a fire of my own, and it waits for its last meal!"

There came a scraping sound and a loud clatter as Hans probed inside the stone oven with a long wooden pole, lifting the heavy clay dome that he used to cover the coals at night and shoving it aside. The sudden rush of air rejuvenated the fire, and the coals glowed with ruby light. Hans tossed the stick aside, grabbed Efi roughly by the back of her dress, and dragged her to the oven's burning maw. The sudden blast of scorching wind lifted her loose blonde curls, and a few stray hairs shriveled and turned brown.

"Please," Efi wept; her tears felt like they were boiling on her cheeks. "Please." It was all she could say. The heat and the terror overwhelmed her. There came a ringing sound in her ears, so shrill and high-pitched that she thought it must be the sound of God's angels beckoning her to the afterlife.

A few tendrils of flame started a demonic dance toward the top of the cavernous oven, casting a hellish light on Hans's face.

Angels and demons. Her thoughts wandered casually across the irony. Oh, Appel would love this.

Again, Hans shoved her violently from him, and her small body came to a stop only when she hit a nearby wall, sending a shower of flaking plaster to the floor. He grabbed her by her hair and flung her again, this time toward a wall stacked with sacks of grain and kegs of wine. Efi tumbled over the kegs while Hans screamed with laughter.

"Think carefully about who you anger the next time you reject a marriage proposal, little kitten. Or perhaps I should call you 'little mouse' instead, for I am the hunter, and I am the one with claws and teeth!" He lunged at her, wrenching her to her feet, but she didn't scream. She had no more strength, and even if her friends outside heard her, no one could come through the barred door and windows.

Hans pulled her close to him, running his hands along her waist and hips, pressing his chapped lips on hers. She gagged with the stench of his breath, but he was kissing her so hard that she couldn't breathe or move her head. When he pulled away, he laughed again and pointed to a corner of the room.

"See him? If you are a good girl and do as I say, you will escape his fate. But if you do not obey me, your fate will be the same as his!"

Efi followed his pointing finger and saw a man slumped against a wall of firewood. In the rapidly growing flames from the oven, she made out the features of Friar Tacitus, pale and unconscious. His head lolled, blood dripping from his mouth and neck. Efi gasped and covered her mouth. One of the friar's hands was gone, and a spreading puddle of blood reflected the flames.

"Now, my little mouse, let us stoke the fire. You shall pump the bellows while I add the wood, and when it is good and hot, we shall take the friar's pieces and burn them until there is nothing left to prove that he was ever born." Hans gestured to the large leather bellows meant for fanning the oven's flames, and Efi took them up, moving the wooden handles timidly while Hans picked up armloads of wood and tossed them into the oven. The fire cast more light into the room, and Efi looked over to the wooden counter where she used to set out her dough for Hans to weigh before he decided how much to charge her for a bake in his oven. Unlike most counting tables, this one had canvas stretched across the front, so it was not possible to see the baker's legs or feet.

Efi swallowed hard. She knew it was mad of her to ask, but she had nothing else to lose. At least she could die knowing the truth about what she suspected had been going on. Nodding her head toward the counter, she took a deep breath.

"So, is that where Gilbert of Sundhoffen used to hide while you were busy cheating the goodwives of Les Tanneurs out of our coins and our dough at the same time?"

Up in smoke

In which the murderer is revealed, but not the method

T HE ROAR OF THE fire as it devoured the thatched roofs of the houses was so loud that the desperate townsfolk could no longer hear themselves yelling as they handed buckets to and from the canal. Appel and Gritta ran around the side of the bakehouse, looking for another entrance. They tried to pry back the shutters from the small window, but Hans had fortified his home like a château. The flames made their way up one side of the house and crawled to the front. As soon as the door caught fire, there would be no escape for anyone inside.

Gritta looked around wildly. Sheriff Werner had joined the bucket line and was heaving water onto another flaming house. "Let us both throw our weight against the door and push it open," she yelled to Appel over the noise of the fire and the shouts of the people around them.

Appel and Gritta counted to three and ran at the door, throwing their shoulders against it. The wood remained fast.

"Let us try again!" Gritta shouted. "One, two, three!" But just as their shoulders were about to make contact, the door opened, and the two alewives fell inside. Hans slammed the door shut behind them and shoved the bar into place.

"Get over there!" he screamed, pointing to the nearly empty partition where he kept his cords of pearwood for the oven. The two women looked around, searching for Efi. They saw Friar Tacitus slumped against the stacked logs, blood dribbling down his forehead, with more pooling on the ground where he sat. His eyes were closed. There were no lamps lit in the house, but coals glowed hot from the yawning mouth of the great stone oven on the east wall of the building. Most alarming was the light cast by the tendrils of flame that slipped along the ceiling beams overhead.

"Appel! Gritta!" They heard Efi scream. She knelt on the sooty floor across the room, her hands bound tightly behind her back.

Gritta picked up a stick of kindling from the woodpile. With a shout, she ran at Hans, but he jerked Efi to her feet and thrust her at the roaring mouth of the oven.

"Put it down, Gritta, or Efi will cook in my oven like a spitted pig! She fanned the flames herself with the bellows, and she knows how hot they are, don't you, girl?" He gave Efi a little shake for emphasis.

When Gritta hesitated, he pushed Efi a little closer. Sweat started to pour down her face from the waves of heat washing over her.

"She will taste delicious, too," he leered. "As delicious as she looks."

"Wait, don't do it!" Gritta lowered her weapon to the ground.

"Hans," Appel said as calmly as she could. "The street is on fire. We must leave this house at once, or we will all die."

"Then we will all die. I was planning to burn them both, anyway!" Hans said, but tears dribbled down his cheeks as he spoke.

"Please, Hans. You can still live! There are things worth living for!"

Hans swiped at his eyes, but more tears came.

"Not for me there ain't. When the city council finds out what I've done, they'll hang me for sure, or worse! I've done terrible things, Frau Appel. And the most terrible thing of all is that I learned to like it. I liked taking hands! I liked taking lives!"

Appel glanced again at Friar Tacitus, unconscious against the woodpile, and felt her stomach heave. One of his forearms ended in a bloody stump.

"All this time I've been serving others. Day after day, I take loaves and bake them. Day after day. Do you know what it feels like to hold and remove the life of a man? It feels like power. It feels like you are God himself." Hans was yelling now in ecstasy, but tears still poured down his cheeks. "The nothingness of your life takes on meaning. You can consume, like the flames of your oven. You can wield power over others."

Fighting against her instincts, Appel nodded in the most knowing way she could.

"Efi still has much to live for. So do Gritta and Tacitus. So do I. Please let us go. You may do what you will with what remains of your life, and we would dearly like to live ours."

Hans pointed at Efi. "This is her fault! Hers! I made her a perfectly reasonable offer. Had she agreed to marry me, none of this would have happened!" He still held her near the fire, and her head sagged as she grew faint from the heat. "Women these days have their heads filled with nonsense, and this one is stupider than all the rest!"

There came a loud crack overhead and Hans dove out of the way just as a flaming beam came crashing down in a shower of smoldering plaster and roof tiles. Appel and Gritta ran forward and dragged Efi back from the fire. Then Gritta leapt at the door, tugging and clawing at the bar, but it was stuck firmly into place as the wood of the doorframe expanded from the heat of the flames.

Dazed, Hans clawed his way across the ground to where Friar Tacitus lay and picked something up – a bloody, severed hand.

"I think I shall take the other hand now. What say you, Brother?" He slapped Tacitus across the face with the man's own hand. Tacitus groaned, but his eyes did not open. By now, the smoke that lingered high up in the rafters infiltrated the entire room. Gritta and Appel's throats and eyes burned, and they crouched low to the ground, fanning Efi's face and gasping for air.

Hans snatched up a long, stained knife and rolled Tacitus onto his back. He stretched out the friar's pale, unmarked arm and bent to his work. Gritta screamed, picked up a stick of firewood, and ran at Hans. Dodging as he swiped the knife at her, she landed a blow on his head so swift and strong that she heard the crack of wood meeting bone above the sound of the fire. A moment later, the barred door to the house was wrenched from its hinges and kicked forcefully into the flaming room.

"Ma!"

Gritta turned. Through the smoke, she couldn't see who had broken the door down, but the voice was unmistakable.

"Lonel?!"

Lonel and Jorges rushed into the room and grabbed her by both arms. They dragged her backward from that flaming inferno until she felt the bliss of cool water on her face. She was in a canal, and overhead a soft rain pattered onto the surface of the water. She took this in for a moment before her husband and son deposited her in the street, ran back in for Appel, and then dragged Efi outside.

The three women knelt in the street, pulling deep drags of fresh, cool air into their smoke-damaged lungs. Father Konrad arrived, running through the dark, escorted by Friar Evart and Friar Stephen. With only a moment of hesitation, the three of them dove through the bakehouse door, which belched out clouds of oily black smoke. They emerged moments later, carrying Friar Tacitus between them.

"Hans!" Appel yelled. "Has anyone seen Hans Bäcker? Is he still inside?"

As if to answer her question, a sooty hand gripped the edge of the open doorframe for a moment. Then, the heavy wooden door was heaved back into place from the inside. Hans had barred the way once more.

The rising sun struggled valiantly to light the sky the following morning but could not penetrate the rain clouds that blanketed the Rhine River valley. Although the smoke had cleared from the air, the smell of charred wood lingered, mingling with the welcome reek of muddy fields and overflowing canals from the much-needed rain. Near the bakehouse on the edge of Les Tanneurs, a few citizens milled about. Some nudged the ruins with a toe, discreetly looking for valuables that might have survived the flames. Others just stood in tight huddles together, gossiping quietly.

The stable had burned itself out, and the house next to it was smoldering, doused with canal water. But the house of Hans Bäcker was too engulfed by flames to be saved even by the rain, and the townspeople eventually stopped their bucket line and watched silently as it burned, and Hans, the baker, burned inside of it.

Fresh air

In which the full extent of the murderer's crimes comes to light

THEY PLACED EFI IN a makeshift bed that Appel hastily constructed of hay and spare blankets on the brewing floor of her house. The girl had taken in much smoke and poison from the fire, and with each breath she rasped and wheezed. Her face was ashy pale, her lips tinged with blue. She only woke when Appel roused her to take a little broth or some weak ale. But mostly, Efi slept, even through the constant stream of neighbors and well-wishers who came to call.

Gritta was there too, fielding questions and shooing people from the door when it became clear that Appel was fatigued. The two of them talked lightly of everyday things – the next set of herbs they wanted to try in a new brew, what they were planning for their summer gardens, all the gossip about the tanners' wives. But one topic they could not bear to discuss was the fate of Hans the baker, or the state of Friar Tacitus.

They had heard from their many visitors that Friar Tacitus lived, but he burned with fever and the Devil tempted him in his dreams. Appel and Gritta also learned that Sheriff Werner's men had removed the charred remains of Hans from the burned-out shell of his house, along with the knife that he used to murder and dismember people. Curiously, the men who recovered the body also found a long, unadorned sword in the wreckage. When Gritta checked the ceiling beams of her house, she discovered that the confiscated sword belonging to Heinrik of Strassburg was missing. Lonel eventually admitted to running back for it during the fire and using it to wrench the door to Hans's house from its hinges. Gritta stopped herself from scolding her son for discovering her hiding place. If he hadn't done so, she and her friends would undoubtedly be dead.

The river of visitors dwindled to a trickle after a few days, to Appel's great relief. As much as she wished to show herself to be a gracious and accommodating host, the company exhausted her, which is why she groaned when there was another knock at her door one afternoon.

"I'll tell whoever it is to come back later," Gritta said, jumping to her feet. But when she pulled the door open, she gasped.

"Friar Wikerus!"

"Greetings, dear alewives," Wikerus said, a pleasant smile on his lips, but his large, blue eyes were serious. "It seems you decided to wait until I had returned to Breisach to discover the identity of our murderer all by yourselves."

"Hans may have confessed to killing and taking hands from his victims before the fire took him, but we still do not know why, Friar," Appel said. "The killer is gone, but the mystery remains."

"I know," a voice rasped. It was the first time Efi had spoken since her ordeal. "I know why he did it because he told me everything."

Appel poured four cups of small ale, and Gritta dragged a few stools to Efi's bedside. Efi drank deeply from her ale cup and sighed.

"I never appreciated how refreshing and good this is until I thought I may never taste anything again."

Her audience of three waited in anticipation while she cooled her throat with the ale. Then she took a deep breath and began.

"When Hans pulled me into his house and shut the door behind me, I was terrified. You see, I had slowly started to realize what had happened, and I knew that he had murdered at least one person: Gilbert of Sundhoffen. I know this because I used to take my loaves to Hans's oven every day. Usually, the only person working was Hans, but one day, as I set my dough down to be weighed, a man rose from behind the counter and greeted me. I was startled because I didn't see him when I came in. Hans seemed very angry and told me that the man, who I now know to be Gilbert, was there to repair a problem with the floor. I thought nothing of it, but I did notice that he had flour on his shoulders and in his hair."

"Just like my Lonel!" Gritta gasped. Efi nodded and continued.

"The next day, Gilbert was gone. When I came to drop off my dough, Hans took my hand in his and told me that he wanted to take me as his wife since his own had died several years back in the Great Pestilence. He told me that I was young and strong enough to work in the bakehouse with him and that he needed an heir since his children had all died along with their mother. Well, I was surprised, and I never viewed the man as a potential husband. I told him no. When I came to pick up my loaves that afternoon, they were burned black. From that day on, Hans burned the loaves every day until I finally stopped going to his oven and walked the extra distance to bake my bread at Frau Ghent's oven instead. And then shortly afterward, I discovered Gilbert of Sundhoffen's hand floating in the mash."

"That doesn't prove that Hans Bäcker killed Gilbert," Wikerus said gently.

"But I am not finished. When Hans held me captive inside his burning house, I asked him about his relationship with Gilbert. It seems that Hans was running a scheme that required an assistant. You see, when the goodwives of Les Tanneurs and La Poissonnerie came to the oven, he always instructed them to place their balls of risen dough upon his counter so it could be weighed, and he would determine a price."

"Aye, this is how all oven meisters do it," Appel said, nodding in agreement.

"Well, Hans hired Gilbert of Sundhoffen to hide underneath the weighing and measuring table. And here is the clever part. Hans would place the dough upon the scales and weigh it so the goodwife could see for herself the exact measurement. Hans would then remove the dough from the scale and return it to the tabletop. But while he and the goodwife haggled over a price for time in the oven, Gilbert, who was hiding underneath the counter, would reach up and pull off a generous pinch of the dough, placing it into a bowl under the table. He did this all morning until he had several bowls filled with dough from households across the city. At the end of the day, Hans and Gilbert mixed them together, baked them, and sold them at the night market. Thus, they never paid for their wheat and salt."

"The absolute audacity!" Gritta jumped to her feet. "Many times I have spoken with Hans, and he has quoted me an outrageous price to cook my loaves. Are you telling me that while I was losing my temper with him, someone was stealing the dough I had brought him – right in front of me?!"

"Yes."

"But how did Gilbert's hand end up in our mash?"

Efi shuddered and took a moment to gather her wits. "Gilbert grew dissatisfied with how little Hans paid him. According to Hans, he acted in self-defense and killed Gilbert when the man tried to rob him. We will never know the truth of it, but when Hans had Gilbert's corpse in his home, the only way he could dispose of the body was to put it in his oven and burn it, and the only way that a big man like Gilbert would fit into the oven was if…if…"

"Was if Hans were to quarter him and put him into the oven piece by piece," Friar Wikerus finished for her.

"Indeed. But in his haste to stuff the body in the oven, one of Gilbert's hands rolled underneath the counter, and Hans discovered it later when the fire was already cold. So, because he was angry with me for refusing his marriage proposal, Hans decided to put it in our ale to ruin our business."

"But when?!"

"I had the branch up alongside the door, and customers had been coming and going all day to buy ale. Hans showed up demanding that I fill a pitcher for him. He must have slipped Gilbert's hand into the brew when I had my back turned, because I discovered it that afternoon. This is my fault, my friends, and I am sorry."

"Ain't your fault," Gritta said. "You didn't kill Gilbert, and you didn't put his hand in our brew. Ain't your fault one bit."

"And the rest of the victims?" Friar Wikerus asked.

"When Margitte came to town, she showed up at the communal oven claiming that she knew his secret and would start talking if Hans didn't pay her. As you know, Gilbert was an occasional lodger in her home in Vogelgrun. Apparently, during a night of drunken fighting, Gilbert revealed his other source of income, which was, of course, stealing dough and selling illegal bread in Colmar."

"But why did he remove Margitte's hands? It was not necessary," Appel asked.

"I think he started to enjoy it, tampering with the bodies of the dead."

Gritta was nodding as Efi spoke. "Aye, he said as much when he had us inside his burning house."

"After that, he just wanted to do what he could to make it seem like we were guilty of a crime. Hans had to travel to

Vogelgrun to conduct some business, and while he was there, he saw Jorges leaving the docks after a day of work. He plied your husband with drink, then murdered Jens Töpfer, an innocent traveler on the road, and put the hands in Jorges' sack to make it look like Jorges had committed the crime. He would do anything to put us on the gallows."

Appel's brow wrinkled in thought. "But what about Heinrik of Strassburg? By all accounts, Heinrik was not only on the road but also acting extremely guilty. And he carried a sword."

"Merchants and tradesmen often carry swords," Wikerus said. "Even though they are forbidden to carry arms, many do to protect themselves and their wares while they travel." He cleared his throat and hesitated for a moment. "It is not permitted for a friar to speak of what he hears during confession, but it may save a life in this case. Heinrik was guilty when he removed himself from Vogelgrun – guilty of putting a child into the daughter of Steppen, the fodder seller."

At this, Appel yelped. Friar Wikerus shot her a questioning look.

"Steppen was the very man I encountered when I met Heinrik in Vogelgrun when I purchased straw and rosemary for my bed in Margitte's house! Are you telling me that Heinrik fathered a child with that man's daughter?"

"Indeed. The young woman had just told Heinrik about the babe in her womb on the day the minstrels came upon the handless body and Jorges sleeping by the road."

"But why did he come to Appel's house later that night?" Efi asked.

"Perhaps he sought a way to relieve his lover of her child," Appel said slowly. "If the so-called 'witch of Vogelgrun' was dead, maybe no one else in the town knew what to do."

"This seems a likely reason," Wikerus said. "Or perhaps he just enjoys your company, Frau Appel." Friar Wikerus's large blue eyes sparkled, but Appel was incensed.

"I relieve the suffering of women. I am not in the business of saving men's reputations," she snarled, rising from her seat.

"Tell us of the last victim, Efi. There was another traveler from Vogelgrun who was found dead but with hands still attached. What was his name again?" Frair Wikerus asked.

"Dieuwert Moune was his name," Efi responded. "It was as I had suggested days ago. Some townsfolk discovered the body on the road to Vogelgrun before Hans could remove the hands and place them in a location that would make us look like killers. He told me he intended to slip the hands inside another pot of ale, but he was interrupted. By then, he had convinced Lonel to become his new dough-stealing accomplice, and as his profits increased from selling bread baked with stolen dough, his thoughts turned away from killing. For a while, anyway."

"Well, my thoughts have just turned toward killing," Gritta growled. "Where is that boy? I shall make him rue the day he clawed his way from my womb to torment the world with his devilry!"

Friar Wikerus patted Gritta on the arm. "Peace, Frau Gritta. Lonel could have been the next victim, and had he not found the sword that you stole and hid from Heinrik of Strassburg and used it to wrench the door from Hans's house during the fire, all of you would be dead. Let it lie."

For a moment, the four of them sat in silence, each absorbing the information about the murders, searching their memories for clues they had missed. Efi slowly rose from her bed, hobbled across the room, pulled the wooden plug from a small cask of ale and refilled her friends' cups with the golden liquid. When it was empty, Efi pried the top off the cask and turned it upside-down. A shower of silver and copper coins jangled to the ground.

"What in the name of Jesu's beard..." Gritta said, flinching under the disapproving stare from Friar Wikerus for her blasphemy.

Efi didn't answer. She stooped to pick up the coins, counting out five of them and placing the rest in the small purse hanging from her girdle. She handed the five coins to Friar Wikerus.

"Please take these and give them to Father Konrad at Saint Martin's with my blessing."

"But Efi, is that not your dowry? Those are five silver coins! Silver!" Gritta yelled.

Efi took the purse with the remaining coins from her girdle and handed it to Appel. "And please take the rest, Appel. We shall use it to buy grain and gruit, more casks, and anything else we require for brewing."

"But Efi, you will have no dowry for your marriage," Appel argued.

"I think there is no need to rush to find another husband. No, I would like to invest my dowry. Let us make something for ourselves."

Appel held up the little purse and felt the weight of coins in it. "I do believe you are growing up, Efi."

"Aye," said Gritta, crossing her arms over her chest. "And if Efi develops into a sensible businesswoman, who can stop her from running this whole city? She will have money, good sense, and her luscious looks. Who could stand against her?"

Efi blushed and then grinned. "Oh stop, Gritta. It will go to my head."

"Very well, if you insist. Efi, you're a silly, spotty-faced bumpkin with bad breath and feet like blacksmith's anvils. How dare you feed your friends ale that contains coins you not only buried in the fireplace, but also removed out of a burned-out privy!"

"It don't mean nothing if the coins were in the privy!"

"Do you want to kill us all with loose bowels and vomiting?!" Gritta swiped at Efi, who jumped away in time to avoid a cuff across the ear.

"Well," Friar Wikerus groaned as he got to his feet. "I had best go. I wish to be present this afternoon when the blacksmith fits Brother Tacitus with a hook over the stump of his hand."

"Must you return to Breisach, Friar? If you leave, Father Konrad may ask Friar Tacitus to minister to Les Tanneurs in your place."

"Then you have not heard?" Friar Wikerus said, his face breaking into a wide grin. "I requested and was granted orders of transfer. I shall continue to live in Colmar – not at Saint Martin's priory but at Saint Matthieu's, where the other Franciscans in Colmar reside. It is small, to be sure, and only a few friars live there, but they have plans to enlarge it and build up the community of brothers of Saint Francis here in this town."

"Then you shall continue to minister to Les Tanneurs?" Efi clapped her hands in excitement, but Friar Wikerus just smiled at her, set his cup down, bowed with a flourish, and walked out the door.

"Friar Wikerus?" Appel asked. "It will be you who tends to this quarter of the city and not another friar of the Dominicans or Franciscans, yes?"

"Farewell, alewives. I shall see you again soon," Wikerus called back to them as he left, and the three alewives stood, bewildered, in the doorway for a moment.

"I have a dreadful suspicion that we may be seeing less of Friar Wikerus and more of Friar Tacitus in our streets, my friends," Gritta said with a scowl.

"Well, Friar Tacitus certainly can't sit all day in a scriptorium and copy texts with a hook for a hand."

"Come then, this ale ain't going to brew itself!" Gritta declared. "I shall go to fetch some clean water from the stream by the church."

Efi placed a hand on Gritta's arm. "No, let me do it. Fetching water is my task."

"But, Efi dear, you're only just recovering your voice after taking so much smoke into your lungs. Stay at home and help me with the gruit herbs while Gritta fetches the water," Appel said, but Efi shook her head.

"I have spent enough time in bed. Drinking a cup of our fine golden ale restored my body. Telling my story to the two of you and Friar Wikerus restored my soul. And now I would like to work."

Appel and Gritta exchanged glances, then shrugged. Efi couldn't be stopped. Somehow, they knew she was no longer the silly girl they took in a year ago, recently widowed, empty-headed, and frivolous. The woman standing before them was no less fair, but now she was resolute, which enhanced her beauty.

Efi picked up her little yoke and readied herself to visit the stream near Saint Martin's church to fetch clean water. The muscles and tendons in her legs tingled as they adjusted to the movement after days of rest. It felt magnificent.

As she balanced the two pigskin buckets across her shoulders, Efi looked about the house and smiled. Sunlight streamed through the unshuttered windows, and a small fire crackled in the new hearth. There was fresh straw on the floor, sprinkled with sprigs of lady's bedstraw and rosemary to freshen the room, and clean linens fluttered in the breeze on the line outside. Standing at the large trestle table, Gritta and Appel were already bickering amicably as they sorted gruit herbs, their insults interrupted with peals of laughter.

"Yes," she whispered to herself. "I can wait a while longer before taking another husband."

Author's note

In which we learn that the author didn't just make this all up

READERS OF *THE ALEWIVES*, the first book in this series, may recall that I conceived the idea of a story about three lowbrow women brewing ale in the 14th century while the world was still in the clutches of the COVID-19 pandemic. Pushed by a desperation to assure myself that there were lessons to be learned from our ancestors who survived past pandemics, I began to study the plague (aka the Great Pestilence, the Black Death, the Great Mortality). Even though germ theory and the contagion theory of disease were both hundreds of years away, in the 14th century, people understood that being in the presence of a sick person could also cause others to fall ill. Sometimes this understanding was applied too far, such as spiritual contagion, or a fear of catching a genetic disease, but regardless, unlike the pandemic of the 21st century, isolating at home was simply impossible. I think often about the bravery of people who survived that world-altering wave of the plague.

Many pages have been written about the horrors of disease, but there are also acts of love, sacrifice, service, and compassion. This is what I learned during COVID-19 – that I wanted to find the love and compassion inside myself and share it with others.

And a miraculous thing happened: it started to return to me. It was a humbling lesson in the old adage that you "reap what you sow." After a lifetime of scrambling to get to the top of my career, I realized that the return harvest was hollow. In a way, Gritta, Appel, and Efi have been my guides. They are the wise and witty women who help me find friendship, community, and heart in a crisis.

Through the plague of the 14th century, people survived, and some of them even thrived. Babies were born and the elderly died of old age. Crops were planted, nurtured, harvested, and composted according to the seasons. People pressed on, adapting to their rapidly changing reality. And then, as now, when humans become desperate, as in times of a global pandemic, charlatans will always appear ready and willing to take advantage of those in need.

Enter the dough-swap con.

Medievalists may have solved this whodunnit a little sooner than the rest of us, because this was a well-known scam, with creative variations that the enterprising merchant or tradesperson could apply to all manner of goods. Although I didn't get into it in this book, medieval towns and cities had inspectors who were charged with making sure that people received the goods they paid for. Food was tested to ensure it wasn't contaminated. Grain and breads were weighed to prove that a penny loaf was, indeed, a penny loaf. But this didn't stop an unscrupulous baker from hiding an assistant to steal a pinch of dough during the process of weighing and measuring, or supplementing his dough with dirt and sawdust instead of flour.

We won't even get into the creative cons and harsh punishments directed at an alewife accused of selling a bad brew. Instead, I'll save that for another book.

E.R.A.

February 2024

Join me!

In which the reader is invited into the community

D ID YOU ENJOY *Sleight of Hand*? Other readers would love to know if the exploits of Gritta, Appel, and Efi are a worthwhile read, and your positive review is one of the most effective ways to support independent authors. Please leave your comments on the bookstore or review site of your choice, or recommend *Sleight of Hand* and *The Alewives* to your book club. You can sign up to receive regular updates on her work and promotional pricing on indie books at www.elizabethrandersen.com or follow her on social media at:

- **Instagram** @elizabethrandersen

- **Facebook** @ERAndersenBooks

- **X (formerly called Twitter)** @E_R_A_writes

- **Threads** @elizabethrandersen

- **BlueSky** @elizabethrandersen

Acknowledgements
In which credit is duly given

SO MANY THANKS NEED to go out to my community of indie and traditional authors who encouraged me to continue with The Alewives of Colmar series. Special thanks to my mom, who read my books despite valiantly battling cancer and chemotherapy (the alewives would have had a lot to say about chemotherapy, believe me!). This book is dedicated to her. Thanks to authors Christine Herbert, James Whittaker, and the other members of the PNW Authors Meetup at Side Hustle Brewing, where I not only spent many hours writing and sipping fine ales but enjoying the fellowship of other authors on their own journeys. My two indispensable medieval mavens, M.J. Porter and Kelly Evans, both formidable authors of early Medieval and Renaissance historical fiction, not only provided encouragement and much-needed jokes but valuable first reads of my manuscripts to steer me in the right direction. My developmental editor, Craig Hillsley, ensured that I tied up all the loose ends and created a cohesive story, and Sarah Dronfield cast her keen eyes over the manuscript a final time to give it the polish it needed. And thanks to Olly from More Visual Ltd., who worked his magic on the cover, as he has for all of my books and to Mallory MacDonald, who took the lovely author photo at the back of this book. The map was hand-drawn by Dr. John Wyatt Greenlee, a medievalist and formidable expert on all things related to eels. Yes, I said eels. Look him up – you won't be disappointed.

Many thanks to my son, who is only 11 years old, but recognizes that writing about obscure long-dead people is important to his mother and always encourages me to keep at it, and to JC, who, despite my complete disbelief, thinks that writing books is not a waste of my time.

Finally, so many thanks go out to the people of Alsace. I've now spent weeks in your cities and towns, stuttering in my terrible French and even worse German, and exploring the countryside in a microscopically small French car. Thank you for joyously sharing your beautiful and unique culture with me. I know that I am an interloper, but you welcomed me with beer, sausages, stories, and good company. Merci vielmols!

Also by Elizabeth R. Andersen

In which we discover that the author also writes other books

The Alewives of Colmar series
The Alewives
Sleight of Hand

The Two Daggers series
The Scribe
The Land of God
The Amir
The Marquis of Maron
The Two Daggers (coming 2025)

About Elizabeth R. Andersen

In which the author introduces herself

Elizabeth R. Andersen is an independent historical fiction author living in the beautiful Pacific Northwest of the United States. She is passionate about reviving (and eating) historical recipes, reading and supporting other indie authors, and exploring the stunning Cascade mountains.

Join Elizabeth's monthly newsletter and receive *Nasira*, the free prequel novella to *The Two Daggers* series for free. Sign up at https://www.elizabethrandersen.com or follow her on your favorite social media sites.

Printed in Great Britain
by Amazon